SCARRED SOULS

THE DEIFORM FELLOWSHIP FOUR

SARAH ETTRITCH

NORN PUBLISHING
TORONTO, CANADA

ISBN: 978-1-927369-44-9

Published by Norn Publishing
www.NornPublishing.com

For Kath and Jim

Acknowledgements

My thanks to Jennifer Brinkman (my lovely partner and beta reader extraordinaire) and Marg Gilks (my fabulous editor).

Chapter One

J ILLIAN THREW A stick away from the water and watched the Fellowship's two black Labradors tear after it. She'd learned not to throw anything into the water. The dogs would splash after it without a second thought, and when the winner returned with the stick, they'd both shake off their coats right next to her. The result: two damp dogs and a soaked, pissed-off human.

Her phone rang. She pulled it from her pocket and glanced at its display. "Yes."

"I'd like to see you," Roberta said. "Can you come back to the house? I'm in the conference room."

"Sure." She hung up and whistled for the dogs. *"Follow,"* she said to them, and her two canine companions enthusiastically raced alongside her as she jogged back to the house. Passing the graveyard, she thought about the freshest grave. Patrick, the cell's former Guide, had passed away in his sleep last week. Ruth had gone looking for him when he hadn't shown up for one of the twice-weekly services those on the island attended.

His death had hit Roberta and Ruth hard. Patrick had been the Guide when Ruth had come in, and Roberta, who'd replaced him, had sometimes sought his advice. She hadn't wanted him to tell her what to do, but when she'd needed a second opinion, Patrick had always been happy to oblige. Now she was on her own.

Jillian and Patrick hadn't been close, but she'd miss the conversations they'd had when she'd bumped into him while out walking. He'd rarely visited the main house, and since she'd stayed away from the services, they'd never struck up a friendship. She felt more for those he'd left behind.

When she reached the house and opened the front door, Puck and Raven took off for the kitchen, probably to see if they could persuade Penny to let them taste whatever she was preparing for dinner. All they worried about was their stomachs. They didn't have a care in the world. Lucky dogs.

The conference room usually meant a new case. Though part of her was enjoying the unusually long break, the other part wanted something to investigate. It had been a while since she'd spent more than a few days on the island. It was time to get back to work.

She wasn't surprised to see Sam already seated at the conference table. Sam had appeared stoic after Patrick's death, but she'd also begged off a jamming session, a sign that she was grieving. Jillian would let her decide when she was ready to play together again, and hoped it would be soon. The first time they'd tried to play a song together, Jillian on guitar and Sam on keyboards, they'd both flushed and apologized every time they made a mistake, but they were past that now. Both instruments were in the basement. Jillian wondered if Sam would take the keyboards wherever they were going.

She pulled out a chair and nodded at Sam. "What's up?" she said to Roberta.

"I was watching TV earlier," Roberta said. She wasn't following her regular routine, an indication of how much Patrick's death had affected her. "I asked Jeremy to find one of the segments on the national news." She pressed a button on the control panel in front of her. The large black screen hanging at the front of the room came to life.

"And now we turn to our top news story of the day," the female anchor said. "Police have arrested a woman in connection with the three murders in Grayhurst that have shocked the entire city. Marcy Abrams is standing by outside the Grayhurst police station. Marcy."

Jillian tensed. Marcy Abrams had covered Jim and Joanna's murders.

Abrams looked earnestly into the camera. "Carol, I'm here in front of the Grayhurst Police Station, where police just held a press conference about the latest developments in the murder spree that has kept everyone on edge—three men found murdered within the same week, all shot to death. Everyone was wondering who would be next, but today the residents of Grayhurst can breathe easier. According to Detective Laura Meyer, a suspect turned herself in to police this morning, apparently without a lawyer. She walked in off the street and told the officer on duty that she had committed the murders."

"I understand that the identity of the suspect is causing quite a stir," Carol said.

Abrams nodded. "She's Sister Catherine, a member of St. Joseph's convent and a nun who's familiar to many who live in Grayhurst. Not your typical murder suspect, for sure."

"She's more than a suspect, isn't she?" Carol pointed out. "She confessed to the murders."

"Well, she did so without legal counsel present. According to Detective Meyer, she now has an attorney, and the court has ordered that she undergo a psychiatric evaluation. But Detective Meyer also said that Sister Catherine provided them with information that led them to charge her with three counts of first degree murder."

"What happens next, Marcy?"

"As I mentioned, she'll undergo a psychiatric evaluation. In the meantime, the police will continue their investigation."

The screen went blank. Roberta blew out a sigh. "She's innocent."

Jillian exchanged a glance with Sam. "Why do you think she's innocent?" Sam asked, her tone neutral.

Roberta was silent for a moment, then she shrugged. "I can't explain it. When I watched the news report, I just knew she was innocent. I want you to go to Grayhurst. Look into the murders. Find out why Sister Catherine confessed to crimes she didn't commit. Figure out who the killer really is."

Jillian drew breath, then decided to keep her mouth shut. Okay, they'd poke around Grayhurst based on Roberta having a gut feeling. How would that be different from poking around because Roberta had received a vision or some other communication she believed was from God? Jillian had never demanded a more tangible reason to leave the island and stick her nose into other people's affairs, so why start now?

Sam shifted in her chair. "Has Jeremy pulled the police reports?"

Roberta nodded. "He's also started a file on Sister Catherine, but we don't know much. She entered the convent when she was forty-two. She's in her early sixties now." She clasped her hands on the table. "One of you will start at the convent. You'll speak to the nuns under the pretense of wanting to write a book about the case. We'll get you in through a contact we have in the local diocese. The other one will start with Sister Catherine. I'll leave it up to you to decide who will do what."

Jillian had an evangelical religious background. "I don't know much about nuns. I'd say Anglican is much closer to Catholic." She looked at Sam, who was, or had been, Anglican. Now she was Fellowship, which was interdenominational. This cell was a Christian one. Catholic, Protestant, and one lone atheist, all working together.

"Sister Catherine is an Anglican nun," Roberta said.

Sam nodded. "I'll start with her."

Deal with one nun, or a bunch of them? Jillian would have preferred just the one, but she didn't protest. After her brief stay in prison, when she was an accused murderer waiting for her court appearance, she wasn't eager to step foot in one again. Speaking of which . . . "What about Marcy Abrams? She worked on Jim and Joanna's murders. What if she recognizes me?"

"She won't hang around in Grayhurst until the next court appearance," Roberta said. "Now that the excitement is over, she'll pack up and go to the next big story. If she does go back to Grayhurst, it'll probably be for the trial, not for a five-minute appearance."

"If we're still there, you'll stay out of her way." Sam quirked a brow. "She probably wouldn't remember you anyway."

"She probably wouldn't," Jillian agreed. Abrams had shouted a question to her as she'd entered the courthouse. She'd also watched her walk from a police station to a car. How many people had she covered since then?

"Hopefully it won't take us long to at least determine whether Sister Catherine is guilty or innocent," Sam added.

"She's innocent," Roberta said flatly.

Jillian resisted the urge to look at Sam. "When she turned herself in, did she say why she committed the murders?"

Roberta hesitated. "She said God told her to do it. That's also why she turned herself in. Because the Lord told her to."

In other company, Jillian would have giggled.

"The police must believe she did it," Sam said. "What do they have? Or maybe I should be asking, what did she give them?"

"The murder weapon, with only her fingerprints on it, but she turned herself in two days after the last murder, plenty of time to wipe other fingerprints away. She also knew a detail about the murders that hadn't been released to the public."

Jillian leaned forward. "What is it?"

"The three murder victims, all men, were shot in the genitals, in addition to the chest. And there's one other thing. Security cameras picked her up in the vicinity of the location where the second victim was shot, at around the time of the murder."

Sister Catherine sounded guilty to Jillian. She looked at Sam, but couldn't read anything from her expression.

"Jeremy is building new identifications for you," Roberta said. "We're retiring the Westwood name. You've used it for a while now."

"Will we still be sisters?" Jillian asked.

Roberta nodded. "Remember when Sam was taken to hospital? If you'd only been a friend or roommate, they wouldn't have given you any information or let you see her."

If it was a matter of having some legal standing in each other's lives, they could be spouses. Jillian didn't dare voice the thought. She didn't want to give Sam any hint of how she felt about her. Sam would interpret the suggestion as a joke and wouldn't appreciate it, and Roberta . . . maybe she'd take it seriously, maybe not. She had dark circles under her eyes and lacked her usual vigour. Jillian didn't want to say anything that might heighten the tension in the room. "Let's go see Jeremy," she said, pushing back her chair before Sam had the chance to leave without her.

Sam stood, but she didn't follow Jillian. She put her hand on Roberta's shoulder and leaned over so that her mouth was almost touching Roberta's ear. "Do you want a coffee?" she asked softly.

Roberta's answering smile was strained. "Please. That would be nice."

Watching from the doorway, Jillian could see the concern in Sam's eyes. She shared it.

* * * * *

JILLIAN SLID HER guitar into the back of the Jeep, then frowned when Sam set her bag next to the guitar and slammed the hatch door. "No keyboards?" she couldn't help asking.

Sam didn't answer until they'd both fastened their seat belts and were driving along the gravel road that led to the airstrip. "We'll be staying in a hotel. I can't see us being on this case for long."

"Do you think she's innocent?" Jillian asked.

Squinting into the sun, Sam lowered the driver's side sun visor. "I don't know. I'm keeping an open mind."

Jillian grunted at Sam's diplomatic response. Sure, Sam sincerely believed that Roberta received visions from God, but Roberta usually had more than a gut feeling when she sent them out on an investigation. Plus, this nun had confessed. If she wasn't bonkers or guilty, why would she walk into a police station and claim responsibility for three murders she hadn't committed, and brutal murders, at that? Because God had told her to do it? Sure.

Last night, Jillian had read over the information Jeremy had collected about the murders. The timestamp on the security footage put Sister Catherine a block away from the second murder location within half an hour of the victim's estimated time of death. The woman had confessed. Maybe she was fragile and had witnessed something that had unhinged her, or maybe she'd pulled the trigger. The psychiatric evaluation would explore the first potential explanation. If the second explanation was true, then Roberta's gut feeling was wrong. What did Sam think? "If she didn't do it, why would she walk into a police station and confess?"

"I don't know," Sam said, her tone neutral.

"But you think we'll figure it out pretty quickly."

"The evidence combined with her confession is pretty damning. She's probably guilty. I know that means Roberta would be wrong, but it's happened before."

If Roberta wasn't grieving, Jillian might have expressed her skepticism, rather than meekly agreeing to go on what felt like a wild goose chase.

As if reading her mind, Sam said, "Roberta's dealing with Patrick's death. I don't think she's sleeping well. It won't hurt us to spend a few days seeing if we can dig anything up. Like I said, I'm keeping an open mind, but I'll be surprised if she didn't do it."

"Even though she's a nun?" Jillian couldn't resist saying.

Sam rolled her eyes. "I've been doing this too long to believe that everyone who appears to dedicate their life to God is a saint. But you already know that."

"What, that not everyone's a saint, or that you won't be surprised if it turns out Sister Catherine did it?"

Sam's mouth twitched. "Both."

Jillian chuckled. So much had changed since the first time she'd driven to the airstrip in this Jeep with Sam. Back then, she'd thought Sam was bat-shit crazy. Now . . . her feelings for Sam hung over every moment they spent together, no matter how hard Jillian tried to suppress them. Things could be worse. Many people pined for someone they hardly saw, or silently suffered because the object of their desire was involved with someone else. Jillian wasn't married to Sam, but they'd be in each other's lives until one of them died. She couldn't decide if that was a blessing, or a curse.

Chapter Two

Sam murmured a thank you to the guard who'd escorted her into an interrogation room at the prison, and sat down. The burly man across the table from her extended his hand. "Dave Greenwood, Sister Catherine's attorney. You must be the PI?"

Sam pumped his hand. "Sam Wright." She pulled a folder from her satchel and slapped it onto the table.

"I'm glad the church believes she's innocent," Greenwood said. "When the bishop asked me to take the case, I got the impression he'd already passed judgement. I was surprised when he told me it had hired a PI."

Sam met his shrewd eyes. "The church wants to make sure no stone is left unturned. It will leave it up to the court to decide whether Sister Catherine is guilty."

"But it would prefer that she be innocent. Reputation, and all that."

Sam inclined her head to indicate that she agreed. "I'm acting on the assumption that she *is* innocent. We're on the same side. What do you have that can help me?"

Greenwood barked a laugh. "I'm hoping you'll be able to help *me*. She insists she's guilty. I've told her she can tell me anything in confidence. I've begged her to give me something to work with. Nothing."

That didn't sound promising. "I'd still like to compare notes. I have the police report, but you might know something I don't, and vice versa."

"I wish I—"

A door clanged shut. Greenwood straightened in his chair. Approaching footsteps grew louder.

Sister Catherine shuffled into the room, with a guard on her heels and her hands cuffed in front of her. The guard motioned for her to sit next to Greenwood, then bent down and uncuffed her. "I'll be right outside," he growled. The door swung shut behind him. Sister Catherine rubbed her wrists.

Sam studied her. The prison jumpsuit the nun wore hung off her slender frame. Salt and pepper hair framed a face with few wrinkles, making the sister appear younger than her sixty-three years. She looked as if she wouldn't hurt a fly, but youth and brawn weren't required to pull a trigger.

Time to get down to business. "My name is Sam Wright. I'm a private investigator. The church has hired me to make sure all the pertinent information related to your case comes to light. Thank you for agreeing to meet with me."

Sister Catherine folded her arms, perhaps because she'd only agreed to this meeting when pressured by a priest she respected.

"The church believes you're innocent, and I'm here to prove it," Sam said, watching the nun closely.

Emotion flickered across Sister Catherine's face, but it wasn't the relief Sam hoped to see. It was fear.

"I'm here to help you. Why did you confess to murders you didn't commit?"

Sister Catherine stared at her.

"It's all right," Greenwood said. "You can answer the question." When the nun didn't speak, he shrugged his shoulders at Sam.

Sam flipped open the folder and slid a photograph across the table. "Why were you on the corner of Grant and Main around the time of the second murder?"

Sister Catherine's eyes remained on Sam.

Sam reached across the table and tapped the photo. "This clearly shows you near the location where Ronald Grabinsky was found dead. According to the timestamp, you were there around his estimated time of death. What were you doing there?"

Nothing.

She exchanged glances with Greenwood, then slapped the crime photo of Grabinsky on the table. Sister Catherine stiffened and looked away.

"You confessed to doing this," Sam said. "Ronald Grabinsky was shot multiple times in cold blood. If you did it, why did you do it?"

Sister Catherine stared at her, stone-faced.

"Is there anyone you'd like to come visit you?" Sam asked, trying a different tack.

No reply. Sam might as well be talking to herself. Greenwood shot her an "I told you so" look and shifted in his chair.

"Are you all right? Are you being treated well?" Sam asked the nun.

Crickets.

"Is there anything you'd like to tell me? I'm here to help you. This is your chance to tell me what happened."

Sister Catherine's lips didn't even twitch. Apart from the fleeting fear in her eyes when Sam had suggested she was innocent, and perhaps shock when she saw the crime photo, she'd conveyed no emotion. The police must have shown her the photo and many more when they'd interrogated her, so surprise hadn't made the nun tense. If Roberta was wrong, Sam was sitting across the table from a woman who'd murdered three men in cold blood. Was she shocked by her own crimes? Did she have no memory of them? Or was she innocent?

Sam slipped the photos back into the folder. "Thank you for your time," she said, flipping the folder shut and sliding it into her satchel. "If you'd like to speak to me, tell Mr. Greenwood and he'll arrange it." Maybe Sister Catherine would be more forthcoming if they were alone, though Sam doubted it.

"I want a private word with my client. I'll meet you outside," Greenwood said.

Sam rose and knocked on the door. A guard took her back to the waiting area. She wasn't surprised when Greenwood joined her a minute later. "She wouldn't speak to you either, eh?"

"Nope. Let's walk out together." He didn't speak again until they were in the parking lot. "I have to confess, I'm at a loss. The evidence is pretty damning. I'd like to mount a defence, but it's difficult when my client won't talk to me." He lifted his finger. "Scratch that. She has talked to me. She keeps insisting she did it. That's all she ever says. Whenever I try to bring up something in the police report, she shrugs. I can't do much when the client won't cooperate."

"Maybe she wants to be punished. If she's guilty . . ."

"You think she went on a murder spree and now she's riddled with remorse?" Greenwood shook his head. "I haven't seen any remorse or regret. I haven't seen any emotion at all. I'm hoping the psych evaluation will give me something to work with. Maybe the shrink can figure out what's going on in her head, because I don't have a clue. All I know is that she's confessed to the crimes and seems determined to go to prison. Have you found out anything?"

"Not yet. I was only hired yesterday."

"If you stumble across anything, let me know. I'll do the same. Like you said, we're on the same side."

Sam nodded. She handed him a business card and accepted the one he dug out of his wallet, then said good-bye.

Strolling to her car, she concluded that her trip to the prison hadn't been a total loss. She'd seen Sister Catherine in the flesh and established a relationship with Greenwood, but what now? She'd hoped the sister would provide her with a lead or two. Jillian would have to fare better at the convent, or they'd be at a dead end before they'd even started.

Jillian found a parking spot across the road from the convent and killed the engine. She peered out the window at the modern brick building that defied the austere stone structure she'd expected. The Supporter who worked at the diocese to which Grayhurst belonged had better have paved the way for her entrance. She had no idea what the nuns would think of a writer who wanted to write a book about Sister Catherine and her alleged involvement in three brutal murders. She suspected more than a few wouldn't be thrilled with the idea, but there had to be one or two who'd want to dish, all in the name of setting the record straight and preserving the reputation of the convent, of course.

She lifted the satchel lying on the passenger seat, then let it go when her phone rang. "I wasn't expecting to hear from you so soon," she said to Sam.

"She didn't say anything."

"Nothing? She wouldn't tell you anything about the murders?"

"No. She didn't say a word. About anything. She stared at me the whole time."

"Wait, you mean she didn't speak? At all?"

"Right. She's giving her lawyer the same treatment. He wants to defend her, but she keeps saying she did it, and that's all she'll say."

"She must be guilty, then. When I was arrested for Jim and Joanna's murders, I would have been all over a lawyer who wanted to help me, and if a private investigator had shown up saying they wanted to prove me innocent, I would have said, yes, please do, what do you need from me? I wouldn't have given her the silent treatment."

"There's still the psychiatric evaluation," Sam said.

"I don't think they ordered it because they think she's innocent and off her rocker. They did it because she's a nun who suddenly went ballistic and murdered three men."

"You're being diplomatic. She also claims God told her to do it."

Yeah, and Jillian supposed that God and Satan were equal when it came to people wondering if someone was crazy. When the Devil came up in court, it was usually because he'd told the defendant to commit the crime. He never told them to confess to it. God, on the other hand, might compel a remorseful nun to come clean—meaning she was guilty, so they were back to square one. She'd leave the question of why God would order someone to kill and then confess to the killing to those who believed in Him.

"There's also the condition of the bodies," Sam said.

"Even if they'd only been shot in the chest, we're still dealing with a nun with no criminal record who confessed to shooting three men when they were wide awake and looking at her. You don't get any more cold-blooded than that. But we're not just dealing with that. There's a sexual component to the crimes."

Sam grunted. "I agree with everything you're saying. She's probably guilty. But when I told her the church believes she's innocent, it frightened her. If she *is* innocent, I could understand relief. If she isn't, maybe smugness or contempt. But why would she be afraid that she might be proven innocent?"

"If she's guilty and remorseful—"

"She wouldn't be proven innocent in that case. The only thing I can think of is that if she's proven innocent, the case will remain open. The police will keep looking."

Sister Catherine having confessed because she wanted to protect someone was the first possibility she and Sam had discussed when they'd reviewed the police report. Jillian repeated the same words she'd said to Sam during that conversation. "But all the evidence points to her guilt, and she confessed. I could understand if she confessed and nothing tied her to the crimes, but that's not the case." She glanced at her watch. "Anyway, I've got to go, or Reverend Mathis will wonder what's happened to me."

"I'll see you back at the hotel."

They disconnected. Jillian blew out a sigh and grabbed her satchel. After jaywalking across the road, she strode up the path to the convent and rang the buzzer next to the door. She'd arranged to meet Mathis in the convent's lobby, so she wasn't startled when the door swung open and a man, rather than a nun, beckoned her inside.

He stuck out his hand. "I'm Reverend Mathis."

Smiling, she shook his hand. "Jillian Wright." She handed him a business card. While he scrutinized it, she glanced around the airy reception area. Plush chairs, bright colours . . . she'd expected dour and austere. She had an evangelical Christian background, for Pete's sake. Her knowledge of nuns came from movies—not the most reliable source. Was it any wonder that, in her mind, nuns were either uptight, unhappy prudes, or musically gifted? To her, the quintessential nun was Julie Andrews singing *Do-Re-Mi*.

Mathis slipped her business card into his suit jacket pocket and cleared his throat. "I told the Reverend Mother I'd let you in because I wanted a few words with you alone."

Here it comes.

"I agreed, and she agreed, to this . . . meeting, because our bishop apparently thinks a book is a good idea. But is it?" His brow creased with concern. "What will writing about Sister Catherine's case accomplish?"

"It will give people more insight into her. Right now, they see her as a cold-blooded killer."

Mathis winced. "It all sounds sensationalistic to me. And she's innocent until proven guilty."

"I've agreed not to turn in my manuscript until after her case has gone through the courts. Depending on what I find out, I might not turn it in at all. I don't want to decimate the woman, or the reputation of this convent and diocese. When I saw the news report about her turning herself in, I called my publisher right away. They agreed that a book might be worth pursuing. They haven't committed to it yet. I'm only doing research at the moment, to see if a book would be viable."

"Oh," Mathis said, brightening. "I'm sure the Reverend Mother will be pleased to hear that. Because this is a family, and we're a tight-knit community. You see the sister as a killer. To us, she's a sister, an advisor, a friend. She may be someone who's lost her way, we don't know. But she deserves dignity."

What about the three men whose genitals she'd obliterated? Jillian was short on sympathy for Sister Catherine, but she could feel for Mathis. She had more experience than she'd ever wanted with discovering that someone wasn't who you thought they were. "As I said, I'm not here to tear the sister or the convent apart. I'm simply interested in examining Sister Catherine's case in more detail. I agree that the coverage has been sensationalistic. It'll only get worse when the case goes to trial. If I go ahead with the book, it'll act as a balance to all the breathless reporting."

"Will it?" Mathis didn't wait for Jillian to respond. "Apparently the bishop thinks so. I'll take you to see the Reverend Mother now."

As she followed Mathis down a corridor, a woman wearing a brown habit nodded as she passed them. No veil or wimple. Just a simple habit that included a cloth belt—and a freaking huge cross around her neck.

Mathis stopped outside an open door and motioned for Jillian to enter the room ahead of him. She stepped into what could serve as a consultation room. A woman wearing the same habit as the nun they'd passed rose from one of the two chairs facing each other. "Reverend Mother, this is Jillian Wright, the, uh, writer," Mathis said.

Jillian extended her hand. The Reverend Mother hesitated a beat, then shook it. "I'm Sister Anne." She sat down again and motioned for Jillian to take the other chair.

"I'll leave you to it," Mathis said. He scampered away. Jillian clasped her hands on her lap and waited for the sister to say something, wondering whether she'd committed a faux pas by offering to shake hands with her. More than likely, the good sister was pissed off about the book that would never be written, at least not by Jillian.

"I have to be honest, I don't know what purpose a book about Sister Catherine will serve," Sister Anne said.

Here we go again. "As I told Reverend Mathis, it'll act as a balance to whatever the media reports."

"If Sister Catherine is found to be guilty, the media will report that a nun committed three murders. If she's found to be innocent, the media will report that a nun was caught up in three homicide cases. Your book won't make a difference." Sister Anne pushed her glasses up her nose. Her expression challenged Jillian to disagree with her.

It would be worse than that when the detail about the victims' genitals became public. "Do you think she's guilty or innocent?" Jillian asked, trying to throw her off balance.

Sister Anne's eyes widened slightly, but she quickly mastered herself. "I find it difficult to believe that the woman I've lived and worshipped with for twenty years could be guilty."

"But you're not sure." Jillian didn't give her a chance to respond. "You mentioned living and worshipping with her. That's why I'm here. If I write the book, I'll want to present a three-dimensional view of the woman, so I appreciate that you'll allow me to speak to everyone and get a sense of who Sister Catherine is." It was more likely that the Reverend Mother hadn't defied powerful people in the diocese who'd strongly encouraged her to let Jillian question everyone.

"You might not write the book, then?" Sister Anne said, failing to mask her hope that Jillian would drop the idea.

"When I get an idea for a book, I do some preliminary research. Some ideas never make it past that stage. The publisher hasn't committed to it yet, and neither have I."

"I see." Sister Anne's brow furrowed. "I looked you up on the Internet. I couldn't find any books written by Jillian Wright."

Now it was Jillian's turn to hide her surprise. "You have Internet access here?"

Sister Anne's laugh echoed around the small room. "Of course we do. If you brought a laptop or some other gadget, we have Wi-Fi in the library. We read newspapers and magazines, keep up with current events, and go outside. This is a convent, not a prison."

Then why did they call their rooms cells?

"Getting back to your books . . ."

"I write under a pen name."

"I see." If the Reverend Mother wanted to ask for the pen name, she resisted her curiosity. Jillian would have declined to tell her anyway. "Now, what exactly do you want from us?"

"I just want to talk to you about Sister Catherine. If possible, I'd also like to see her . . . room."

"There are twenty-two of us. Well, twenty-one, while Sister Catherine is away."

"You expect her back. You do think she's innocent. Can I start with you, or do you want me to speak to the other sisters first?"

Sister Anne frowned. "I don't want your presence here to disturb anyone. This is our home."

"I understand that."

"We value peace. When you're in the corridors, please don't speak. If someone greets you, merely nod."

"Okay."

"We have a rest period every afternoon. You can speak to the sisters then. I'll draw up a schedule for you. You can speak to me today and start meeting with the others tomorrow. I'll also show you Sister Catherine's cell today. Will that suit?"

Jillian smiled. "Perfectly."

Sister Anne offered her a strained smile in return. "Now, what would you like to know about Sister Catherine?" She squared her shoulders and waited, looking as if she expected to be interrogated.

Jillian pulled a tablet from her satchel. "Do you mind if I record this interview?" she asked, pulling up the app on her phone.

"Yes, I do. I assume you'll take notes on there." Sister Anne jutted her chin toward the tablet on Jillian's lap. "That'll have to do."

All righty, then. Jillian turned off her phone, to make it clear that she was following the nun's wishes. "Let's start with how she came to join your community."

Fifteen minutes later, she'd tapped in tons of notes, but only for the Reverend Mother's benefit. She already knew the factual information Sister Anne had provided. What she hadn't known—Sister Catherine's spiritual journey, personality quirks, interests, and habits—didn't point to any potential avenues for investigation, but maybe Sam would spot something that would make a lightbulb go on.

"I happen to know that Sister Catherine was in the vicinity of where the second murder was committed at around seven o'clock in the evening," Jillian said. "Would you know why she was there?"

Sister Anne shrugged. "Grayhurst General is just around the corner from there. Sister Catherine visits parishioners in hospital every Tuesday and Thursday evening. Parishioners from the church next door to us," she clarified.

Really? If Sister Catherine had told the police, they would have checked, but Jillian bit her tongue. "Have you visited her since she was arrested?"

Sister Anne's mouth pinched. "No."

"Why not?"

"She refuses to see me. She won't see any of us."

So, Sister Catherine was giving everyone the silent treatment, including women she'd lived with for twenty years.

"I think she feels guilty, or maybe she's afraid we'll judge her, or look down at her. She should know that we won't."

Jillian found it interesting that the Reverend Mother felt compelled to explain. "Well, I think that's enough for now." She slid her tablet into the satchel.

"I'll take you to Sister Catherine's cell, then, though I'm not sure how it will help."

Several minutes later, Jillian glanced around a small bedroom containing a single bed and the usual furniture: a bureau, desk, end table, and lamp. She'd love to peek inside the desk and bureau drawers. She also wanted to ask whether the sisters were leaving Sister Catherine's room as she'd left it because they believed she'd soon be home, or because they were waiting for the outcome of the court case before they packed her things away, but she'd already covered that ground with the Reverend Mother. She didn't want to irritate the woman too much. She still had twenty nuns to see. "Thank you," she said, turning toward the door.

Sister Anne led her back to the reception area. "Is 1:30 tomorrow afternoon a good time for you? That would work the best for us."

"That's fine." Jillian pulled a business card from her pocket. "If you need to reschedule, my cell number is on there."

Sister Anne peered at the card through her glasses.

"I'll see you tomorrow."

As she left the convent and crossed the street, Jillian figured it would take her and Sam less than five minutes to go over what she'd learned. Except for the tidbit about Sister Catherine visiting parishioners in hospital, a big fat nothing just about summed it up. But did it matter that they hadn't come across anything to suggest that Sister Catherine wasn't guilty of the crimes she claimed to have committed? A guilty nun would go to prison—as she should.

Chapter Three

IN SAM'S HOTEL room, Jillian swallowed the last bite of the sandwich she'd picked up from a deli near the hotel and washed it down with several gulps of water. She balled up the sandwich wrapper and tossed it into the wastebasket under the desk. Not the ideal place to eat, but they could have a private conversation here. "I didn't find out any more than you did, but at least the Reverend Mother spoke to me and I have permission to talk to everyone."

"But will they tell you anything?" Sam asked from her perch on the edge of the queen bed.

"I don't know."

Sam's knitting needles clicked away. Jillian had grown used to watching a future sweater, scarf, blanket, or mitten grow line by line. "What are you knitting?" she asked, realizing that the light blue wool was a new colour.

"A sweater for Roberta," Sam murmured. "I noticed there's a hole in the one I knitted her a few years ago."

Jillian grunted and watched her for a minute. The thought that Sam would be comfortable in a convent sprung to her mind, but she quickly rejected the notion. Stuck with the same people day in and day out with no chance of escape? Sam would go crazy. Sure, the Fellowship was akin to a religious vocation, but Deiforms didn't live in the same place year-round. Sam had spent most of her life working alone, until Jillian had come along and the joint gifts had bound them together. Sam managed to hide her dismay at their situation—most of the time. It helped that Jillian wasn't the type who wanted to constantly be in someone's face, though she wouldn't mind more time with Sam, especially time that had nothing to do with whatever investigation they were conducting. At least they jammed together now.

She cleared her throat. "You know, when I was at the convent, I kept wondering if the nuns were there because they truly felt called to it, or because they were running or hiding from something. What purpose do they serve, shutting themselves off from the world? It seems kind of selfish to me."

Sam looked up. "Why does it seem selfish?"

"What are they contributing to society?"

"They serve God."

"But they don't do anything for anybody else." Jillian lifted her hand. "I know some communities are more open. These nuns, the ones at St. Joseph's, they venture outside and try to help others. But the ones that don't participate in society outside the convent . . . it seems self-indulgent to me."

"Because you don't believe in God, so you think they're not doing anything important." Sam lay her knitting on the bed. "The Lord calls people in different ways. He's called them to be in constant communion with Him. You think they don't do anything, but they pray for us, for the world."

"Rather than praying, it might be more effective to actually be out there helping people."

Sam frowned. "What did you do when you weren't working a case for the agency? Were you out there saving the world?"

No, she'd sat around watching TV, and gone to Mom and Danny's twice a year—where she'd sat around and watched TV.

"Do you think most people out there are making a real contribution to society? Most of them are spinning their wheels working jobs that don't mean anything. It's busy work that only has meaning within the systems we've created—existing so people will have money to go shopping and think they're doing something important."

Jillian barked a laugh. "Watch it. You're sounding as cynical as I am."

"I'm not cynical. I just don't understand it. But those nuns . . . they get it. They're not wasting their lives. They figured out what's important." When Jillian drew breath, Sam quickly continued. "I'm not saying everyone should be in a convent. Not all are called to that. But they saw through society and what it thinks is important, and they rose above it."

"Maybe not. Sister Catherine insists she killed three men."

"So let's get back to her." Sam chewed her lip. "You still have the rest of the nuns to speak to. Maybe one of them will give you a lead. As for me, I doubt Sister Catherine will ask to see me, so I'll take another look at the victims. I know Jeremy's already gone through everything, but I want to do it again. Maybe he missed something. If she did kill them, there has to be a connection between her and them. I doubt she chose three men at random."

"That depends on the results of the psych evaluation. If there's something wrong upstairs, she might have chosen them at random."

"Or she's innocent and her confession is bogus." Sam raised her right index finger. "Mentally ill and killed them. Mentally ill and confessed to murders she didn't commit." She continued ticking options off on her fingers. "Sane and killed them, or sane and confessed to murders she didn't commit. We need something that'll point to one of those possibilities."

Jillian's phone rang. "Hi," she said to Jeremy.

"I've checked all the hospital security footage for that evening. No Sister Catherine. She was there on the Tuesday night, though."

"What time?"

"She arrived around 6:30 and left just before 8:00."

"Thanks." She disconnected. "Sister Catherine didn't go to Gray-hurst General on the night of the second murder. She was there on the night of the first one, but she left an hour before the police believe the murder was committed."

Sam didn't look surprised.

"Do we think she killed them? The answer to that question will eliminate two possibilities."

"I don't know. It's too early to say, but given that she confessed and refuses to help her lawyer or me, I'd say she's sane."

"Why?"

"Because if mental illness drove her to confess, I think she'd continue to tell the story to anyone who'd listen. But she just sat there." Sam made the motion of zipping her lip. "She's keeping her mouth shut for a reason."

Jillian was inclined to agree with her. "Okay, so she did it and maybe confessed out of remorse, or she's protecting someone, because I can't think of any other reason why a sane person would confess to murders they didn't commit."

"It has to be someone she loves."

"Or maybe she was forced into confessing because . . ."

Sam's brows rose. "Because . . ."

"Because, I don't know," Jillian said, chuckling. "I'm not even sure about her doing it for someone she loves. You'd have to love someone a hell of a lot to take the fall for them. And you'd have to be confident that the person's murder spree is over. Otherwise what would be the point? The moment they murdered again, your confession would be called into question."

"There haven't been any other murders."

"She only turned herself in a few days ago."

"True, but the killer took out three men in a week. There was a murder every second day, until she turned herself in."

"Assuming the spree has ended, either she knew the killer wouldn't murder again . . ."

"Or she did it." Sam picked up her knitting. "And we're back to square one."

Guilty, in which case Roberta's gut feeling had led her astray. She'd be proven wrong, but the killer would already be off the street. What if she was right? If the nun was innocent, the killer was still out there. But then why had the murders stopped? The answer to that question could be the key to everything.

Five days later, Jillian stifled a yawn as she sat in the same room in which she'd spoken to the Reverend Mother, waiting for her next interviewee. Only two more nuns to go, and she hadn't learned anything that would help her and Sam get to the bottom of Sister Catherine's confession. None of the nuns had painted Sister Catherine as a saint, but the tiny sins they'd told Jillian about didn't scream killer, or offer any clues as to why she would have gone on a murder spree or confessed to crimes she hadn't committed. Most of them were convinced, or at least told themselves, that Sister Catherine had suffered some type of breakdown. They'd noticed that she'd been more irritable and distracted than usual just before she confessed to the murders, the only tidbit that had made Jillian lean forward with interest. Yeah, obvious and thin, but at this point, she'd take anything. Could the nun's state of mind before she'd walked into the police station indicate a mental health issue, or had she been struggling with whether to own up to three murders that she may or may not have committed?

A soft knock at the open door broke into Jillian's thoughts. She smiled at the nun who sat opposite her.

"I'm Sister Susan," the nun murmured.

"Pleased to meet you." Not expecting to tap anything into the new note she created on her tablet, Jillian asked her first question. "How long have you known Sister Catherine?"

Ten minutes later, she straightened in her chair and blinked at Sister Susan. "Are you sure?"

"I am," Sister Susan said. "I read the paper in the library every evening at 7:15. I'd only just started when Sister Catherine came in. I remember looking up to see who it was. She wanted a book. A minute later, I could sense that someone was hovering nearby—you know how you can feel it?"

Jillian nodded.

"I lowered the newspaper, and Sister Catherine was standing a few feet away from me. She was shaking. I asked her if she was all right, but she left. Ran out of the library as if her feet were on fire." Sister Susan grimaced. "I didn't know what was wrong."

"Did you go after her?"

"I did. I found her in the chapel. Her head was bowed. I didn't want to disturb her, so—"

"Did you ask her about it later?"

"Well, I asked if she was all right, and she said she was, but she changed after that. She wasn't the same. Something was bothering her. She wasn't at peace anymore."

"And you're sure the incident in the library happened when news of the first murder was on the front page of the paper you were reading?" Jillian asked.

Sister Susan nodded.

Jillian's mind raced as she tapped the information into the note. She should have recorded the interviews, but written notes were searchable, and the Reverend Mother hadn't been keen on the idea when Jillian had suggested it. So, why had seeing a headline about the first murder agitated Sister Catherine? Remorse? No, because if she was guilty, she'd murdered two others after that. If it was a mental health issue, perhaps she'd blacked out and committed the murder. Seeing the news story might have brought back what had happened during the missing time the previous evening. "Do you remember if the story had any photos?"

The nun's face scrunched up. "No. I'm sorry."

"It doesn't matter." Jillian would find the article online.

Sister Susan frowned. "Are you going to put it into the book?"

Jillian repeated the words she'd said to several of the others. "I'm in the research phase right now. When I've completed it, I'll decide whether to write a book. I'll only do it if I think I can offer some insight into Sister Catherine and why she committed the murders—if she did. What's interesting about your account is Sister Catherine's visit to the chapel right afterwards."

"She spent quite a bit of time in the chapel after that."

"Did she?" Jillian said, keeping her voice even.

"Yes. We could see that something was bothering her. When she went out and didn't come back, and then the police arrived . . ." Sister Susan looked down at her lap.

"It must have been quite the shock for everyone."

"It was," she whispered.

"I'm sorry your community has been touched by this," Jillian said, meaning it. She'd come to appreciate how surreal it must have been to have police searching Sister Catherine's cell, questioning everyone, and taking away the computers from the library. They'd found nothing to help their case or enlighten them regarding Sister Catherine's motive.

If the nun hadn't committed the murders and was protecting someone, why would the newspaper article about the first murder have disturbed her? Her reaction suggested that the article was the first she'd heard of the murder. Or was it? "Did Sister Catherine leave the convent much?" She'd asked all the nuns this question and received pretty much the same answer.

"Every now and again, to do her hospital visiting." Sister Susan pursed her lips. "She used to teach at a local community centre. She was a teacher before, you know. But she stopped a few years ago and focused on her visiting."

"Do you know why she stopped?"

"I don't think she liked teaching adults as much. She was teaching English as a second language."

"So she was teaching ESL to adults," Jillian said, trying not to show her excitement. Nobody else, including the Reverend Mother, had mentioned this, probably because it was in the past and they hadn't thought it important. One victim was an immigrant. Could he have been a student? Could the other two have taken classes at the same place?

"Yes. At the community centre on Jones Street. She gave it up about five years ago."

"Did she do any other teaching before then?"

"She did before she joined our community."

"But not while she was here?"

"No. But I just remembered something else."

"What?"

Sister Susan hesitated. "I saw her talking to a man the day after the incident in the library."

Jillian leaned forward. "Where?"

"Near the hospital. I remember thinking she didn't normally do visiting that day, but one of the parishioners next door—" Sister Susan shook her head. "Listen to me. I'm jumping at shadows, now. We talk to people all the time. Next I'll be telling you that Sister Catherine had supper."

"Are you sure you didn't mention it because it struck you as strange for some reason?"

"Positive." Sister Susan looked down at her lap. "There was absolutely nothing unusual about Sister Catherine speaking to people when she was out. I'm getting carried away, that's all. We're all on edge. Since the police came, everyone's been spending more time in the chapel, including me."

Jillian asked more questions, but the rest of the interview didn't bring anything else interesting to light, and the last nun she spoke to didn't reveal anything new.

If the Reverend Mother was elated that Jillian had completed her interviews, she hid it well. "What will you do now?" Sister Anne asked when Jillian told her she was leaving.

"I'll read everything over and see what picture I can paint. I might have more questions."

"Our door is open to you." Sister Anne motioned for Jillian to walk with her. "If you do decide to go ahead with the book, can I read it before it's published?"

"Sure." It was an easy gesture to make, given that there wouldn't be a book.

They entered the reception area. Jillian turned to the Reverend Mother. "Before I go, Sister Susan mentioned a chapel. Would you mind if I saw it and perhaps sat there for a bit?"

"Of course not. I'll show you the way."

Jillian entered the carpeted room Sister Anne took her to and settled in one of the many chairs. A sister sat several rows ahead, with her head bowed. Jillian set her satchel at her feet and slumped in her chair. Not an ideal position, but she'd learned that when she projected, her body would sometimes start to tip forward while her consciousness was having a look around. She'd also learned the hard way that she could feel her body falling and snap back to it in time to sit up. Doing so disoriented her and made her nauseous, but it was better than drawing attention or cracking her head open.

She closed her eyes, relaxed, willed herself to float from her body. Her first stop: areas that had been off-limits to her. No skeletons lurked within them. The community was guilty of having a couple of storage rooms packed with dusty furniture. Okay, she'd seen one of the sisters stuffing her face with cookies in the kitchen, but otherwise everyone appeared to be carrying on with their daily routine. Back in the chapel, she stretched and yawned, then returned to the reception area and left, having said her good-bye to Sister Anne when they'd parted at the chapel door.

THE MOMENT JILLIAN got back to her hotel room, she turned on her laptop and found the newspaper article that had spooked Sister Catherine. It contained a large photo of the victim, one that the sister could have seen from a few feet away. Sister Susan hadn't said that Sister Catherine had moved closer to read the article, so the photo must have set her off, but why? Because she saw the man she'd brutally murdered the night before, or because she recognized someone she knew but hadn't killed?

Jillian pulled out her phone. "I might have something," she said as soon as Sam answered.

"Really?" Sam said, hope lifting her voice.

"Well, nothing earth-shattering, I guess. It won't get us any closer, but . . ." She told Sam about the article and Sister Catherine's reaction.

"It could have been the headline, not the photo," Sam pointed out.

"True, but I'm sure it wasn't the first time Sister Catherine had read a headline about a murder."

Sam didn't respond. Jillian could hear voices. "Where are you?"

"I'm just picking up a tea and doughnut at Tim's. I needed to get some air, get away from the hotel for a bit."

Yeah, three days cooped up in a hotel room would get to anyone, even Sam.

"Do you want anything?"

"Yes, please. Get me a tea."

"Okay." Sam's voice dropped. Jillian had to strain to hear her. "I haven't found anything. I've pored over the police reports and searched online for anything about the victims. Checked social media profiles, followed every search engine link. I can't find any connection between them."

"I found out one other thing," Jillian said. "Sister Catherine taught adult ESL classes until five years ago. One of the victims was an immigrant."

"I didn't see—just a sec." Jillian listened as Sam put in her order. "I didn't see anything about Boris Vasiliev taking a class," Sam said, referring to the first victim.

"It was at a community centre, not at a college or anything like that. I mean, he probably wasn't a student, but it's something else to look into."

"Ask Jeremy to see if he can find out who took her classes. Even if Vasiliev didn't, we should speak to the students, see if they can tell us anything."

"There will be a lot of students, and her ESL classes probably have nothing to do with the murders."

"I know, but . . ."

"Yep," Jillian said. What else did they have? "I'll call him."

"Getting back to the photo in the newspaper, maybe she recognized the victim," Sam said. "It doesn't mean she killed him."

"But it brings us back to her knowing the victim, maybe all three of them."

Sam sighed into the phone. "I haven't found any connection between her and the victims."

"We're missing something. All we can do is chase down leads until we find it. I'll call Jeremy."

They disconnected. Yes, they had the ESL class lead, but bringing up Jeremy's number felt like a futile gesture. They hadn't learned anything to suggest that Sister Catherine hadn't done exactly what she'd confessed to doing. Maybe there wasn't a connection between the victims. Maybe Sister Catherine had simply lost her mind and killed three men she didn't know.

Chapter Four

Sam parked the car in front of a red brick townhouse and double-checked the house number with the one she'd written down. She'd spent the last two days talking to Sister Catherine's former ESL students; this was the second to last student on her list. So far, nobody had told her anything useful. She assumed Jillian was having the same luck today with her list, otherwise she would have called. They hadn't been able to track down all the students and some had declined to speak to them, but talking to them was a long shot, anyway.

None of the murder victims had taken Sister Catherine's ESL classes. If no new information came to light, Sam would have no choice but to call Roberta and discuss closing the investigation, something she wasn't looking forward to. Roberta wasn't always right, but she was grieving over Patrick and more fragile than usual. Knowing she'd sent two of her Deiforms on a wild goose chase wouldn't make her feel any better.

With a sigh, Sam got out of the car and climbed the cement steps to the front door. She pulled a business card from her pocket and pressed the doorbell. The door quickly swung open. "Daisy Chen?"

The woman nodded.

Sam handed her the business card. "I'm Sam Wright. I spoke to you on the phone."

Chen gave the card a cursory look, then motioned for Sam to come inside. "Sit down. You want coffee? Tea?"

Sam dropped into an armchair. "No, thank you."

"You here because of murders, right?" Chen perched on the edge of the sofa. "That nun, she like men too much."

Sam struggled to hide her shock. "What do you mean?"

"They supposed to be, uh, you know, no men, but she liked one. Showed too much attention. It wasn't right."

"Was the man a student in your class?"

"Yes. From Russia, I think." Her brow furrowed. "Nikita. No." She smiled and pointed at Sam. "Nikolay. That's it. Nikolay."

"Do you remember his last name?" Sam couldn't remember more than one Nikolay on the student lists, but she could be wrong.

"No. We never give last name."

The first victim was Russian, but Grayhurst had a population of over half a million people. There might be no connection between Boris Vasiliev and Nikolay. "So Sister Catherine paid a lot of attention to Nikolay?"

"Yes. Too much. Always spending more time with him. Always checking his work. Always helping him. And he stayed after class sometimes. I don't think that's proper, do you?"

"Maybe he was asking her about an assignment."

Chen snorted. "She always explained the assignments to everyone in the class. And one day I stayed longer outside to make phone call. Nikolay came out twenty minutes later. What did they talk about for twenty minutes?"

Good question. "How many of you were in the class?"

"Five of us."

Sam would check the lists to see if she or Jillian had spoken to any of Chen's classmates. "Any other men?"

"Two others. She didn't care about them."

"Do you think Sister Catherine knew Nikolay before he took the class?"

Chen shrugged. "I don't know."

"Did you ever see them together outside of class, away from the community centre?"

Chen shook her head. "You know what I think about the murders?"

"What?" Sam said, genuinely interested.

"She was lovers with them, and they were going to tell everyone. The nuns would have run her out of the convent. They would have disgraced her."

Sam nodded, even though she didn't believe Chen's theory. Killing three men to cover up three affairs would only have dug Sister Catherine a deeper hole. And why would the men have suddenly decided to go public—all three of them? Then again, some people would do anything to preserve their reputations and keep up appearances. But if that had been Sister Catherine's motive, she wouldn't have walked into the police station and confessed to the crimes.

"I hope she rots in there," Chen said.

"You didn't like her."

"She shouldn't have paid him so much attention." Chen's eyes flicked to a rosary coiled up on an end table. "She was a disgrace to the church."

Sister Catherine wasn't Catholic, but that didn't matter. "Have you seen Nikolay since you took the class with him?"

"No."

"Did anyone else notice that Sister Catherine paid too much attention to him?"

"I didn't talk much to anyone. I listen in class and then leave. I wasn't there to make friends."

"Did you ever see Sister Catherine with anyone who wasn't in your class?"

"Only other people at the centre. Other teachers, staff . . ."

"Well, thank you for your time." Sam rose. "If you think of anything else, you have my card."

"I hope she rots in there," Chen said again, as she opened the front door to let Sam out. "Murder always bad, but for a nun . . ." She tutted and shook her head. "She didn't belong in a convent."

Sam murmured a good-bye. In the car, she pulled out the student lists and found Chen's class, then cross-referenced the other four names with her and Jillian's lists. Sam had spoken to one of the students yesterday, Jillian had spoken to another, and a third was the last person on Sam's list. As for Nikolay, they'd left him two messages. He hadn't called them back.

They'd have to call the two students they'd already questioned and ask about Sister Catherine and Nikolay. It could have been innocent, a harmless flirtation, or something deeper. But if Sister Catherine had violated her vows, it didn't mean she'd killed three men. And why not Nikolay? He was still alive. Maybe the last student on her list could tell her more about him.

Her phone rang. Roberta. Chen's information had postponed the conversation Sam had dreaded. Nikolay was a thin lead, but she wouldn't have to butt heads with Roberta just yet. "Yeah."

She knew something was wrong when Roberta said, "When it rains, it pours. First Patrick, then . . ." She trailed off.

Sam's heart pounded. "What's happened?" Her thoughts immediately turned to Ruth, Brian, and Warren. "Is everyone okay?"

"It's my brother. He went to be with the Lord today."

Her shoulders sagged. It wasn't one of them, but still. "I'm sorry."

"I didn't expect it to hit me this hard," Roberta said softly. "I haven't seen him or spoken to him in years."

"But he was still your brother," Sam said, her throat suddenly tight. If—when—Mom or Dad died, she'd be beside herself.

"Yes, he was. Only Mom is left now. I wish I could go to her."

"I'm sorry," Sam said again, wishing she could think of something comforting to say that wouldn't sound trite. "How did it happen?"

"Heart attack. It was quick. He didn't suffer."

"Have you told Ruth or Brian?"

"Brian's coming back to the island for a couple of days."

"Good."

A pause, then, "I'm sorry, I didn't call you to tell you this."

"It's okay. I'm sorry I'm not—"

"You're a good listener."

Sam grunted. That was her. A good listener. Someone who never knew what to say.

"How is the investigation going?" Roberta asked.

Shit. "Great. I just spoke to one of Sister Catherine's former ESL students and got a new lead. Jillian's out there speaking to others. She might find out something, too." Thank goodness Roberta couldn't see her face.

"Keep me posted."

"I will." Not wanting to rush Roberta off the phone, Sam waited for her to say good-bye. "You okay?" she asked, when Roberta didn't speak.

"Yes. Well, no, but I will be." She blew out a sigh. "Do you mind if I give you some advice?"

Surprise made Sam hesitate a beat. "No."

"I know you like to keep to yourself. I respect that. But let Jillian get to know you."

What? "Has she said something to you? We jam together now. We talk." She swallowed. "I don't know what you mean."

"I mean that we don't know when the Lord will call us home. You two share a connection. She's not going away."

Sam wanted to snap at her, but she kept her voice level. "I know that."

"Just let her into your life a little more, past and present. What harm will it do? The connections we make with people . . . that's what it's all about."

"I thought it was about doing the Lord's work."

"It isn't an either/or choice, Sam," Roberta said gently. "We're limited in who we can form lasting bonds with, so don't pass up an opportunity. I think you'd regret it."

She would if Jillian got herself killed, but she'd already figured that out, and it wasn't what Roberta meant. "I'm trying."

"I know. I guess losing people we love is always a reminder that our time on this earth isn't infinite, and we never know when . . . how long." Roberta paused. "Take a chance and tell her about who you are. And not because she complained to me. She didn't. She hasn't said a word. *I* want to see you open up a bit. I don't want to see you miss out."

Sam didn't want to miss out, either, but she wasn't all that interesting a person, and she didn't understand why Jillian wanted to know details about who she was before she joined the Fellowship. It was ancient history. Jillian's life had been much more interesting. She'd grown up, made her own choices—until the Lord had decided it was time. But Sam would tell Roberta what she wanted to hear, and she *would* try harder. Maybe a few autobiographical details about a life that didn't exist anymore wouldn't matter. "I'll try harder."

"That's all I want you to do. I'm not telling you to be her best friend, just to open up a bit more to someone who's always going to be in your life."

Sam still wasn't sure how she felt about being bound to Jillian. She was no longer upset about it, but they *were* growing closer. That was the problem. The loss would be greater. "Thanks for the advice."

They said good-bye and disconnected. Sam gazed out the windshield, reflecting on Roberta's loss. Hopefully she wouldn't have to tell her that the investigation was a dud. As for Jillian, Sam would make the effort to share a little more about her past. With luck, Jillian would be bored to tears and stop asking.

Jillian gazed out the seventeenth floor window while she waited for Sam to arrive. The cars and trucks below looked like toys puzzling their way through a maze. How many more nights would she sleep here? She turned away from the window when someone knocked on the door.

"It's me."

Jillian let Sam in. "I struck out. How about you?"

Sam rolled the chair from underneath the hotel room's desk and sat. "Apparently Sister Catherine paid a lot of attention to a male student who just happens to be Russian."

Jillian's jaw dropped. "Really? How much attention was she paying him, exactly?"

Sam motioned for her to calm down. "It might not mean anything."

Sam was right; the Russian student might not lead anywhere, but he could also be the break they'd been searching for. Maybe Sister Catherine was taking the fall for a secret Russian lover. The possibility didn't shock her. The first hypothesis they'd come up with for Sister Catherine's confession was that she was protecting someone, and they'd included "a lover" on the list of suspects. "If it turns out to be nothing, at least we'll be able to tell Roberta we dug and dug and chased every lead down."

"Speaking about Roberta, she called me earlier. Her brother died."

"No." Jillian sank onto the end of the bed. "How is she?"

Sam took a moment to consider the question. "Sad. Philosophical."

Death was one of those events that turned everyone into Plato. "It must be rough, hearing about it, but not being able to do anything." If it were Mom or Danny, Jillian would want to race to the other one's side. She remembered her shock when Roberta told her they wanted to "kill" her, meaning fake her death. She'd understood the concern that Deiforms and other critical Fellowship members might feel torn between their family and friends, and the demands of the Fellowship. But a small part of her had always wondered whether forcing members to sever ties in such a drastic manner was really necessary. They were all responsible adults. They knew what they had to do.

But now she realized that if something happened to Mom or Danny, her first impulse would be to drop everything, hop in a car, and floor it home. The small part of her stopped wondering. "Her brother was younger than her, right?"

Sam nodded.

"How did he die?"

"Heart attack. He didn't suffer."

He didn't suffer. And that was all that counted when someone died, right? It was easier to bear knowing that they hadn't screamed or fought, but had hit the floor already dead, or quietly stopped breathing.

She leaped to her feet and went to the window. The cars and trucks weren't so fascinating now, but she folded her arms and stared down at them. "We should check in on her more often."

"Brian's going back for a few days."

"Good," Jillian murmured. "I'm glad he'll be there for her." Did Roberta have regrets concerning her brother? When she'd told Jillian about how she'd come into the Fellowship, it had sounded like she'd left abruptly, and the circumstances surrounding her disappearance had eventually led to a ruling of suicide. Had she understood how guilty her family must have felt? Had she wanted to tell her parents and her brother that she was okay, that it wasn't their fault?

Jillian was glad she'd "died" accidentally. She never would have agreed to stage her death as a suicide. No way would she have done that to Mom. It didn't matter that they'd never see each other again. Mom was one of her northern stars. To Jillian, she'd always be there, always be in front of the TV, watching her silly shows. Mom was one of the two people who'd been with Jillian when her life had undergone a confusing transformation. The second person was in this hotel room with her. She fought the urge to turn around and look at Sam, and forced her mind back to Mom.

Unless a Beguiler or something else killed her first, she'd get the dreaded news about Mom one day. Why had she always been in such a hurry to get away and rush Mom off the phone? Between assignments, she'd sat in her apartment and brooded about how she and Mom never connected emotionally, for Christ's sake. What the hell had she expected, when she'd never tried to have a meaningful conversation with her? They'd both been so traumatized by Dad's suicide and the ensuing revelations that they were afraid of what would happen if they poked their heads out of the defences they'd erected around themselves. So they'd smiled, and nodded, and said, "I'm fine. Everything's okay." But it was never okay, not after Dad. Danny's love had helped Mom to trust again, but her relationship with her daughter had never recovered.

She was getting maudlin. She tore her eyes away from the window and plunked onto the bed again. "I'll call her later. Tell me more about this student."

"There's not much to tell at the moment. His name's Nikolay. He's on our list, but he didn't return our phone calls. Apparently Sister Catherine paid him a lot of attention in class and he sometimes hung around afterward. I called Jeremy. He's going to get as much information as he can about the guy."

"At least it's something." Jillian looked down at her hands, then back at Sam. "I've been pretty skeptical about this case from the start. I don't want to have to tell Roberta she was wrong."

Sam's face conveyed her agreement. "Me either, but if this student doesn't pan out . . ."

"Yeah. We have nothing."

They lapsed into silence. Sam shifted in her chair. "I want to tell you something."

"What?" Jillian asked.

"You've asked me about my last name a few times. I've hoped you'd read my file, but you're not going to, so . . ." She met Jillian's eyes. "It's—it was—McDougall."

"Seriously. Your last name was McDougall."

Sam nodded.

Well, hello, Sam McDougall. "Why now?"

Sam clasped her hands on her lap. "We'll be working with each other for the rest of our lives. After talking to Roberta . . ."

"All this death is getting to you."

"No. It's more than that." Sam searched for words. "We're friends, right?"

"Yes," Jillian said emphatically.

"That means something to me, maybe more than you realize. I was alone for a long time. I wasn't lonely, but I'd forgotten what it's like to, I don't know, have someone there all the time. For years, it's been go in, do what has to be done, leave. I never saw most of the people I worked with again, or if I did, only years later." Sam's words tumbled out. "I worked with the others—Jim, Brian, Warren—a few times, and I see those like Jeremy several times a year, but we're not close. We worship together and they know my habits, but I don't share things with them. They don't *know* me. Roberta's our leader and more like a mother to me. Ruth is my mentor. I haven't had anyone around my age who's always with me and understands this life. I never thought I would. If we didn't have the joint gifts, we wouldn't be working together now."

Jillian hadn't thought it possible for her to feel shocked and warmed at the same time. She could see the vulnerability in Sam's eyes, and wanted to say something that wouldn't sound lame or corny. Honestly, she wanted to grab her and— She sat on her hands.

"I guess I've accepted that we'll be working together," Sam continued, "and that it's not too bad, and that being friends means trusting each other, which I'll admit frightens me a little, because I'm not used to it. I'm not used to any sort of emotional intimacy."

"I haven't been that great at it myself."

"We should be closer."

Jillian's heart thumped. She stared at Sam. Did she mean closer, or *closer? Slow down.*

"You should know more about me. I should know more about you. Your file contains facts, not . . . you."

"There isn't much to tell. Life behind the facts was pretty boring," Jillian said, still not sure what Sam meant by "closer."

"So was mine."

Jillian smiled. "No, no, you don't get off so easy. When it comes to your life, I don't even know the facts. So, Sam McDougall, do you have a middle name?"

"Susan. Alex used to call me the S.S. McDougall."

Jillian chuckled. Her stomach grumbled.

"Dinner?" Sam said quickly.

Damn. "Yeah. We can continue this conversation over dinner."

Sam pushed herself up from the chair. "I don't know. I don't want to discuss my life when we're out in public."

"That's okay," Jillian said, wanting to yell at her stomach. "I'll ask questions another time." Man, she'd make a list, but she'd have to pace herself. Too many questions and Sam could balk.

Were the reminders that life was short behind Sam's sudden willingness to share, or was Sam finally opening up because she thought their friendship could become more? Jillian wanted to believe the latter, but she wasn't sure. She'd follow Sam's lead, and hope that Sam led them to where she wanted to go.

Chapter Five

HER EYES STILL closed, Jillian lay in bed and listened to the beeps and whirrs around her. She felt as if she'd emerged from a fog. She went to scratch her arm, then gasped when she touched something foreign. She opened her eyes and blinked at the white walls.

"Her eyes are open," a female shrieked. "Jillian. Jillian, honey, can you hear me?"

Jillian slowly turned her head. Mom swam into view. "Mom?" she croaked.

Mom's eyes welled with tears. "Thank god. Thank god."

Danny took Jillian's hand and smiled. "Welcome back, sweetheart."

Jillian looked down at the tubes snaking from her left arm. What? "What's going on? I—where—am I in hospital?"

"Don't you remember?" Mom said. "You were in a car accident."

"You went straight into a tractor trailer," Danny added. "The car went up in flames. It's a miracle you survived. You've been in a coma for three days."

What?

"A couple of good Samaritans pulled you out before the car exploded." Danny peered at her. "You don't remember any of it?"

Well, she remembered the Fellowship faking her death that way, but . . .

Mom gave her a strained smile. "I knew you shouldn't have left that night. I said you could stay and leave in the morning, but you didn't want to. You said you needed to get home."

Jillian struggled to understand. "So I was visiting you, and I was in this accident on the way home."

They both nodded.

"And I've been in a coma since then."

They nodded again.

"Then it was all a dream," she whispered.

"What was all a dream?" Mom asked.

"Everything. The Fellowship. Deiforms." She was a regular person with a boring life, a life she thought she'd escaped. What now? She tried to sit up, but couldn't. Her head pounded.

"Take it easy," Danny said, his forehead creased with concern. "Lie down. Rest."

Someone knocked at the door. "Good morning," a cheerful voice said.

Shocked recognition made Jillian prop herself up on her elbows, despite her protesting head.

"How's Jillian doing today?"

"She's awake!" Mom said.

A woman in blue scrubs and with a stethoscope hanging around her neck rounded the bed. "That's great news."

Jillian stared at her. "Sam?"

Sam grinned. "See, that's why I told you to keep talking to her," she said to Mom and Danny. "We're never quite sure if they can hear us. There's no harm in assuming they can."

"Dr. Sam has been great," Mom said.

"How do you feel?" Sam asked.

Confused. As if she'd stepped through a portal and entered another world. But if she'd been in a coma . . . "I'm a little disoriented, to be honest."

"That's to be expected." Sam looked across the bed. "Do you mind giving us a few minutes? I'd like to examine Jillian."

Danny squeezed her hand. "We'll be outside," Mom said.

Sam closed the door behind them. "I'll just ask you a few questions. What's your name?"

"Jillian."

"Jillian, what?"

"Jillian Elizabeth Campbell."

"Good. What year is it?"

She hesitated. In her dream, she'd joined the Fellowship in . . . "2013?"

Sam nodded. "What do you do for a living?"

"I, uh, work for a bank."

"Good." Sam pulled the stethoscope from around her neck.

"I had this dream," Jillian felt compelled to say. "I lived years of my life, and . . . it was so real."

Sam's eyes sharpened with curiosity. "What was it about?"

Jillian chuckled. "You wouldn't believe me if I told you." She paused. "You were in it. I saw you."

"It's not unusual to incorporate what you're seeing and hearing into a dream. Your eyes fluttered open a few times. I didn't think you were actually seeing anything, but I guess you were. Can you sit up?"

Jillian pushed herself to a sitting position.

"Now that you're ready to go, I'll discharge you."

What? Jillian looked down at herself. She was wearing a long-sleeved blouse, jeans, and sneakers. When had they removed the IV?

"Now that you won't be my patient anymore, I can do this," Sam said.

Jillian met her eyes. "Do what?"

Sam took Jillian's face in her hands and leaned toward her. Their lips touched. Jillian closed her eyes. Sam's kiss was so gentle, so tender. She'd always known that Sam would be a gentle kisser.

When Sam's lips left hers, Jillian savoured the moment. Then she opened her eyes—dead eyes gazed back at her.

Lilibeth smiled. "Hello, Jillian."

She screamed

And bolted awake. Blinking into the dawn light, she slowly recognized the familiar hotel room. Damn, it had been a wonderful dream, until Lilibeth had shown up and spoiled it. Would she ever get that freaking Beguiler out of her head?

Okay, so she hadn't dreamed years of her life. She was a Deiform. So was Sam. Jillian was letting yesterday's conversation get to her and needed to drag herself back to reality. The probability that they'd ever kiss was smaller than her chance of winning the lottery. Yippee.

She shuffled into the bathroom, looked in the mirror, and cringed when she saw Dad. She'd always looked more like Dad, and the similarity was growing more pronounced as she aged. Sometimes she felt as if she were in Dad's skin. Occasionally she'd lean a certain way, or gesture in a manner that made her think, *I look exactly like Dad when he did such-and-such.*

After splashing water on her face, she left the bathroom and slumped into one of the chairs. It was 6:42, but there was no point in going back to bed. It had taken her ages to fall asleep, and she'd tossed and turned all night. She'd be like a zombie today, sitting in the car brain dead and drooling while Sam did all the work.

She couldn't stop turning their conversation over and over in her mind. Nothing unusual had happened at dinner, or afterward. They'd discussed the local news, which they often did when eating out. Then Sam had gone to her room, presumably to read or knit or whatever else she did in there.

Nothing had changed, and everything had changed. Had Sam been trying to tell her something, or had Jillian read what she wanted to hear into Sam's words? She wouldn't push anything in case she was wrong, but it would constantly be on her mind. Well, Sam always was, but now there might be a chance . . .

She had to be careful, because their conversation had made her more prone to tell Sam about her feelings. If Sam responded with anything but "I'm crazy about you, too," Jillian would be devastated. If she ever told Sam, she'd have to be at her strongest, not her weakest.

Jillian shook herself. Tell Sam? *Don't even go there.* Yesterday Sam had spoken about friendship. She wasn't interested in anything more. Then again, she'd said they should be closer . . . Jillian rarely made tea in hotel rooms because she despised the artificial milk she had to use, but she made an exception this morning and drank the tea while she gazed out the window, watching the maze below.

From across the street, Jillian observed Nikolay Kozlov bound down the front steps of the apartment building where he lived and stroll down the sidewalk. Next to her in the driver's seat, Sam dialed a number. Nikolay stopped, pulled out his phone, and peered at its display. He tapped his phone and shoved it back into his jacket pocket.

Sam disconnected without leaving a message. Nikolay clearly wasn't interested in speaking with a private investigator working Sister Catherine's case. According to Jeremy, Nikolay was single and more than fifteen years younger than the nun. He'd become a citizen not long after he'd taken the ESL class. Since then, he'd had several brushes with the law. Petty stuff like shoplifting, but maybe something had driven him to kill three men and his lover was taking the fall for him. "None of the sisters mentioned him," she murmured. "And according to them, Sister Catherine only left the convent alone when she was going to the hospital to do her visiting. She had the odd appointment, but . . ."

"They probably weren't still involved, if they ever were." Sam chewed her lip. "Maybe they had something, he broke it off, and she never stopped loving him. Do we know why she stopped teaching ESL?"

Jillian shrugged. "They said she got tired of it."

"She taught right up to when she entered the convent. She must have enjoyed it."

"Maybe teaching a group of adults was different. One of the nuns suggested as much."

Sam sighed. "If only she'd talk to me."

Jillian reached for the tea in the cup holder and gulped some down. Real milk made all the difference. "So what are we going to do about Nikolay?"

"Well, he's not going to call us back." Sam tapped the steering wheel. "He's on his way to work. Let's pay him a visit there. He might talk to get rid of us."

They drove to the garage where he worked as a mechanic and waited for him to show up. He got off a bus twenty minutes after they'd arrived. "Do you want to come with me or wait here?" Sam asked Jillian.

"I'll come. Two of us will draw more attention from everyone else." Nikolay would be more eager for them to leave.

As they approached the garage where Nikolay worked, Jillian wrinkled her nose. Oil and gas fumes were already filling her nostrils. A mechanic fiddling with something inside an engine looked up. "Can I help you?" he asked, his hands still under the hood.

"We're looking for Nikolay Kozlov."

"Over there," the mechanic said, tipping his head.

Even though Nikolay had only just arrived, his hands were already dirty, or maybe oil stains always dotted them; Jillian couldn't recall them from when she'd seen him answer Sam's call.

"Nikolay Kozlov?" Sam said.

His eyes narrowed. "Who are you?"

She offered him a business card. "Sam Wright, and this is my associate, Jillian Wright. We've been leaving you messages."

Nikolay shoved the card into a pocket without looking at it. He wiped his hands using an oily rag, which made absolutely no sense to Jillian. "What do you want? You said Sister Catherine. I haven't seen her for years." His Russian accent wasn't thick and his English was good.

"Were you surprised when she was arrested for the murders?" Sam asked.

"What do you think?"

"I don't know. I'm asking you."

He went over to a wooden worktable and picked up a clipboard with a work order clipped to it. Seconds ticked by.

"Look, we just want five minutes of your time and then we won't bother you again," Sam said.

Nikolay tossed down the clipboard, strolled to a red Buick, and lifted its hood.

"We think Sister Catherine is covering for someone. You're on the list of possible suspects."

He whirled to them. "You think I did it?"

"We heard you and Sister Catherine were close."

He snickered. "Who told you that? One of the others in the class? They were all stupid. I flirted with her, that's all. I flirt with all the ladies."

"Including nuns?"

"Nuns are pure. There's something—I don't know, alluring about them. They're sexy. They're so innocent."

Jillian wanted to roll her eyes. She wouldn't tell him that Sister Catherine had been married and divorced before she entered the convent.

Nikolay's eyes raked Sam from head to toe. "You, you're a strong woman, yes? I like strong women. You have pretty eyes."

He reached out to touch Sam's face. Jillian slapped his hand away, then wanted to slug him when he grinned at her. She should have stayed in the car.

"If you didn't do it, then tell us where you were on the nights of the murders," Sam said evenly. "We'll check into it and you'll never hear from us again."

"That would be a shame. I was thinking the three of us could have some fun together."

Jillian's fingernails dug into her palms. Normally he wouldn't get to her, but . . .

"What the hell's going on?" A man in a clean set of overalls marched over to them. "We're backed up already today and you're standing there gabbing," he growled at Nikolay. "Get back to work, or you'll be looking for another job. And you two." He jabbed his finger toward Jillian and Sam. "If you're not here because your car broke down, get lost."

A vein pulsed in Nikolay's temple, but he kept his mouth shut. Sam pulled out another business card and thrust it toward Nikolay's supervisor. "We're part of the investigation into the triple murder case. Nikolay used to know Sister Catherine, the nun who confessed to the killings. We're just here to ask him a couple of questions. We'll leave as soon as he's answered. Unfortunately he's not cooperating."

The supervisor's face darkened. "Get your thumb out of your ass and cooperate," he bellowed. "Don't you want to help keep the psycho in prison?" He slipped the business card into his overall's top pocket. "If he gives you any trouble, come to me." He stalked off.

Nikolay gave the supervisor's back the finger. "Hurry up and ask, and then leave me the fuck alone," he snapped at Sam.

"If your alibi checks out, we won't contact you again. Where were you on the evenings of April 7, April 9, and April 11?"

"Where were you?"

Sam turned to Jillian. "Think we should go talk to his boss?"

"Fuck you." Nikolay rubbed the back of his neck. "Tell me the days. Monday, Tuesday. Not dates."

Sam pulled out her phone and brought up a calendar. "Tuesday April 7, Thursday April 9, and Saturday April 11."

"Tuesday I was at group. For drug addiction."

"Where?" Sam asked.

"The detox centre on Lawrence. I was at a party on Saturday. Yes, I was. A birthday party." He gave Sam the host's name and phone number. "I don't remember where I was on Thursday."

"What about Sister Catherine? Can you tell us anything about her?"

"What's the matter with you, you don't talk?" he said to Jillian.

Not to morons. "Just answer the question," she said.

"She was a good teacher," he said, keeping his eyes on Jillian. "I made her smile every class. What can I say? I could make you smile, too."

Oh, please. She wanted to gag.

"Another student said you used to stay after class," Sam said. "Why?"

"She was helping me with my citizenship test." He winked at Jillian. "She was nice like that."

"Have you seen her since you took the class with her?"

He shook his head.

"Were you surprised when she confessed?"

Nikolay finally turned his attention to Sam. "Of course."

"Do you think she did it?"

"Why would she say she did, if she didn't?" He spat on the concrete floor.

"Were you two having a relationship?"

He tapped his head. "Only up here. I thought of her a lot when I was having fun by myself, if you know what I mean. I like it better with a lady, though. Or two ladies." He waggled his eyebrows at them.

"Thank you for your time." Sam whirled and walked away.

"I feel like a shower," Jillian said, falling into step with her.

"Yeah, charming fellow. Let's hope his alibis check out, or we'll have to talk to him again."

"I'm sorry I reacted the way I did when he looked like he was going to touch you. I should have let you handle it however you wanted."

"That's okay. If you hadn't stopped him, I would have." In the car, Sam dialed a number. "I'm calling the party host. Then we'll head to the detox centre."

When the host picked up, Sam switched to speakerphone and told him who she was and why she was calling. "Was Nikolay Kozlov at a party at your place on Saturday, April 11?"

"Yes, he was," the guy said.

"Are you sure?"

"It was my birthday. Nikolay hit on my girlfriend, threw up on my bathroom floor, and passed out on my couch. So, yeah, I remember."

Jillian shook her head. Yep, it sounded like Nikolay was there.

"Thank you." Sam disconnected. "We'll check with the detox centre, but it's looking like he wasn't the murderer."

"Can you imagine Sister Catherine taking the fall for him? If she's protecting someone, it's got to be someone else."

Sam fired up the engine. "Maybe she was in love with him. People in love can do some strange things."

Jillian wanted so badly to ask whether Sam had ever been in love. But if she said no . . . Jillian slumped down in her seat and folded her arms. She didn't want to hear it from her. Not today, when she believed for the first time there was a chance their friendship could evolve into more. She wanted to enjoy the prospect a little longer.

The social worker who ran the Tuesday night group was at the detox centre. After calling Nikolay to get his permission to talk to Sam and Jillian, he confirmed that Nikolay had been at group the night of April 7 and had left around 9:30, which would rule him out. The first murder had taken place around 8:00 p.m.

"You're certain?" Sam asked.

The guy nodded. "I have them sign in. Attendance is a parole condition for some of them." He held up the sheet he'd pulled from a drawer. "Nikolay was there, not because he has to be, though. He's working hard to turn over a new leaf."

"Too bad he can't get a new personality," Sam murmured as they left the centre, making Jillian snort.

They turned to face each other on the sidewalk. "I think we're at the end of the road with this one," Sam said.

Jillian nodded her agreement. "Let's face it, everything pointed to her guilt from the beginning, and we haven't heard a shred of information to suggest that she didn't do it."

Sam grimaced. "I'll call Roberta."

Jillian rocked on her heels as she listened to Sam's side of the conversation. "There's not much I can do when she won't speak to me," Sam said. "She's either guilty, or she's determined to go to prison for something she didn't do." Silence, then, "She might have a mental health issue, or she could be protecting someone. She could also be guilty. The police wouldn't have taken her confession seriously if there was no evidence pointing to her. They arrested her with good reason. She had the murder weapon, remember, and she knew about where they'd been shot."

Another pause. "Yeah, I know. But sometimes it happens. You know that. It's not your fault." Sam nodded. "Okay, see you soon." She hung up. "We're going back to the island."

Jillian wanted to pump her fist into the air, but it would feel disrespectful of Roberta, especially with everything she was dealing with right now. "So, back to the hotel to get our things, then?" She couldn't wait to get back to the island. She hadn't touched her guitar since they'd arrived in Grayhurst and wondered why she'd brought it with her. On their way home, she'd suggest to Sam that they meet in the basement and play for a while. Should she pepper Sam with questions about her past life on the plane, on the way to the plane, or between songs? What a beautiful morning!

Just because Sam's letting you in doesn't mean she wants to marry you. Yeah, well, tell that to her heart.

Chapter Six

JILLIAN INWARDLY SIGHED when they passed a sign that read *Duncan Airport 37 km*. Taking a Fellowship plane always meant driving to an airstrip outside of town. Normally she wouldn't mind, but today she felt cooped up in the car. Her eagerness to get back to the island was making her antsy. She turned to Sam. "So, your middle name is Susan. Is that a name that runs in your family? My middle name comes from my great-grandmother on my mother's side."

"Susan is my paternal grandmother's name," Sam said, her eyes on the road.

"What are your parent's names?"

"Emily and Arthur."

Emily and Arthur McDougall. Wait a minute. Jillian straightened. Arthur McDougall? "Is your father in real estate?"

"Yeah. He's an investor, or at least he was when I left. He could have retired now. I don't know."

"Arthur McDougall Enterprises. He provides venture capital to start-ups sometimes, too, right?"

Sam raised her brows. "You know about him."

"Only because a couple of companies I investigated did business with McDougall Enterprises." The transactions had involved millions of dollars. McDougall Enterprises was a family-owned, private business. Arthur McDougall—Sam's father—was respected by the financial community. He had a knack for investing in the right companies, and the last time she'd had a reason to notice, the real estate arm of his business was booming. She'd never heard so much of a whisper that the man was crooked or took shortcuts. He was one hundred percent above board.

"My paternal grandfather emigrated from England to the U.S.," Sam said. "He made a killing on the stock market down there and my father got it all."

"He doesn't have any siblings?"

"No."

Jillian hesitated. "This is crass, I know, but how much is he worth?"

Sam's mouth twitched. "You mean, how much money does he have?"

"Yes, that's what I mean."

"When I left them, he was worth about $450 million."

It was a good thing she wasn't driving because the car would have gone into the ditch. "Are you serious?"

"Yeah, and that was twenty years ago. I know everything crashed around 2008, but I'm sure he came through it all right."

Jesus. Sam could be living in luxury and sitting in the back of a limo. Instead she was driving a family sedan up the highway and lived in what could be characterized as a group home. "And you walked away from it."

"I didn't exactly have a choice." Sam waited until she'd passed the slow car in front of them to continue. "Not that the money would have stopped me from joining the Fellowship. I don't miss the money."

Something in her voice made Jillian ask, "What do you miss, besides your family?"

"We've talked a little about this already. I used to wonder what it would be like to live a normal life. I used to wonder what my life would have been like. I've gotten past that. And as far as the money goes, we're not exactly living in poverty. All our needs are taken care of."

Jillian couldn't argue with that. When they were on an investigation, they stayed in decent hotels or a safe house and ate whatever and wherever they wanted. She had a credit card with a high limit. Whenever she went to an ATM, it spit out cash.

"I also miss not knowing about the depraved crap I know about now," Sam said. "There's something to be said for being blissfully ignorant. What do you miss?"

The question gave her pause. She knew Sam meant apart from her family. Frankly, she didn't miss anything, and that embarrassed her. She'd left no friends and hobbies behind. Her normal life had consisted of pretending to be others and watching TV until she could be someone else again. By the time the Fellowship had shown up, she'd grown tired of it and was starting to worry about losing herself. She'd hoped there was more to life but hadn't known how to break free of her slumber. If the Fellowship hadn't arrived, would she have woken up, or would she still be sleepwalking through her life? "Life is better for me now. I was at a crossroads. I knew something had to change, but I didn't know how to change. Then the Fellowship came along and forced me to take a long, hard look. If it hadn't, I don't know what would have happened. Maybe I would have hit a crisis point and made some changes. Maybe not."

"You fought it. Coming into the Fellowship."

"I know," Jillian said, remembering how adamant she was about never stepping foot on the island again, and how she'd intended to use the Fellowship to clear her name, then leave it behind. She'd wanted to cling to a dead life, whereas Sam had leaped from one decent life to another. Well, her involuntary shifting had thrown her and her family for a loop, but before then, it sounded like she'd been happy. Jillian had the impression that Sam's family was religious, but had Sam actually told her that, or had she assumed it? "Was your family—"

Her phone rang. She peered at its display. "It's someone calling through my Jillian Wright number." She picked up the call. "Hello."

"Yes, hello. Is this Jillian Wright?"

"Yes, speaking."

A pause, then, "It's Sister Lynn, from the convent."

"It's one of the nuns," she told Sam. "Yes, I remember you. How are you?"

"Fine, thank you." Silence, then, "I've agonized over whether to call you about this. I still don't know if I'm making the right decision. I think it might help Sister Catherine, then I think it'll make things worse. And I don't know what will happen to me if the police find out. Will they arrest me? It might not have anything to do with anything, but then why did I—"

"Slow down, slow down. Why are you worried about the police?"

Sister Lynn's breath came in quick gasps. "I did something. I don't know why, and I don't know if it has anything to do with the murders, but I have to tell someone. I thought I'd tell you, and if you think the police should know, then you can tell the police."

"What did you do?"

"No, I need to tell you in person."

"Okay. Would you like to meet today?"

"No, tomorrow. Can you meet me outside the community centre on Jones Street at about two?"

Sister Catherine had taught her ESL course at that community centre. "Sure."

"All right. Oh, dear, I hope I'm doing the right thing."

"You sound like you need to get it off your chest."

"I do. I'll see you tomorrow, then. Bye-bye." She disconnected.

Jillian looked at Sam. "Turn around. It looks like we're not at the end of the road, after all. One of the nuns wants to meet with me tomorrow. She might know something."

Sam nodded, and pulled off the highway at the next exit. Jillian turned the radio on and gazed out the passenger-side window. Sister Lynn's call had scuttled her conversation with Sam. She'd ask Sam about her family another time. For once, she wouldn't expect to be rebuffed.

Jillian tried not to pace as she waited for Sister Lynn to emerge from the community centre. Sam was nearby. While they didn't believe that Sister Lynn was worried about being arrested because she'd committed the murders, they couldn't rule it out. If Jillian suddenly found herself threatened by a homicidal nun, Sam would jump into the fray. They'd use translocation as a last resort. Jones was a busy road.

She tried not to appear too eager when Sister Lynn finally stepped onto the sidewalk. "Sister Lynn? It's good to see you again."

Sister Lynn's face was etched with worry. "I'm still not sure I'm doing the right thing."

"Do you want to talk here?"

The nun shook her head. "Let's go to the coffee shop on the corner."

Five minutes later, Jillian sat self-consciously across a table from Sister Lynn. Everyone was staring. Nuns apparently drew attention. She sipped her tea and forced a smile. "So what are you worried about?" she asked.

"Oh, I don't know." Sister Lynn picked up her tea, then put it down. "I wish I hadn't known."

"Known what?"

"When the police came—they searched her cell, you know. That was the first we knew. We didn't know that she'd gone to the police station and confessed. We found out when the police showed up with a search warrant. I don't believe it, you know."

"What did the police do when they came to the convent?" Jillian asked, struggling to keep her frustration out of her voice. This couldn't be easy for Sister Lynn.

"They searched her room, like I said. But first they waited in the reception area while the detective, or whatever she was, spoke to the Reverend Mother. They were respectful, at least. They didn't just barge in and go where they pleased without any warning."

"I assume they spoke to you," Jillian said, knowing she was correct because some of the other nuns had told her the police had interviewed everyone.

Sister Lynn gulped. "I hope I did the right thing."

"What did you do?"

The nun lifted her cup and clung to it. "When they first came in, I heard one of them mention Sister Catherine's name. As soon as the detective finished speaking with the Reverend Mother, I went to her. I was wondering why we had police on our doorstep. I could tell she was in shock. I thought something had happened to Sister Catherine, but they wouldn't have sent a group to inform us, would they? The detective was talking to the other police officers, giving them instructions, I suppose. The Reverend Mother told me what Sister Catherine had done and that the police wanted to search her cell and take the computers from the library. She'd asked them to give her a few minutes and then she'd take them where they wanted to go. She was in shock, like I said. So was I." She put her tea down.

"So what did you do?" Jillian prompted.

"I don't know, I—I went to Sister Catherine's room and took something from it. I didn't think, I just went. I'm sure she didn't do it."

"What did you take?"

Sister Lynn patted her folded napkin, then leaned to her left and flipped open the bag she'd had slung over her shoulder. "This." She handed Jillian a photo.

It looked like a boy's school picture. She flipped it over. Someone had written *1985* on the back. "Why did you remove it from Sister Catherine's room?"

"I didn't want the police to find it."

She'd gathered that. "Why not?"

"Because Sister Catherine had it hidden inside a drawer."

"How did you know about it?" Jillian asked, wondering if Sister Lynn rummaged through the others' belongings when they weren't around.

"Sister Catherine fainted a couple of years ago and was taken to hospital. It turned out not to be anything serious, but they wanted to keep her overnight, just to be sure. The Reverend Mother asked me to take her a change of clothes, for when they let her out. That's when I found it."

"Did you ask her about it?"

Sister Lynn nodded. "As soon as she came home from the hospital. She told me it was her favourite nephew."

"Why would she hide it?" Jillian asked. "Are you not allowed family photos in your rooms?"

"No, we're not. We have contact with our families, but we've also left them behind."

They had one up on the Fellowship as far as families went. "Did you tell anyone about the photo, like the Reverend Mother?"

"No. I'm not a tattle-tale. Everyone has their weaknesses. I leave such things up to each sister's conscience and God."

What were Sister Lynn's weaknesses? Jillian chuckled to herself. Obstructing police investigations, for one. "I don't understand why you took the photo."

"Neither do I," Sister Lynn said, her brow furrowed. "As soon as the Reverend Mother told me why the police were there, I just knew I had to go and get it. Do you think it was God?"

Jillian wasn't touching that question with a ten-foot pole. "No, I meant why would it have been bad for the police to find it? They wouldn't have cared that she had a photo of her nephew."

"But that's just it. I'm not sure it's her nephew."

"But—"

"Some time after that, I asked her about him. The nephew. The boy in that photo must be in his forties now. I asked her how her nephew was and what he did for a living. She'd never mentioned him before I found the photo, you see, and she never mentioned him afterward, either. And if he was her favourite, why did he never visit? Why did she never see or hear from him?"

"Maybe she didn't want to remind you of him, in case you changed your mind about telling on her."

"Maybe, except when I asked her about him, she gave me a strange look and said that she didn't have a nephew, only nieces."

"Exactly how long after you found the photo did you ask her about him?"

"Oh, a year or so. It had bothered me, you see. It had built up. Now that I knew about him, I expected her to mention him now and then, but she never did, and I realized that was strange. She mentioned other family members now and again, and her nieces. Why not him? Especially if he's her favourite."

Good question. "How long ago did you ask her from today?"

Sister Lynn's face scrunched up. "A few years ago now."

If Sister Catherine had confessed to the murders because of a mental health issue, could forgetting that she had a nephew have been one of the first signs of her condition? Or had she forgotten about her lie? The problem with telling a lie was that you had to keep telling it.

"When you asked her about him and she said she only has nieces, did you ask her about the photo?"

"No. I didn't want to push. I thought it best to let it drop."

"Does anyone else know about the photo?"

"No." Sister Lynn looked down at her napkin. "I don't know what to do about it. I suppose I should give it to the police, but they'll arrest me, won't they?"

Jillian doubted it. "I don't—"

"More importantly, I've let down everyone, and myself, and God. Unless He guided me to take the photo, in which case I shouldn't give it to the police, should I?"

"Why don't you leave the photo with me? I'll see if I can find out who it is, and then we'll decide what to do."

Relief flooded Sister Lynn's face. "Would you do that? Oh, thank you. I'd hidden it among my own clothes. Every time I'm in my cell, I think about it. I know it's there."

"You don't have to worry about it anymore."

Both eager to get away, they quickly drained their cups. After bidding Sister Lynn good-bye, Jillian took a closer look at the photo. *Who are you?* She was determined to find out.

BACK IN SAM's hotel room, Jillian compared a photo of Sister Catherine with that of the boy. "I don't know, but I'm not good at this. I don't see a resemblance, but there isn't anything that makes me think they can't be related."

Sam grunted. "She doesn't have a son."

"Not one we know about."

"Jeremy hasn't found a birth certificate with Sister Catherine listed as the mother."

"If she gave him up for adoption or wanted to hide the relationship for some reason, maybe she kept her name out of it."

Sam frowned. "She was married when—"

"I know. It's far-fetched."

"She doesn't have a nephew, either, but she was a teacher."

"He might be a friend's child."

"Then why keep the photo? Out of all the photos she could have kept, of her parents and siblings and friends, why this one?" Sam chewed her lip. "We need to talk to the ex-husband."

They'd hoped to keep him out of it. According to everyone they'd spoken to, Sister Catherine and her ex-husband hadn't seen or talked to each other since their divorce. He'd remarried and had three children. They'd figured he wouldn't know anything about the murders, but the photo put him squarely back into their investigation.

"I'll call her attorney, too," Sam said. "I want to show the photo to her."

"Won't he have to tell the prosecution about the photo, too? I told Sister Lynn we'd decide what to do about the photo after we found out who the boy is."

Sam pursed her lips. "He'll only have to tell the prosecution if he knows it's evidence someone took from Sister Catherine's cell, so I won't tell him that. I'll tell him that someone I spoke to gave it to me, saying it's a boy Sister Catherine once knew, and showing it to her might break through her defences."

"She'll probably refuse to say anything again."

Sam shrugged. "It's worth a try. The photo obviously means a great deal to her. It could be the key to everything."

"Or she could have kept it for a reason that has nothing to do with anything," Jillian said, even though she didn't believe it. The photo seemed so out of place. Her gut told her it would help to shed light on Sister Catherine's involvement in the murders, but that didn't mean it would exonerate her. When Jillian had shown Sam the photo, they'd discussed the possibility that the boy had grown into the person Sister Catherine was protecting—or had killed for. As Sister Lynn had said, the boy in the photo would be in his forties now.

Sam rummaged through her satchel, pulled out Greenwood's business card, and dialed his number. She hung up five minutes later. "We're going tomorrow," she said, telling Jillian what she'd already gathered from Sam's side of the conversation.

"I'll arrange for us to see her ex," Jillian said, wanting to be useful. The ex-husband had left Grayhurst after the divorce. He was only an hour's flight away. "The police spoke to him, right?"

Sam nodded. "He didn't tell them anything useful, but they didn't have the photo."

"Hopefully he won't mind talking to a couple of private investigators."

"Sister Catherine's motive for turning herself in, or committing the murders, could be in her past. Let's review everything we know about her." Sam poised her fingers over her laptop's keyboard, then relaxed them. "I feel like ice cream, probably because of the Dairy Queen we keep passing a few blocks away. Do you want to walk over there and have a sundae or something? We can talk about

Sister Catherine as we walk. When we get back, we'll check her file to make sure we didn't miss anything."

"That sounds like a great idea. I'll get a dip cone, though. I love those at Dairy Queen." Feeling a grin coming on, Jillian ducked her head. Sam had never suggested going for a stroll and discussing a case. Something had definitely changed. Jillian was starting to see a white-picket fence.

Chapter Seven

SAM AND GREENWOOD sat in the same room they'd occupied when she'd last seen Sister Catherine. The attorney didn't have any new information and didn't know who the boy was. "How could I?" he'd said, when Sam had shown him the photo in the parking lot. "She doesn't talk to me." The conversation with him hadn't been a total loss, though. He'd told her that the results of Sister Catherine's psych evaluation would be delivered to him the following week. The judge would decide the next step in the case soon afterward.

Sam felt a sense of déjà vu when Sister Catherine shuffled into the room and dropped sullenly into a chair. The prison guard uncuffed her. "I'll be outside," he said. The door closed behind him.

"I won't waste time on pleasantries." Sam pulled out her phone and brought up the photo she'd scanned into the Fellowship's system. "Who is this?"

Sister Catherine's eyes widened. Her lips parted—then closed.

"You obviously know who it is. What's his name?" Sam wanted to swear when Sister Catherine's mouth set. "I *will* find out who he is, so you might as well tell me."

Nothing.

Greenwood shook his head and looked down at his hands.

"When I find out, he'll be dragged into this case, because it will take time to figure out if and how he's involved. Do you want that? If he's not involved, just tell me who he is. Spare him the hassle."

Sister Catherine drew a deep breath. Her hands were underneath the table, but her arms weren't still. Was she wringing her hands? Clenching them?

"I don't want to bother him if—"

"He's dead," Sister Catherine blurted.

Sam gaped before she could stop herself. Greenwood turned to Sister Catherine, his brows raised. "What's his name?" Sam asked. She'd have to confirm that he was deceased. The nun could be lying.

"He's dead. He can't help you."

"If he's dead, telling me his name won't hurt him."

Sister Catherine's chin trembled. She blinked rapidly and lowered her head.

Sam softened her voice. "If you tell me his name, it'll be a simple matter of confirming his death. If you don't, then I'll have to dig. I might upset people who were close to him, dredge up memories."

The nun raised her head. Her moist eyes met Sam's, but she didn't speak. Sam could guess what she was thinking: even if she divulged the boy's name, the private investigator across from her would dig, anyway. Sister Catherine was right. She must be hoping that the digging would lead nowhere, that the boy's name would remain a mystery.

"Did he go to the school where you taught?" Sam asked, carefully watching the nun.

No reaction.

"Did he live near you? Did he go to the same church as you? How old was he when he passed away?"

Nothing. Sister Catherine's eyes were now steel and her body still.

"Do you want me to start picking through lives? To speak to your ex-husband? To visit the school where you taught?"

The nun remained a statue. Did that mean she was confident Sam wouldn't get anywhere with those lines of inquiry, or was she adept at hiding her emotions? She'd spent years in a convent, practicing peace and focusing on God.

"The prosecution will try to find out who this boy is, too," Greenwood said. "It would be better if we found out who he is first. Why don't you tell us?"

Greenwood's lie didn't help. She wasn't going to tell them anything about the mystery boy. He shot Sam a questioning look. When she tipped her head toward the door, he went and knocked on it.

Five minutes later, Greenwood turned to Sam in the parking lot. "Where did you say you got the photo?"

"From one of the friends who knew her before she entered the convent. Sister Catherine had distributed her worldly goods, I guess you could say. This friend got a box of books and found the photo inside one. She thought maybe seeing it would break through Sister Catherine's defences. According to her, Sister Catherine loves children."

"So it has nothing to do with the case. It's not evidence."

"Not as far as I know," Sam said, half-lying. Sister Lynn had removed the photo from Sister Catherine's cell so the police wouldn't find it, but the boy might have nothing to do with the case.

"And this friend doesn't know who the boy is?"

"No."

Greenwood scowled. "In all my years of doing this, I've never represented anyone so determined to be found guilty."

"Maybe the psych evaluation will help you."

"Maybe. I'll let you know."

Sam climbed into her car and looked at the photo again. *Who are you? Are you really dead?* If so, he wasn't the killer, and Sister Catherine wasn't protecting him, which would bring them right back to square one.

"It wouldn't necessarily bring us back to square one," Jillian said when Sam told her that the boy might be dead. "He must mean something to her. Like you said, why keep his photo and nobody else's?"

"We need to find out who he is."

"Too bad she wouldn't tell you when he died, but we know approximately how old he was in 1985." The boy appeared to be around ten or eleven, too young to be one of Sister Catherine's students in 1985. "Assuming he went to school in Grayhurst, a teacher might remember him. We could look through class photos."

Sam nodded. "If the ex-husband doesn't know who he is, we'll have to go that route. We'll start with schools where she taught, and near to where she lived."

Jillian went to her hotel room window and looked down at the street. She was on the twentieth floor now, still high enough to see a maze.

"Are you ready for dinner?" Sam asked.

"Half an hour, maybe?"

"Sure. I'll meet you in the restaurant."

Jillian waited for the door to close behind Sam, then she sat at the room's small desk and opened her laptop. She probably shouldn't do what she was about to do, but her curiosity was too strong, and frankly, she couldn't resist her desire to learn more about Sam. Not by reading her file, though. Jillian had a more interesting idea in mind.

She brought up a search engine and typed, *Samantha McDougall drowned.* A few search results appeared on the screen. She stared at them. Damn that inner voice of reason telling her to close the browser and walk away! Sam was thawing. Jillian was certain that Sam would eventually tell her the details of how her death was faked, about Brian bringing her in, about her training and how she felt the first few months. *Patience!*

She moved to close the browser, but one of the search results caught her eye, an article in an investment magazine. *Peter Stanton: A Conversation with Investor Arthur McDougall.* The snippet underneath the link said, "Arthur McDougall reveals why he invested in the company everyone thought would fail, and speaks publicly about his daughter's tragic death for the first time."

She clicked through to the article. Her eyes immediately went to a family photo, one that had obviously been snapped by a professional photographer in a landscaped garden. Unlike the Campbell family, the McDougall family hadn't trekked to Sears every year to sit in front of the same background as everyone else in the neighbourhood. Dad shouldn't have wasted the money. Nobody had looked at those photos since he'd offed himself.

She didn't have any trouble picking out Sam in the photo that must have been taken within a year or two of her joining the Fellowship. Since then, she'd put on a couple of pounds and Jillian had noticed a stray gray hair or two popping up, but otherwise, she pretty much looked the same. She was cute back then. She was cute now. And she looked a lot like her mother and sister, and not so much like her father. She had his nose, though. It hadn't been the milkman.

Had Sam already started to involuntarily shift when she'd smiled for the camera? Had Brian made contact? Or was this the calm before the storm for the McDougalls? Were there more family photos with only three people smiling?

She shifted her attention to the interview with Sam's father. A few years ago she would have read the parts about his company, his investments, and his reasons for throwing money at a venture everyone else had predicted would be a stinker, but today she couldn't care less and skimmed past it all.

Stanton: Two years ago, you took what you called a time-out after your daughter Samantha suddenly passed away. You dropped everything for over three months. Did you consider retiring?

McDougall: When I stepped back, I wasn't thinking about retiring or the business. I wanted to be with my family. Sam's death hit us very hard. Only someone who's lost a child can understand how we felt—how we still feel. It doesn't go away. Everything felt so meaningless, and we were in limbo. We didn't have closure.

Stanton: Because her body was never recovered. It was a tragic accident. She fell through ice and drowned.

McDougall: Yes. Part of me still wonders if she's out there with amnesia. I don't know if that will ever go away.

Stanton: What brought you back?

McDougall: There was never any question of retiring. Investing is in my blood. We've suffered a terrible loss and things will never be the same for us, but at some point, you have to force yourself to live again. Life moves on with or without you. Our faith in God helped us tremendously. Knowing that Sam is with God is a great comfort to us, especially to my wife.

Stanton: You took over the business from your father. When you do eventually retire, who will you pass the torch to? Will your daughter Alexandra take over?

McDougall: Alex has always wanted to be a vet. She's never shown any interest in the company. I was intending to pass the reins to Sam. Now that she's gone, I'm considering other options. I'm not prepared to say what they are. I still have a lot of years left in me.

Sam, an investor? Jillian found that hard to believe. Sam had wanted to serve God. Okay, maybe you could do that by investing in ventures that furthered Christian values or helped those in need or something along those lines, but no. She didn't think that was what Sam had in mind.

Stanton: So if Sam hadn't died, she would have followed in your footsteps and taken over the company?

McDougall: Yes. When she passed away, she was doing a religious studies degree. It was something she wanted to do before she came to work with me. Some kids go to Europe right after high school. Sam went to university. If she was still with us, she would have been going into the office with me right about now. I wish she was.

Stanton's next question changed the subject. Jillian scanned the rest of the article, then closed the browser. Sam had never said anything about going into investing. Hell, she showed zero interest in anything related to it. Why would her father believe that she was going to take over from him? Had Sam told Jillian what she would have liked to happen, rather than what was going to happen? Jillian would love to ask her about it, but she'd have to admit that she'd indulged her curiosity and tell Sam what her father had said. Looking into Sam's past had been stupid. Now a question would constantly be on Jillian's mind—one she couldn't ask without admitting to snooping.

Chapter Eight

S AM CLIMBED THE stairs to the chiropractor clinic where she'd meet Sister Catherine's ex-husband and pushed the glass door open. A smiling receptionist told her to take a seat in the waiting room. Following the instructions printed on a colourful sign on the wall, Sam removed her shoes, padded to an empty seat, and glanced around the cozy room. Glowing testimonials scrolled across a large flat-screen TV suspended from the ceiling. Dr. Dave was doing okay for himself.

Jillian had flown with her to Farmington, a city almost 400 kilometres away from Grayhurst, even though they'd decided that Sam would speak to Dave Donovan alone. Jillian was wandering outside while Sam met with Donovan, a meeting she didn't expect to be very long. They could have cancelled Jillian's ticket, but Sam was glad they hadn't.

She was starting to appreciate Roberta's advice. Talking to Jillian about Dad hadn't felt awkward, like she'd expected it would. She was out of practice when it came to talking about herself, and especially about life before the Fellowship. She hadn't wanted questions, and she realized now that she'd partly held back because she was afraid of how talking about Mom, Dad, and Alex would make her feel.

She didn't like returning to the years when she believed she'd have a say in what she'd do when she grew up, and every time she spoke about her family, the longing returned . . . the longing to know how they were, what they looked like, what life had done to them . . . the longing to tell them she was sorry. Maybe answering the many questions she was sure Jillian would ask would help to put that longing to rest. Maybe guilt would no longer taint Sam's memories. Having a friend she trusted was a great gift. She hoped Jillian would forgive any awkwardness. She needed to learn how to be a friend again.

A man strode into the waiting room and stopped in front of her. "You must be Sam Wright. I'm Dave Donovan."

Sam rose. "Pleased to meet you."

"You said on the phone that you want to speak to me about Cathy," Donovan said, after ushering Sam into one of his adjustment rooms and shaking her hand. He dropped onto a rolling stool and motioned for Sam to sit in one of the two chairs against the wall. "Terrible business. I had the shock of my life when I heard she'd confessed to three murders."

"Do you think she did it?"

Donovan's eyes bulged. "No. Or at least, the Cathy I knew couldn't have done it. I haven't seen her in years. But the Cathy I knew wouldn't have entered a convent, either. I don't know her anymore."

"You'd already been divorced for a few years when she made that decision."

He nodded. "She was always religious, but she'd never once expressed any interest in becoming a nun. She never once said, 'Before we got married, I was thinking about entering a convent.' But I don't know. I know things were hard on her."

"You mean the divorce?"

"More what led up to the divorce. By the time we called it quits, we were both ready. It was amicable. Sad, but amicable."

Sam glanced at the photo standing on a shelf. Donovan, his wife, and three grinning kids. "I know this is personal, but I'm trying to understand why Sister Catherine would have committed murder, or confessed to murders she didn't commit, depending. She won't speak to me, so I'm talking to everyone who can offer any insight into who she is." She paused. "Why did your marriage break down?"

Donovan smiled sadly. "We couldn't have children. We tried, then went for tests. It was her. She couldn't conceive. At the time, in vitro fertilization was still fairly new, and it was expensive. We looked into adoption, but . . . " He lifted his hands and dropped them to his lap. "Something changed for me. I've always wanted children, and I wanted them to be mine. Biologically. There was nothing wrong with me. It was her."

Sam struggled to keep her expression neutral.

"I had an affair," Donovan continued. "I guess it was my way of leaving the marriage. It had been strained anyway, long before we got the test results. Trying for a baby and never succeeding . . . it sucked the joy out of everything."

Had Sister Catherine left teaching and entered a convent because she couldn't bear to work with children anymore?

"You have to understand, we both really wanted children. We'd discussed it before we got married. We were more than ready. I loved her, but . . ."

He loved the idea of having kids that looked like him more. Sam kept the thought to herself. "Did she enjoy teaching?"

Donovan nodded. "She loved it. She saw it as her vocation. That's another reason I was surprised when she gave it all up for God."

"You don't think being around children was perhaps painful for her?"

Donovan frowned. "No. In fact, she always said, 'At least I have my students.' And when we divorced, she was teaching high school, not little kids."

Sam doubted that had made a difference. "And she didn't talk to you at all about why she gave it up."

"We'd been divorced several years by then. I'd married Pat, we'd had our first son. We'd moved here. I hadn't talked to or seen her since we'd signed the papers."

"How did you find out she'd entered the convent?"

"A mutual friend told me."

"Can I have that friend's name?"

Donovan grimaced. "She passed away a few years ago. Breast cancer."

"How about other friends?"

He fell silent for a moment. "You could try talking to Ellen. Ellen Young. She and her husband lived next door to us during those final years. But they had a falling out."

"Ellen and her husband?"

"No, Ellen and Cathy." His voice dropped. "It was Ellen. The affair."

Despite the fact that Sister Catherine might have committed three brutal murders, Sam felt sympathy for her. A husband who'd viewed her as inadequate because of something beyond her control, and a friend next door who'd betrayed her. Had dealing with a broken marriage and a disloyal friend brought her closer to the Lord? Was that why she'd entered the convent?

"Do you have Ellen's address and phone number?"

"No. I lost touch with her."

If she wasn't still living next door to the house where Sister Catherine and Donovan had lived, Jeremy would track her down. Sam brought up the photo of the boy on her phone and showed it to Donovan. "Do you know who this is?"

Donovan leaned forward and peered at the display, then shook his head.

"Are you sure?"

"Yes. Who is it?"

"I don't know his name. I'm trying to find him."

"He's connected to Cathy in some way?"

"That's what I'm trying to find out. She started out teaching elementary school, right?"

"Yes."

"When would that have been?" Sam asked, to see if Donovan's recollection would match the official record.

Donovan's eyes grew distant. "Oh, sometime in the late seventies. She only did it for a couple of years."

"At which school?"

"St. George, on Radley Park." Donovan paused. "She babysat sometimes. Not for her students, though. She had a rule that she wouldn't babysit a student. She mainly babysat babies and preschoolers."

"Do you remember who she babysat for?"

Donovan gave her an incredulous look. "No. It was a long time ago."

If the boy was a child she'd minded, they'd have a difficult time finding him, unless Ellen Young could point them in the right direction. "Thank you," Sam said, handing Donovan a business card. "If you think of anything else, please call me."

Donovan blinked down at the card, then raised his head and met Sam's eyes. "I can't see Cathy killing anyone. I said I don't know her anymore, but how much do people change?"

"Why would she confess to doing it, then?"

"I don't know."

"Could she be protecting someone?"

Donovan's brow furrowed. "Who?"

That was the sixty-four-million-dollar question.

Jillian pushed herself away from the car when she spotted Sam striding up the sidewalk. "How did it go?"

Sam blew out a sigh. "He hasn't had any contact with her and didn't recognize the boy. He gave me the name of one of Sister Catherine's friends, or should I say, former friends. They stopped talking to each other when Donovan had an affair with her."

Jesus. "There's a park not too far from here. You want to go find somewhere to sit, and you can tell me all about it?"

"Sure."

Five minutes later, they found an empty bench facing a fountain. Water shot from cement fishes' mouths and splashed into the pool at the fountain's base. "So, what did Donovan say?"

"Like I said, he had an affair. Oh, and they couldn't have children."

As Sam recounted her interview with Donovan, the splashing from the fountain faded away. Sam's voice mesmerized her. Jillian had always thought it was pleasant, and then she'd heard Sam sing . . . Christ, she felt like a lovesick teenager. She'd wanted Sam to loosen up a bit, and now that Sam had, she was having a hard time clamping down on her feelings. She couldn't shut down when she was with Sam, couldn't slip into her armour and slam down her helmet's visor, which both exhilarated and frightened her. This was what all the freaking love songs were about. *And the rejection songs, when someone's heart has been ripped from their chest and stomped on.*

Her annoying voice of reason—again. She imagined herself throttling the thing and drowning it in the fountain, then forced herself to pay attention to what Sam was telling her. "So apart from the affair and Sister Catherine being infertile, he didn't tell us anything we don't already know," she said when Sam finished.

"We'll have to talk to Ellen Young."

"Yeah."

They sat in silence and watched the water—comfortable silence. A silence Jillian could revel in all day, but also the kind of silence that allowed guilt to intrude. "I did something I shouldn't have done," she said impulsively, but knowing in that moment it was the right thing to do.

"What?" Sam asked.

Jillian shook her head at herself. "I searched online and read an interview with your father. He gave it a couple of years after you died. But that's all I read, I swear. I still want to hear it from you."

Sam's face tightened. Jillian swallowed and waited for her to say something. Was she struggling with whether to ask? Jillian wished she'd paid attention to her wise inner voice and closed the browser. She should have known that once she'd read the interview, she wouldn't be able to keep it from Sam. It would have tipped the balance of their friendship in a way that would have nagged at her. Since reading the interview with Arthur McDougall, she'd understood why Sam had let her read Dad's file against Roberta's wishes. She also remembered how she'd felt when she'd discovered the Fellowship knew a whole bunch of stuff about Dad that she didn't. "I should have known better, but I was curious. I didn't want to keep it from you. It would have been unfair for me to know, but not you."

Her heart sank at Sam's silence and taut face. "Do you want to know what he said?" she asked, not wanting to force Sam to ask.

"Well, yeah, of course I'd like to know what he said." Sam's voice was level, but Jillian could sense her anger. "I don't know if I should hear it."

"You should hear it, or you'll keep thinking about it. And that's my fault. I shouldn't have read it, but the genie is out of the bottle now."

Sam took a deep breath and slowly exhaled, but she didn't ask. Maybe she thought that asking would displease God or show a lack of dedication to the Fellowship, that she shouldn't want to know. She was wrong. It would only eat at her. "You told me you were taking religious studies, and you didn't know what you were going to do with the degree, but you knew you wanted to serve God," she said, deciding to relieve Sam of the decision she was struggling with.

"You didn't mention that you'd be taking over the business from your father when he retired."

Sam's brows shot up and her mouth hung open. Jillian had never seen her look so shocked. "You weren't going to take over from him," she said slowly.

"No. Did he say that?"

"Yeah."

Sam's shoulders slumped. She clasped her hands on her lap. "That's disappointing," she said, her knuckles turning white. "I thought he'd accepted it. He was disappointed, but I thought he'd accepted it." She sounded bewildered.

"He was probably hoping you'd change your mind. I'm sure everyone's parents smile and nod at times, while they're secretly hoping it'll be a phase."

"A phase." Sam shook her head sadly. "See, this is why you don't dredge things up from the past. Because there's nothing you can do about it. I can't talk to him now." She bolted from the bench and whirled to Jillian. "I've lived all these years thinking he'd accepted it. That's what he wanted me to believe."

"He could have just answered that way because it was easy. If he'd said that you were planning to dedicate your life to God in some way instead of following in his footsteps, the interviewer may have asked him questions that he was afraid he wouldn't be able to answer, because those answers died with you."

"Or maybe he honestly thought I'd change my mind, even though I told him over and over again that I wouldn't." Sam turned and gazed at the fountain.

"He took three months off after you died. That's how hard it hit him."

Sam didn't move.

"He said his faith got him through. He said your mother was particularly comforted by the thought that you're with God."

"My mother knew me," Sam said, so softly that Jillian had to lean forward to catch what she said. "My father didn't know me. Not really. I love and respect him, but we're very different. He wouldn't have wanted me taking over his company. When it came to investing, all he cared about was whether he'd make money. He didn't worry too much about what the company was all about. He'd say, 'Jesus said to give to Caesar what's Caesar's, and give to God what's God's.' So the economy, money, fell under Caesar's purview. If he invested in a company that used sweat shops to manufacture its goods, or that encouraged children to develop a bad habit, it was only business. I couldn't have done that. But I benefitted from it." She turned back to Jillian. "It's what put food on the table and a roof over my head."

"Don't beat yourself up for that," Jillian said, relieved to see that Sam's eyes were dry. She would have hugged her and probably made things worse. "You would have changed that. All kids are dependent on their parents until they leave the nest." And Sam had made up for it a hundredfold since then. Why was it that the people who flagellated themselves the most usually had the least to beat themselves up over? "You've spent the last twenty years serving God in the best way that you can."

Sam nodded, but Jillian doubted she'd let herself off the hook that easily. "I take it that your parents were always religious."

Sam nodded again.

"Did they know you were gay?"

"No. I didn't accept it myself until I was in the Fellowship. I suspected, but I was still hoping that maybe I wasn't."

Jillian stared at her. Had Sam been involved with someone after she'd joined the Fellowship? She wouldn't get involved with an outsider. There would be no future in it, and she'd have to constantly lie to them. So was it a Fellowship member? Who? "What made you accept it?"

"One day I admitted to myself that only women would ever interest me in that way. Until then, I'd told myself that I just hadn't met any men I'd want to date. You know what we tell ourselves until we're finally honest about it."

Yeah, she did, but Jillian was still dying to know whether Sam had dated someone in the Fellowship. Her stomach knotted. She forced out the question. "Did you finally accept it because you were involved with someone?"

Sam frowned down at her. "How could I have been involved with anyone? I'm a Deiform."

Jillian let out her pent breath, but dismay mingled with relief. In a flash of insight, she understood why the prospect of Sam having been in a relationship with a Fellowship member had frightened her. It would have meant that she could no longer tell herself the lie that Sam would never get involved with her because she was dedicated to the Fellowship, and not because she simply wasn't interested, though Jillian wasn't sure if the latter was still true. But at least she could use the lie when she needed it, and she wouldn't have to ever see Sam involved with someone else. She couldn't take that. At the same time, her fantasy of them being together was fantasy, fantasy, fantasy. Right? For Sam, God came first. Everything and everyone else was a distant second.

"You just know who you're attracted to," Sam said. "For me, it's not men." She dropped back onto the bench. "It's funny how when you get older and you understand life a little more and become your own person, you wonder how you came from your parents, or in my case, my father. Do you ever wonder about that?"

Jillian would forgive her the change of subject; she'd stood too close to the edge. She raised her hand and wiggled her fingers. "Hello? My father. Yours pales in comparison. He obeys the law."

"What about your mother?"

"We didn't have a close relationship. I'd like to say I would have liked to be closer to her, but I don't know. I never tried. If that's what I wanted, why didn't I try?" She didn't expect Sam to answer. How could Sam tell her why when she herself had no clue? "I respect my mother. I love her. But I blamed a lot of stuff on her. We both should have tried to let things go and move on together, rather than trying to be so damn stubborn and strong." They were the same in that regard. If one of them had been weak, if one of them hadn't tried to pretend, to appear as if everything was okay, would things have been different, or would the other one have looked down her nose in disdain? "I should have talked to her. We should have supported each other. But we shut each other out."

Jillian had shut everyone out. She couldn't trust. She couldn't allow herself to be vulnerable. How many times had Dad said 'I love you'? How many times had Dad said 'I care about you'? How many times had Dad told her that he was proud of her? Hundreds, no, thousands, of times. She'd believed him. But all those words had been just that: words. Everything he'd said had turned out to be bullshit. He hadn't cared. Every word out of his mouth had been a lie. Jillian had vowed to never let anyone pull a fast one on her again. Trust? Ha!

Sam was an exception. Somehow she'd slipped through Jillian's defences without trying or wanting to. "I gave up on having any type of meaningful relationship with her, and now we'll never bridge the gap. We can never fix it, never have the conversation we should have had a long time ago."

Sam nodded. "Sometimes it's what you didn't say, and sometimes it's what you did say."

They grew silent. Jillian knew Sam regretted not saying a proper good-bye to her family. "Thanks for letting me go home for those few days. I know you had to convince Roberta and she wasn't happy about it. Things would feel a lot worse right now if I hadn't had the chance to say good-bye to her and Danny."

"I'm glad you benefitted from my mistake." Sam stared at Jillian. "Don't leave important things unsaid. You never know if you'll have another chance to say them. Especially in the Fellowship. People do die."

Jillian's throat tightened. She used to tell herself that she didn't need anyone else, but that had been a lie, a lie that had deprived her of too much for too long. She could feel now. Hell, she was in love. Unrequited love ached relentlessly, but she was grateful for it. She'd rather be in pain than feel nothing.

Chapter Nine

J ILLIAN PULLED INTO the school parking lot and got out of the car. This was the third school on her list for today. She'd started with the one where Sister Catherine had last taught, but she hadn't had any luck. Nobody at the first two schools had recognized the boy in the picture, and sifting through class photos hadn't turned him up, either. If they couldn't figure out who he was, they'd be back to having nothing to investigate. Yesterday Sam had called Ellen, Sister Catherine's former friend and neighbour, and the one who'd cheated with her husband. Beforehand, she'd sent Ellen the photo of the boy. Ellen didn't know who he was and had offered terse answers to Sam's other questions.

Jillian strode up the path to the school's main entrance and pressed the door buzzer. Man, times had changed. These days, schools were like fortresses. She sounded like an old fogey, but she preferred the good old days when kids had walked or biked to school by themselves and hadn't worried about being sexually assaulted in the bathroom or a gunman blowing them all away. She and her classmates hadn't spent all day inside a locked building, protected from the big bad world. It was a wonder kids didn't grow up terrified to leave their homes.

"Yes?" a voice crackled from the intercom.

She looked directly into the security camera. "Hi, I'm Jillian Wright. I spoke to someone on the phone about coming in and taking a look at class photos."

The voice lifted. "That was me. When you come inside, turn left. The office will be the first door on your right."

The door buzzed. Jillian pulled it open and followed the directions. A smiling woman came to the counter and stuck out her hand. "I'm Marie Goodwin, the assistant principal. I spoke to you on the phone. You said you're doing some research about the murders."

"I might write a book about Sister Catherine," Jillian said, pumping Goodwin's hand. "She's the one who's confessed."

"I know. Imagine, a nun," Goodwin said breathlessly. "You can't trust anyone these days. The papers said she used to teach, but she didn't work here."

"I have a photo of a boy, but I don't know who he is. All I know is that he's somehow connected to Sister Catherine. So I'm going to the schools—"

"And looking at class photos. Makes sense." Goodwin unlatched the half-door attached to the counter and swung it open. "Come on through."

Jillian followed her into a small room containing a round table surrounded by four chairs.

"Can I see the photo?" Goodwin asked.

She pulled out her phone and swiped to the photo of the boy. Goodwin's brows drew together. "Do you know when it was taken?"

"1985, I think. I don't know how old he is. Ten or eleven, maybe?"

"He looks like he'd be in grade four or five. Mrs. Henshaw and Ms. Gibson were two of the teachers who taught those grades back then, and they're still with us. Do you want me to call them down?"

"That would be great!"

"I'll have to wait until recess. It's in twenty minutes."

"That's fine. I'll look at photos until then."

Goodwin pursed her lips. "I'll bring the ones for grades four to six, those that were taken from 1984 to 1986. Sit down. I'll be back in a tick." She bustled away. Jillian stared at the empty white wall in front of her.

Goodwin returned and set a pile of photos on the table. "Have you been to many schools?"

"Yours is the third." Sam was also out there looking at class photos, and must be on her second or third school by now.

"I'll leave you to it. Shout if you need anything."

Jillian pulled out a magnifying glass and lifted the top photo from the pile. *Grade 4, 1985.* Starting with the boys in the back row, she held the magnifying glass over each face, pausing longer over those boys whose hair and skin colour matched the boy in the photo. Nope, he wasn't in this grade four class. She struck out with the next photo as well, and was examining the third when a bell rang. The sound of excited voices filtered into the office area.

Goodwin peered into the room. "Any luck?"

Jillian shook her head.

"I'll go see if I can round up Mrs. Henshaw and Ms. Gibson."

By the time Goodwin returned with two women in tow, Jillian had finished with the third photo and was studying the fourth.

Goodwin gestured to the younger of the two teachers. "This is Mrs. Henshaw, and this is Ms. Gibson." She pointed over her shoulder. "I need to be out there right now. Show them the photo."

Yes, Ms. Goodwin. Jillian smiled to herself. Goodwin was clearly accustomed to telling children what to do. She handed the phone to the teacher standing the closest to her. Mrs. Henshaw scrutinized it, then grimaced. "No, sorry, I don't know who this is." She gave the phone to Ms. Gibson and slipped from the room.

The second teacher looked down at the phone and sucked in her breath. "It's Michael Atkins."

Jillian straightened in her chair. "You know him."

Gibson nodded and clucked her tongue. "Terrible business."

"What do you mean?"

Gibson lifted her head. "You really don't know?"

"No."

"He killed himself," she said, handing Jillian back the phone. "His mother found him hanging in his bedroom closet." She shook her head again. "It was awful. He was a few years older than he is in that picture. Fifteen, I think." She smoothed the back of her skirt and sat in the chair opposite Jillian. "He didn't go to school here. I knew the family, in passing. We lived on the same block."

"Do you know why he committed suicide?"

"No. The media was respectful for once. One of my friends knew a cop who worked the case. He said that Michael didn't leave a note or anything, but I don't know if that's true. I do know it came as a complete shock to his parents. They were devastated. He was an only child. They moved away not long after that. Who'd want to live in the house where your son hung himself?" Gibson drew a shaky breath.

"Do you know where they moved to?"

"Hawksville, I think." Gibson's eyes went to the phone Jillian had set on the table. "I heard they split up. Suicide shatters families. The guilt, the grief . . ."

Tell me about it. "What school did Michael go to?"

"St. Jude's. Well, that's where he was when the photo was taken. He was in high school when he died. Notre Dame High School."

"Do you know if the family knew Sister Catherine?"

Gibson's gaze sharpened. "Right, you're doing a book on her. I don't know. I never saw her with them. But then, I didn't know her. I've only seen her picture in the paper."

"Thank you. You've solved a mystery for me."

"Glad I could help." Gibson pushed her chair back. When she reached the doorway, she turned around and frowned. "You're not going to bother his parents, are you? They've been through enough."

Jillian hoped they wouldn't have to track them down and force them to relive the horror yet again. "I'm going to visit St. Jude's and Notre Dame to see if I can find out who Michael's friends were."

"Sounds like a plan. Good luck with it."

The moment Gibson stepped from the room, Jillian tidied up the pile of photos. She'd leave them on the table for Goodwin to collect and say good-bye to her on the way out.

In the parking lot, she called Sam and got her voice mail. Sam must be poring over photos, and at the wrong school. Jillian had St. Jude's and Notre Dame on her list. "Hey, it's me. I got him. Michael Atkins. He went to St. Jude's and Notre Dame High School. I'm heading to St. Jude's now, to see if he had any best friends and if the teachers there know anything. Why don't you take Notre Dame?" She paused. "He committed suicide when he was fifteen, so I'm sure a few people there will remember him vividly."

Jillian drove to St. Jude's, excited that they'd finally identified the boy in the photo, but dreading the conversations with teachers and staff who may have known him. She wasn't looking forward to seeing the same bewilderment in their eyes as she'd seen on so many faces after Dad's suicide.

* * * * *

Two DAYS LATER, Jillian strode up the path to a typical single-family home in the burbs and rang the doorbell. A dog barked inside the house. A twenty-something woman opened the door. "Jillian Wright," Jillian said loudly, hoping the woman could hear her over the dog.

"Come on in. I'm Tara." She whirled. "Settle down, Lincoln!" The mutt behind her gave one final squeaky bark, then wagged his tail. "Don't worry about him. He's harmless, but he'll bark at you again when you go into the living room. I don't know why he does that. Looking out for us, I guess." She gave Jillian a sheepish smile.

Jillian smiled back at her and stepped into the house. She looked at Lincoln. *"Friend, Lincoln. Quiet."*

Tara led her into the living room. "Sit down." When Lincoln silently padded into the room and sat wagging his tail, she raised her brows. "Huh. He usually only does that after he's barked up another storm. Do you want tea or coffee? Kyle called. He's in traffic. He should be home in five or ten minutes."

"Tea would be nice, please."

"I'll be back in a sec."

While Tara was in the kitchen, Jillian surveyed the bright and cozy living room. Sam was sitting in another living room right now, talking to Drew, one of Michael's closest friends. Kyle had been his other best buddy at the time he'd ended his life. The staff at St. Jude's and Notre Dame hadn't offered any new information that provided insight into why Michael had killed himself, or how he was connected to Sister Catherine. Nobody had seen his suicide coming. His high school teacher had told Sam that he'd always been a quiet boy, albeit one who occasionally cut class and usually got *Cs* and *Ds* on his report card. But there hadn't been any warning signs, even with 20/20 hindsight. Why the hell had Sister Catherine hidden a photo of him in her convent cell?

Tara returned with the tea. They made polite conversation until Kyle came home and dropped onto the sofa. He loosened his tie. "I was surprised when you called me about Mike. Not because I'd forgotten about him, though. I still think about him every day."

Jillian could hear the shock that must have jolted through him when he'd received the news back then. Lincoln jumped onto the sofa, lay down, and rested his head in Kyle's lap. Maybe he could sense his master's distress.

"You mentioned that nun, the one that confessed to those killings," Kyle continued. "I have no idea who she is or what she might have to do with Mike. I've thought about it, and I can't remember ever seeing any of my friends with her."

"You and Mike were best friends?" Jillian said, quashing her disappointment. She should never expect it to be easy.

"Yeah, we hung out together."

"What was he like?"

Kyle absently stroked Lincoln's head. "He was fun to be with, once you got to know him. He wouldn't say boo around authority figures and those he didn't know, but he wasn't shy when he felt comfortable with someone." He smiled as the memories rushed back. "He was a typical kid, a bit of a joker. He loved skateboarding, he collected comics. He tried smoking in the park behind the school. Didn't like it, though. Everything seemed to be going okay. When I heard . . . I didn't understand it."

"There was nothing different about him? Nothing at all?"

He hesitated. "The only weird thing was that he suddenly had money to throw around. He said his parents had raised his allowance, but unless they were giving him a hundred bucks a week, that couldn't have been it, and I doubt they were. The Atkins were a typical middle-class family."

"So where do you think he got the money?"

"At the time, I thought maybe he was dealing drugs or something. You know how it is when you're that age. Your imagination runs away with you. It's always something big. But he couldn't have been. I mean, he would have been on drugs, too, right? I'm sure I would have seen that."

So where had he been getting the money, and why did one of his best friends have no clue? At that age, best friends told each other everything, and in graphic detail, or so she understood. She'd had a couple of friends in high school, but she'd also been wrestling with her sexuality. She hadn't shared all her secrets with anyone. She'd also been a good girl. No naughty details to breathlessly recount, no smoking behind the school. Unless she'd embellished or made stuff up, she would have bored a best friend to death. "I understand he cut class."

Kyle nodded. "I didn't. I wanted to get into college."

"And Mike didn't?"

"He talked about it until he started to hang out with Brandon."

"Brandon?"

"Yeah, his new best friend," Kyle said, sounding bitter.

"Nobody at the school mentioned Brandon."

"That's because Brandon didn't go to Notre Dame. He was older, too. Seventeen, maybe? I think he went to East Brook High, but I could be wrong."

Jillian tapped the information into her phone.

"To be honest, we'd kind of started to drift apart. We still hung out, but those two were getting closer and I was starting to feel squeezed out. I felt guilty about that . . . feeling mad at him for drifting. And I've always wondered . . . if we'd stayed as close as we used to be, maybe I would have seen something, or he would have told me something that would have tipped me off that he was going to kill himself. Maybe I could have stopped it."

"I doubt it would have made a difference," Jillian said, feeling like a hypocrite. How many times had she blamed herself and wondered if she could have stopped Dad? "His teachers didn't notice anything. Neither did his parents."

"Still."

Yeah, still.

"I guess I'd gravitated toward the good crowd, and Mike had joined a cool, older crowd."

"What about Drew?" Jillian asked, wondering if Sam was listening to a similar story.

"We stuck together. I can see why the teachers told you about us two. We hung out with Mike when we were at school. After school, Mike preferred to spend time with his new buddies. He was cutting school more and more, though. Drew and I told him he was going to fail if he didn't stop."

Was Brandon also cutting classes? If he and Mike and who knows who else were meeting up, what were they doing? "Did Brandon also have money to throw around?"

Kyle shrugged. "I don't know."

"Do you know Brandon's last name?"

"Yeah, and you might have seen it, too."

Jillian gave him a curious look. "Why?"

"Brandon MacIntosh, realtor. You might have seen his name on a for sale sign."

If she had, it hadn't registered.

"I think we have his card somewhere," Tara said, piping up for the first time.

"Did you know Mike?" Jillian asked her, even though Tara would have been a toddler around the time Michael had killed himself, assuming Jillian had guessed her age correctly.

Tara shook her head. "I only moved here a few years ago." Tara smiled at Kyle. "We met online."

"Oh. That's interesting."

"What is it, hun, about twenty percent of couples meet online now, or is it twenty percent of couples who get married met online?"

Kyle shrugged again. "I'm not sure."

"How did Mike get along with his parents?" Jillian asked, wanting to get the conversation back on track.

"Okay, I guess," Kyle said. "They weren't thrilled with him cutting class. They wanted him to do better at school. He didn't kill himself because of them, though. They weren't horrible to him."

Jillian didn't have anything more to ask. The conversation hadn't uncovered Michael's connection to Sister Catherine, but she had another lead. "Thanks for your time." She handed Kyle a business card. "Call me if you remember anything else."

At the door, Tara told her to wait while she looked for Brandon's card. "He's one of the top-selling agents, I think," she said when she handed it to Jillian.

"He didn't go to college, but he ended up doing all right for himself," Kyle added.

"Thanks." Jillian slipped the card into her pocket.

In the car, she called Sam. "I just finished talking to Kyle. Nothing about Sister Catherine, but I have the name of another guy we should talk to. Michael's newest best friend, apparently. Brandon MacIntosh. He's a real estate agent."

Sam chuckled.

"What?"

"I'm looking at a sign with his name on it right now."

"That's not all I found out," Jillian said. "Michael had money to throw around when he died."

"You did better than I did. Drew wasn't as willing to talk."

"He was cagey?"

"More like protective of Michael's memory," Sam drawled. "Call Jeremy and tell him to look into MacIntosh. I'll call MacIntosh's office and set up an appointment."

"Do you need his number?"

Sam chuckled again. "No. I'm looking right at it."

Chapter Ten

JILLIAN UNBUCKLED HER seatbelt and gazed out the window at the bungalow with the for sale sign out front. Figuring that the quickest way to see Brandon would be to express interest in buying a house, Sam had set up an appointment to view the one she'd been outside when Jillian had called her the previous day. Jeremy had dug into Brandon's background and discovered a minor charge for marijuana possession. He hadn't found a connection to Sister Catherine.

A sedan pulled into the bungalow's driveway. Brandon jumped out and immediately pulled out his phone.

"We're on," Jillian said.

The sound of the car doors closing alerted Brandon to their presence. He shoved his phone into his blazer pocket and strode up to them. "You must be the Wright sisters." He stuck out his hand. As Jillian shook it, he said, "Let me guess. You're in the airline industry." He chuckled at his quip. Sam rewarded him with a small smile right away. By the time Jillian got it, the moment had passed.

"Sorry, you must get that all the time." Brandon swept his arm toward the bungalow. "So, you're interested in this home. Did you take a look at the listing I sent you?"

"Actually, we're not here to look at the bungalow," Sam said.

Brandon's brow furrowed. "I don't understand."

Sam offered him a business card. "We're private investigators. We're looking into the triple murder case on behalf of Sister Catherine's defence team."

"I still don't understand," Brandon said, studying the card.

Jillian shifted her weight. "Our investigation led to a boy named Michael Atkins."

Brandon's head shot up. "Mike?"

"Yes, we—"

He thrust the card back at Sam. "I'm sorry, but I don't appreciate you wasting my time like this. Unless you're interested in buying or selling a house, don't contact me again." He marched back to his car.

"Wait!" Sam hurried after him.

Jillian planted herself right behind Brandon's car. He'd have to run her over to leave. She prepared to time shift, just in case.

"All we want to know is whether Michael knew Sister Catherine," Sam said.

Brandon got into the car and slammed the door shut. He fired up the engine and blew the horn, making Jillian jump. Nope, she wasn't moving.

Sam knocked on the driver-side window. "Just one question," she shouted.

The window whirred. Brandon leaned toward it. Jillian strained to listen. "Even if I wanted to talk to you about Mike, I can't," he said. "So tell her to get out of my way, or I'll call the police."

"Did Mike know Sister Catherine?" Sam said. "Do you know why Mike committed suicide?"

Brandon lifted his phone and waved it in Sam's face. "Five seconds, and I'm calling 911."

Sam glared at him, then backed off. She motioned for Jillian to let him go. They watched Brandon back out of the driveway and floor it, tires screeching. The smell of burned rubber filled Jillian's nose. She coughed, then walked over to Sam. "That was a total loss."

Sam was staring down the street, in the direction in which Brandon had raced away. "Maybe not. Did you notice that he said, 'I can't talk to you'?"

"Do you think he's worried about his safety? Maybe someone's threatened to break his legs if he talks."

"Or perhaps an order from the court?"

"Sealed court documents, which could mean—"

"A settlement," Sam finished for her. "Or you could be right and he's afraid to talk."

"Could he know the murderer, then, if it's not Sister Catherine?"

"He knows something. The question is, what? Come on."

They returned to their car. Sam pulled out her phone. "Hey," she said a moment later. Jillian gazed out the passenger-side window and listened. "Can you check into Brandon again, this time looking for any signs of a settlement? It might have happened when he was a minor, so check his parents, too. If you find anything, see if you can get the case file." Sam paused. "Yeah, thanks." She hung up. "He'll let us know."

Jillian turned to her. "I guess we'll have to wait for him, then." She jutted her chin toward the windshield. "This street reminds me of my mom's. Similar houses."

Sam's phone rang. "It's for Sam Wright," she said. "Hello." Silence, then, "I guess that wasn't completely unexpected. Have they set a trial date?" Another pause. "Not much. I'm following a lead, but frankly I don't know whether it has anything to do with Sister Catherine. It's related to the photo I showed her. I'll let you know if I find out anything that can help . . . I know, I don't understand it, either. You've tried talking her out of it?" She frowned. "I'll keep digging. Bye."

"That was Greenwood," Sam said, shoving her phone back into her pocket. "Sister Catherine has been declared fit to stand trial. They've set a date. We have three weeks. Otherwise she's going to stand up on the first day of the trial and plead guilty."

Jillian groaned. "Then again, she could be guilty, right? We haven't found anything to suggest that she's innocent."

"True, but we have unanswered questions now."

"Well, we don't have to stop looking when she's convicted," Jillian pointed out. "We can still bring anything that proves she didn't do it to the attention of the authorities. But we might not find anything. And don't forget, if she didn't commit the murders, she's protecting the person who did. She's protecting a brutal killer."

"She must have a very good reason," Sam said. "Let's find out what it is."

"You sound like you believe she's innocent, of committing the murders, at least."

"I'm still keeping an open mind. If she is protecting someone, I want all the facts before I judge her."

Jillian bit her tongue. A Christian who wasn't leaping to judgement. What next? World peace?

* * * * *

SAM STOPPED KNITTING for a second to glance at her watch. She still had ten minutes before she had to meet Jillian in the lobby. She might finish the arm for Roberta's sweater before then. Tired of the hotel restaurant, she was looking forward to going somewhere else for dinner. They'd probably try the family restaurant they'd seen a few blocks away.

Her phone rang. The arm would have to wait. "Yeah."

"We can't find Brandon's name in any court files," Roberta said. "The file is buried deep, or he accepted a private settlement to stay out of it, not one reached through lawyers."

"Police files?"

"Nothing there, either, except his own juvenile record."

Sam grunted. "We searched online, looked at what's there for the local paper. We didn't find him, either. Since you didn't come up with anything, we're going to go to the newspaper's office and see if any reporters working around the time Michael died can give us information that didn't make it into print."

"That's a good idea."

Sam waited for Roberta to say more, then said, "So why are you really calling? Jeremy or Emma could have called me."

"I wanted to know how Jillian is."

"Why?"

"Did she finally read your file, or did you tell her more about yourself?"

Sam's surprise quickly died. The Fellowship would be monitoring searches related to its members, especially its dead ones. "I told her my last name and what my father does for a living. I know she searched for me. I know she read the interview with him."

Roberta's voice sharpened. "Did she tell you, or were you with her?"

"She told me," Sam said, bristling. "She knows she shouldn't be looking us up online. I'm pretty sure she won't do it again."

"But you discussed the interview."

"Not at length. She told me what he said about my death, that's all." Sam had bounced between wishing she didn't know, and being grateful that she did. She'd believed a lie for the past twenty years. Now she knew the truth, even though it hurt. The worst part was that she couldn't talk to him, couldn't pick up the phone and say, "Hey, Dad, you were wrong, it wasn't a phase. I was never going to take over the company. That's not how I wanted to spend my life." Maybe he'd been saving face when answering the question. Would it have been that terrible to admit that his daughter would rather serve God than make oodles of money? He'd said his faith had comforted him, but he'd always relegated God to Sundays and charity fund-raisers. It sounded like his three-month sabbatical hadn't changed anything. "She didn't tell me anything I didn't already know," she said to Roberta.

"You should have let me know."

"Why? I'm not her babysitter. Why are you talking to me about this? You should be talking to her."

"I thought you could talk to her about it."

"We've already talked. She won't do it again. It was partly my fault, anyway."

"Why?"

"Because she's very curious and I never tell her anything." When Sam had told her about her father, Jillian hadn't badgered her with tons of questions about her family's life, or teased her about being born with a silver spoon in her mouth, but she would. She would.

"She can read your file."

"She wants me to tell her." And maybe Jillian had a point. Sam's file was factually correct, but facts were open to interpretation. "Look, I'm taking your advice. I'm answering her questions about my life. She shouldn't have gone online and looked me up. She knows that. Leave it be."

"All right," Roberta said mildly. "Let me know if you find out anything at the newspaper office."

"I will."

They disconnected. Sam shook her head. Roberta had forced them together. Then she'd been pleased because they'd received the joint gifts. Then she'd suggested that Sam open up about her past life. Now she was upset because Sam had followed her advice. Good advice, as it had turned out. The joint gifts had tied her and Jillian together. The only path had been acceptance. Anything else would have been wishing for a life she couldn't have. Sam had already travelled that route and learned that it led to a dead end.

So she was trying, trying to be more forthcoming about herself, learning how to be a friend again. Letting someone in, having someone to worry about . . . it still frightened her, but she'd realized that she missed talking about regular stuff. Not Fellowship business, not faith and God, but regular stuff. It was one of those things that had disappeared from her life in such a way that she hadn't noticed it was gone and had forgotten what it was like.

Jillian had come into the Fellowship when she was thirty-six years old. She'd led a normal adult life. She expected to have conversations about regular stuff. There was nothing unusual about asking someone where they were from, what school they went to, whether they liked fries with that—or whether Sam's parents had known about her sexual orientation. That part of the conversation about the interview with her father had surprised Sam the most, not only Jillian's questions, but her willingness to answer them.

Jillian was the first lesbian she'd talked to about her sexuality. Sure, she'd come across lesbians over the years when working cases, but she'd never talked to them about herself. As she'd told Jillian, she hadn't been sure until after she'd joined the Fellowship. She'd noticed that the odd time someone turned her head, it was always a woman, and that she wasn't attracted to men. She'd had a few mild crushes, always on girls and then on women, but she'd never seriously considered acting on them. She'd been too afraid of how her parents would react if they found out, and she'd wanted to focus on her studies. Plus, she'd learned that when you had money, you never knew if someone liked you for you, or for the money. She'd worried that if she dated someone and they broke up, the ex would blackmail her. That was another good thing about Jillian. She hadn't known about the money. Her friendship, and her curiosity about Sam's life, had always been genuine.

Sam hadn't struggled to reconcile her sexual orientation with her Christianity. She'd never doubted that God loved her and had made her exactly the way she was, sexual orientation and all. When she'd admitted to herself that she was gay, she'd told Ruth and Roberta and everyone else on the island, but only because she didn't want to hide it from them. Nobody had judged her. Sam wasn't the first gay Deiform, but she was the only living one she'd known of—until Jillian had come along. If Sam was honest with herself, Jillian being a lesbian had made her wary of her. There was also her atheism, and the fact that she was older when she'd come in had intimidated Sam a bit. Getting to know her—being forced to spend time with her—had allowed a friendship to blossom. Sam could be honest with her. There was trust between them. It was kind of nice.

Chapter Eleven

Jillian felt like a football player dodging her way down the field as she strode through the newspaper's bustling lobby toward the reception desk. Unimaginatively called *The News*, the local rag had been in business for almost a century. She put on her best smile and leaned on the counter. The woman behind it said, "Can I help you?"

"Yes. My name is Jillian Wright. I'm hoping to speak to the reporter who covered court cases between 1988 and 1991. I'm writing a book," she added, voicing the reason she'd come to the newspaper office instead of Sam. They didn't want to tip the paper off about their real reason for hanging around Grayhurst, asking questions.

"I'm sorry, the reporter who worked during that time is no longer with the paper."

Jillian gave the woman a mildly skeptical look. Was the receptionist's memory so brilliant that she could recall the name and beat of every reporter who'd worked here?

"Would you like to look at our archives?" the receptionist asked. "Not all of the articles from that time period are available online."

She wouldn't know what to look for. If they were right and Brandon had received a payoff, there may never have been a court case, or any smoke to attract reporters. It would depend on whether the settlement had ended a case, or stopped it from going forward. "Can I have the reporter's name?"

The receptionist pushed her glasses up her nose and peered at Jillian. "Well, you can, dear, but I doubt she'll talk to you. She's a busy woman."

"What's her name?" Jillian asked, resisting the urge to reach over the counter, grab the woman's shoulders, and shake her.

"Marcy Abrams."

Shit.

"She got her start here, you know," the receptionist said. "Now she works for News World Five, but I'm sure you know that. She was here not too long ago, because of that crazy nun. Took me and a few others that were here back then out for lunch. She's never forgotten those who were kind to her when she was a nobody. Lovely woman, but busy. She doesn't have time for just anyone."

"Thank you," Jillian said, her smile tighter.

Outside, she called Sam. "You'll never guess who the court reporter was. Marcy Abrams. She started out here."

"Small world," Sam said.

"I can't talk to her. I know you think she won't remember me, and maybe she wouldn't if she saw me for five seconds on the street. But having a conversation with me—my photo was in the paper. I'd have a difficult time explaining why my first name is Jillian and I look exactly like the Jillian Campbell who was arrested and then released for a double murder she covered, the Jillian Campbell who's now dead." She wouldn't want to have to talk her way out of that one. Abrams wouldn't just accept whatever Jillian told her. She was a reporter. She'd probe further, perhaps look into the police report about the accident that had killed Jillian Campbell.

Sam chuckled. "I still think she won't twig, but let's not push it. I'll try to set something up with her."

"Use another name."

"Yeah, I'll call Jeremy, have him throw something together."

"The paper's receptionist knows her. According to her, Abrams is busy and my chances of talking with her are slim, but she could be exaggerating. She seems quite proud of her connection to her."

"I'll leave her a message she can't resist."

"Okay. You know, the receptionist mentioned looking at the archives. Apparently not all articles from back then are online. I think I'll go back in and take a look. Something might jump out at me, and I have nothing else to do."

"There's always Michael's family," Sam said.

"Yeah, but—"

"I know. I don't want to bother them unless we have to." Sam paused. "I'll get going on setting up something with Abrams. Talk to you later."

They disconnected. Jillian squared her shoulders and returned to the reception desk. The receptionist raised her brows.

"Hi again. I've decided I will look at the archives."

The woman nodded. "She doesn't have time for you, eh? I told you."

"The archives," Jillian said through clenched teeth.

"Third floor. But wait, you need to sign in and wear a visitor's badge." The receptionist plunked a clipboard onto the counter. Jillian picked up the pen attached to it with an elastic band and added her name and *9:48* to the visitors sign-in sheet.

At 11:52, she handed in her guest badge and signed out. "I'll be back after lunch," she said, hoping the receptionist couldn't hear her grumbling stomach. So far, combing through old newspapers hadn't yielded any new information, and the in-house search engine was crap. She'd only just started looking at articles for the year 1990, but her gut told her that she wouldn't find anything that would help the investigation. Someone had buried whatever had happened back then. It was up to her and Sam to dig it back up.

SAM STOPPED ON the sidewalk outside News World Five's head office and took a moment to drill her temporary identity into her head. Sam Rivers, author of true crime books—under a pseudonym, of course, one she hadn't revealed to Abrams's assistant. Under other circumstances, that probably would have meant no meeting, but she'd mentioned Michael's photo and its possible connection to Sister Catherine. As she'd suspected, Abrams couldn't resist the bait.

Jillian had returned to the hotel bleary-eyed after spending hours searching old newspapers. She hadn't come across anything useful. If Abrams didn't know anything or wasn't willing to share, they'd have no choice but to speak to Michael's parents. Sam would not look forward to those interviews.

As she walked to the elevators inside the building, she wondered what Jillian was doing. This time she'd remained in Grayhurst. Movie? Guitar? Book? Sam would ask her over dinner; she'd be back at the hotel by then.

She rode the elevator to the seventh floor. The receptionist smiled. "Can I help you?"

"I'm Sam Rivers. I'm here to see Marcy Abrams."

The woman squinted at her screen. "Take a seat, please."

Sam dropped into a chair and watched people boarding and leaving the elevators. She recognized a man who couldn't stand still while he watched the floor numbers above the elevators change. He looked exactly as he did when doing the science reports, minus the lab coat. She wanted to wave to him, but reminded herself that while he was familiar to her, she wasn't to him. TV acquaintances were one-way affairs.

She straightened when she saw Marcy Abrams striding toward her.

"Sam Rivers?" When Sam nodded and stood, Abrams stuck out her hand. "Marcy Abrams. Pleased to meet you."

They shook, then Sam followed Abrams into a cozy office with numerous awards adorning its walls. She motioned for Sam to sit at a round table and pulled out the chair opposite her. "You said you wanted to talk to me about the Sister Catherine case in Grayhurst," Abrams said, getting straight to business.

Sam pulled a business card from her pocket. "Yes. I'm writing a book about the case."

Abrams took the business card from her. She glanced at it, then tossed it on the table and lifted a brow. "My assistant told me you write under a pseudonym."

"Yes."

Abrams' mouth turned up at the corners. "Sam Wright, perhaps? A private investigator who writes true crime—or pretends to, any-way."

Sam blinked at Abrams, her mind racing. How did she know? *And what should I say?* Protesting would only make things worse. She forced a smile. "You got me. I didn't think you'd agree to meet with a private investigator. How did you know?"

"I grew up in Grayhurst and started my career there. I have a lot of connections back home. When you told me you were doing a book, I called the convent to see if you'd spoken to them yet, and I found out something interesting." Abrams leaned forward. "An author had interviewed everyone, but her name was Jillian Wright, which I found interesting, because my source at the prison had told me about a Sam Wright, a private investigator who's visited Sister Catherine a couple of times with her attorney. The thing is, you don't look anything like the description of the author that sniffed around the convent. You're a dead ringer for the PI, though."

"Uh, wow, maybe *you* should be a private investigator."

Abrams grinned. "I sort of am. I'm guessing Jillian Wright is a private investigator, too? Well, I'm not, actually. I found the Wright and Wright website. I understand the stock photography. You can't pretend to be others when your pictures are all over the company website. Are you sisters, or . . ."

"We're sisters." Jillian was right. They'd better keep her out of Abrams's sight. The woman was as sharp as a tack.

"Don't worry, I won't blow your sister's cover at the convent."

Abrams' assurance only increased Sam's apprehension that the reporter would get in her and Jillian's way. "Why not?"

"As I said, Grayhurst is home to me. My mother is still there. Two of my siblings are there. I used to go to the church next to the convent. I know a lot of people. Don't get me wrong, I don't know the sister well, but we've talked. Unless a switch flipped in her brain that turned her into a homicidal maniac, I don't think she did it." Abrams folded her arms. "According to the psychiatric evaluation, she's fit to stand trial."

Sam hid her surprise. The results of the psychiatric evaluation hadn't been released to the public yet.

"No switch flipped," Abrams continued. "So either she's guilty, or she's taking the fall for someone else. My money's on the second option. I volunteered to cover this case because I wanted to dig into it and find the truth. I'll be honest, I haven't found anything. So I won't blow your sister's cover. I'm hoping you'll find something. I won't even ask you to give me an exclusive."

"I appreciate that, Ms. Abrams."

"Call me Marcy."

"All right, Marcy. I'm glad I didn't come all the way here so you could see my face when you told me you'd figured me out."

Marcy's eyes danced. "No, you didn't. So now that I've had the satisfaction of seeing you squirm, how can I help?"

Sam brought up Michael's photo on her phone. "I'm here because I'm trying to figure out the connection between Sister Catherine and this boy." She handed her phone to Marcy. "His name is—"

"Michael Atkins. He committed suicide. I remember." Marcy stared at the photo, then shook her head. "I don't know of any connection. Sister Catherine used to be a teacher. I'm sure you know that."

"We've looked into that angle." Sam took her phone back. "We haven't found a direct connection, but someone named Brandon MacIntosh came up. He was one of Michael's friends around the time he died. We tried to talk to him, but he wouldn't tell us anything. He said he's not allowed, which made us think that maybe he signed a non-disclosure agreement as part of a settlement. But we can't find the court case. We don't know if there is one. You were the court reporter back then."

"So you're wondering if I might have heard anything off the record." Marcy leaned back in her chair and folded her arms. "Let me think. Around 1988, 1989?" Her eyes widened. "There was one rumour going around. I could never pin it down. Nobody wanted to talk specifics, but it had to do with sexual abuse and boys. And someone powerful, maybe a judge, or a politician. I had a great source in the prosecutor's office, but even he wouldn't talk. Probably afraid his career would take a nose-dive." She frowned in thought. "You know, I think he's retired. Maybe he'd be willing to talk now."

"What's his name?"

"No. Not you. I'll talk to him."

Sam wasn't thrilled with that idea. She didn't want their investigation to depend on what Marcy was willing to give them. "I'd rather do it."

Marcy shook her head. "I'm not giving you his name. Even if I did, he wouldn't talk to you. He doesn't know you."

But they could look around the man's house for old files and notes. "You think he'll be willing to talk to a journalist?"

"I won't talk to him and then report on what he says. I volunteered to cover this case. It's personal for me. I won't do anything that'll hurt the convent."

"Even if you can scoop all the other stations?"

Marcy was silent for a moment. "I wasn't going to tell you this, but I'm hoping we can work together to get to the bottom of this case. Sister Joan is my aunt. She's been a nun since before I was born. That's why as soon as I heard about Sister Catherine, I said I wanted to fly to Grayhurst."

"You've spoken to all the nuns about it, then?"

"Yes. They couldn't tell me anything."

It was interesting that Sister Lynn had come to Jillian about the photo . . . or maybe it wasn't surprising. She might have worried that confiding in Marcy would result in Michael's photo appearing on the six o'clock news. "We didn't find anything out, either."

"Why are you focusing on Michael Atkins, especially if you haven't found a connection to Sister Catherine?"

"Because someone we interviewed said something that suggested he might be important to her."

Marcy's eyes narrowed. "I suppose you won't tell me who the someone is."

"No."

"Fair enough. I understand the need to protect sources."

Sam pocketed her phone. "Getting back to the possibility of sexual abuse, you said you'd heard it was only boys. Was it one abuser, or a pedophile ring?"

"I don't know. There were only whispers. It was very hush-hush and could have been a juicy, but false, rumour. Let me talk to my guy."

"When will that happen?"

"I'll call him today, but unless he's willing to talk to me over the phone, the earliest I'll get anything is Friday." Marcy blew a stray hair away from her eyes. "I'm going back to Grayhurst on Friday. I'll be doing a few lead-up pieces to the trial. We can get together and compare notes."

"Sure," Sam said, not entirely comfortable with teaming up with a journalist, especially a sharp one who'd covered Jillian's case. But Sister Catherine's trial was fast approaching. She and Jillian couldn't afford to turn down help. "When you were in Grayhurst to cover Sister Catherine's arrest, did you hear anything that could shed some light on why she'd confess if she's innocent?"

"If I had, I would have given it to the police. Have you spoken to any of the detectives on the case?"

"No. They don't like private investigators poking around, trying to prove them wrong." A lie. The Fellowship preferred to keep the police out of it as much as possible. Jeremy and Emma could usually get access to police reports and files. "If they had anything to prove Sister Catherine's innocence, she'd be free."

Marcy snorted. "You think? Most prosecutors and cops don't want to see innocent people take the rap for crimes they didn't commit, but I've covered cases where evidence was suppressed or blatant leads ignored because someone was in a hurry to close a case."

Sam was aware of innocents who'd been found guilty. If she didn't have access to the police files for Sister Catherine's case, she would have contacted the police.

It was time to go. Marcy didn't know anything else. Sam didn't want to sit here and be grilled by a journalist. She pushed back her chair. "I'll let you get back to work. My number is on the card."

Marcy's eyes glinted. "Ah, so the number's real, then. Good to know." She beat Sam to the door and blocked her from leaving. "I said I wouldn't ask you for an exclusive, but I wouldn't turn one away."

Sam chuckled. "If your source comes through and his information helps us figure out Sister Catherine's real involvement with the murders, you'll be the first to know."

"Excellent." Marcy swung the door open. As Sam walked past her, Marcy patted her back. "You'll hear from me soon."

In the elevator on the way down to the lobby, Sam relaxed. Marcy was friendlier and more down to earth than she'd expected, and having a reporter helping them out could be fruitful, as long as they were careful to keep Jillian out of Marcy's sight. But she felt disappointed. She still had no idea how Sister Catherine and Michael were connected.

Chapter Twelve

Perched on the end of one of the beds in her room, Jillian chuckled when Sam told her that Marcy Abrams had figured her out. "So the woman has brains." She raised her finger. "But she didn't uncover who you really are. Now *that* would be a story."

"It's too bad you weren't with me," Sam said. "I'm sure we would have had an interesting telepathic conversation with each other."

"Yeah, too bad." She wanted to say that she'd never expected to hear Sam say that she wished her sidekick had tagged along. What a difference from when they'd first started working together, when Sam was counting the days until she could work alone again. Then the joint gifts had tied them together. Sam must have figured that fighting it would be a waste of energy. Or maybe . . . Jillian sipped the tea Sam had brought up from the hotel restaurant. She longed to say, "So, Sam, what exactly are we doing here? Are we working on a friendship, or something else?" She didn't know what was worse: living with the certainty that she'd be the last woman Sam would date, or ping-ponging between "I'm reading too much into it; she only wants to be friends" and "She's trying to tell me something."

Sam took a gulp of her own tea and set it on the desk. "Abrams is resourceful. Let's hope her source comes through."

Jillian nodded, then searched for something to say to fill the silence. Normally she didn't feel awkward sitting with Sam, but the part of her that hoped—believed—there was a chance for more was shouting down her rational side. "So your parents were religious," she blurted. "I mean, are religious. Well, I guess you don't know what's going on now, but . . ." Time to shut up before she devolved into a babbling moron.

Sam cocked her head. "Yeah, they were religious. My mother and Alex are—were—no, are involved in the church. My father is a Christian." She quirked a brow. "I have to talk about them in the present tense, otherwise it sounds like they're dead."

"Yeah, I know. It's weird."

"My father is a busy man. He always makes time for church, and I know he believes, but he's not as involved."

"A church on Sundays kind of guy?"

"Yeah."

Jillian knew the type. Dad had complained about the people who showed up week after week, but never had time to participate, to help out. Right up to when she'd tossed the church from her life, she'd made a point of doing more than putting in her obligatory hour every week. "At least he isn't a baptism, wedding, and funeral type of guy," she said. Dad had complained about them more, about those who didn't give a shit about religion or God, but wanted to marry in church or have their kid baptized. *Well, hey, Dad, at least they didn't rip off the church and bang vulnerable young women while their wives sat at home, you know?* She wished Danny was her biological father. Seriously.

"I think he's good at compartmentalizing his belief, though," Sam said.

"What do you mean?"

"I told you he invests in stuff he probably shouldn't."

Jillian leaned forward. "Like what?" she asked, even though Sam had provided some examples in a previous conversation.

"Casinos. Businesses that are probably tied to organized crime. Companies that use sweat shops. Other stuff I'm sure I don't know about." Sam gazed at Jillian. "I couldn't have taken over from him, even if investing interested me, which it doesn't. It never has."

"You fully intended to finish your studies and then find something to do that would serve God."

"Yeah." Sam's mouth turned up at the corners. "But it turned out that God took care of the problem for me, and here I am, right where I'm supposed to be. I was always destined to join the Fellowship. You told me that, remember?"

"I do," Jillian whispered, suddenly wanting to reach for Sam's hand. There had to be a way to find out if Sam would grasp her fingers or jerk her hand away. They were adults, right? Jillian should just ask. *Right, it should be that easy.* And she was Mary Poppins riding a freaking rainbow unicorn. Still, there had to be a way to gauge where Sam stood without confessing her feelings for her, because the uncertainty was driving her nuts. It was difficult to think about anything else. She had to know.

She drained her tea and tossed the empty cup into the wastebasket. "What do you think you'd do if the Fellowship suddenly went away?" she asked Sam.

"What?"

"What would you do if Roberta called and said, that's it, we're done."

Sam gave her an incredulous look. "It won't happen. The Fellowship has been around for thousands of years."

"Okay, but pretend that it ceased to exist. What would you do? Would you go home to your family? Would you complete your studies?" She took a deep breath. "Would we stay in touch?"

"It's not going to happen."

"Hypothetically speaking."

Sam's jaw set. "I don't see the point."

Jillian's frustration rose. "Just answer the question. Would we stay in touch and hang out, or would it be, nice working with you, Jillian, have a nice life?"

"I haven't thought about it. It's not going to happen."

The rational part of her withered. She had her answer. Sam hadn't thought about it. She didn't lie awake at night imagining what their life could be together if they weren't Deiforms. She didn't search Jillian's every word and gesture for hints that they had a connection beyond friendship. She didn't struggle not to gaze at Jillian when a love song came on the car radio. But Jillian's heart, the stubborn part of her that refused to give up, wanted to press on. It wanted to know beyond a shadow of a doubt. It wanted to bleed. "Just imagine that it does," she snapped.

"Why? It won't happen."

Jillian's ears rang. Her surroundings faded away. She shot up from the bed. "Can't you play along and answer the question like any normal human being would?" she shrieked. "It's always pulling teeth with you. You eventually open up, but after I've hounded you for months. You can't imagine anything, hypothetically, for five seconds? Seriously? All I'm asking you to do is imagine, for a freaking second, that the Fellowship went away and you actually had to make a decision for once in your life, but no, you're incapable of imagining yourself outside your freaking bubble. You've belonged to the Fellowship all your life and been told what to do, where to go, who to speak to. You're not capable of having a conversation with another human being that doesn't start with "yeah" and end with "okay, I'll do that."

Her vision cleared. The ringing in her ears stopped. Shocked silence took its place. She looked at Sam and winced. Sam's taut face, and the hurt in her eyes . . . Jillian wanted to crawl into a hole. *Congratulations. You've sabotaged the most important relationship you have.* And wounded the person she cared about the most. *What's wrong with me? Why am I never satisfied?* Why did she always have to destroy what she had? "I'm sorry," she whispered. "I'm really sorry. I didn't mean it, any of it."

"No, you're right," Sam mumbled, her shoulders stiff. "I can't—I'm no good at this friends thing. I should go. I—" Her voice caught. She stood and reached for her tea. Her hand bumped the cup; it fell over. Tea spilled onto the desk. "Shit. I'm sorry."

"Don't worry about it. I'll deal with it."

Sam absently nodded. "I'm sorry I disappointed you." She turned to leave.

Jillian grabbed her sleeve. "Don't go. I can't have you thinking that you're doing something wrong. It's not you. It's me." She was the one incapable of being friends, not Sam. Anger flared again, this time at herself. "Just listen to me for a minute. Please."

Sam didn't say anything, but she didn't move.

Jillian was stricken by how miserable Sam looked. She couldn't salvage what she'd just blown to smithereens, but she could make damn sure Sam knew it wasn't her fault. "What just happened . . . it had nothing to do with how good a friend you are. You're a great friend. I'm the one who's screwing up." She closed her eyes for a moment. *Shit. Shit, shit, shit!* What had happened to patience? "I—you—like I said, I'm the one who isn't doing it right. I value our friendship. I love that we're friends. I just behaved like an immature moron because I . . . I want more."

Surprise—or was it shock or anger?—flickered across Sam's face. "More in what way?" she asked levelly.

"Do I have to spell it out?"

"I want to make sure I understand what you're saying. I don't want to misinterpret."

Like she had? This conversation was already a train wreck, and it was about to get worse. "I have feelings for you. I want us to be more than friends."

"You mean you want us to be a couple?"

"Yeah, I want us to be a couple."

Sam's voice shot up an octave. "Why? Why would you want that? We're Deiforms. We have to focus on our work."

"I don't remember taking a vow of celibacy."

"Is that what it's about? Sex?"

"Give me a break. You know what I mean. What about Roberta and Brian? They're together."

Sam blew out an exasperated sigh. "They're not with each other all the time. They don't work together like we do."

Jillian wanted to retort that yes, nobody ever got together because they worked and spent time together, but what was the point of arguing with Sam? She already felt like crap. Their friendship was already ruined. Did she want Sam to hate her, too?

"Why can't you focus on your work?" Sam shouted. "Our priority has to be our work. We have the gifts. We're called to dedicate our lives to serving the Fellowship."

Bullshit. Roberta and Brian; and Jillian had spent time in the undercroft, reading about the Fellowship's history and other Deiforms. Sam knew damn-well that if they were to pair up, they wouldn't be the first Deiforms to do so. Far from it. She was hiding behind this bullshit about duty and obligation, rather than having the courage to twist the knife in Jillian's heart. Or maybe she was just being kind. Jillian would have trouble telling someone she wasn't interested, too, especially someone she worked with and had to see all the time. Still . . . "Are you telling me that God wants us to only work, work, work? What about life? Joy? Love? Do you really think God wants you to be that one-dimensional?"

Sam's eyes flashed. "No, Jillian. You do *not* get to go there."

"I suppose I *was* dreaming in Technicolor, thinking there was any possibility you'd get involved with an atheist."

"That's not fair."

No, it was bitchy. She wanted to take away all the ammunition from the part of her that would still hope, that would whisper in her ear that there was still a chance.

"You're a Deiform. You know that means something to me," Sam said.

It meant they would never be more than friends, assuming they managed to rebuild the trust she'd shattered.

Sam shook her head. "I should have trusted myself instead of listening to Roberta."

"Listening to Roberta? What do you mean?"

"She said I should open up more, tell you about my past." She swung her arms toward Jillian. "And look where it led."

Jillian felt as if she'd been slapped. She'd thought Sam had started to answer questions she'd previously rebuffed because she was interested. But no, she'd forced herself to share because Roberta had told her to. Her eyes welled with tears. To Sam, she was just an obligation. An inconvenient obligation. How could she have been so stupid? The fight went out of her. She sank onto the edge of the bed. "I've had feelings for you for a long time." Her voice quavered. "When you started opening up, I thought maybe you felt the same. I was obviously mistaken."

Sam stared at her. "How long?" she asked softly.

"I don't know. Not too long after we met."

Sam's eyes widened.

"I haven't said anything because contrary to what you probably believe now, our friendship is important to me. I hope . . . I hope we can put it back together at some point." She rubbed a tear from the corner of her eye.

Sam grabbed the tissue box on the desk and held it out to her.

Jillian took the box, snapped a tissue from it, and dabbed at her eyes. "Do you hate me?"

"No."

Jillian wanted to say, "Do you think I'm stupid? Because I do." She wanted to pour her heart out to Sam, tell her how terrible she felt, and how she wished one of the gifts could reverse time so she could keep her mouth shut. But Sam wasn't her confidante, and maybe not even a close friend. She was a co-worker. A freaking co-worker.

"I think we should focus on the case," Sam said.

Yep, message received. She nodded, not trusting herself to speak. An awkward silence stretched out.

"I should go," Sam said. "Will you be okay?"

The concern in Sam's voice—or was it pity—made it more difficult for Jillian to hold it together. "I'll be fine," she whispered. "I think it's best that you go."

"I'll see you tomorrow, then." Sam looked as if she were going to say more, but then she turned and left, closing the door quietly behind her.

Jillian stared at the wall between her and Sam's rooms, the wall that would separate them, the wall that would never come down. She crushed the tissue in her hand, then picked up the tissue box and flung it against the wall. She wasn't angry at Sam. The woman wasn't required to reciprocate her feelings. She was upset with herself for being so stupid, and selfish, and impatient.

Being quietly in love with someone was tough. Having them reject you was devastating. But her tears suddenly flowed for a different reason. They flowed because she was drowning in an endless sea, because a little voice whispered to her, "Sam didn't actually say she doesn't feel the same way." Her love wasn't going to die. She would never be free.

Chapter Thirteen

Sam disconnected from her conversation with Emma and turned to the book she'd put aside when the phone had rung. She didn't pick the book up. Reading was difficult tonight; she was reaching the end of too many paragraphs without absorbing anything. She couldn't stop agonizing over whether to call Jillian or knock on her door, to see if she was all right. They hadn't eaten supper together. Sam had figured Jillian needed space, and what would they talk about?

What a mess. She should have kept her distance, but how? They'd work together until one of them died or they retired to the island in twenty or thirty years. They were bound together more tightly than married couples were. They couldn't discuss the weather forever. They couldn't not care about each other. But there was caring, and then there was *caring*.

She'd had no idea. It had never crossed her mind that Jillian cared about her in that way. It certainly hadn't sounded as if Jillian cared when she'd flown off the handle. Her words had stung. If she'd meant to hit Sam where she was vulnerable, she'd succeeded.

Sam didn't need anyone to tell her that she wasn't good around people, and that she'd been told what to do for her entire adult life—for the most part. She made plenty of decisions when she was on an investigation, but what to investigate and where she'd live for a while was up to Roberta. But what about everyone who worked a regular job? They were hardly masters of their own destiny. Still, Sam used to wonder how her life would have turned out if she hadn't entered the Fellowship, and Jillian had known that and used it. If her subsequent confession hadn't taken Sam completely by surprise and cast Jillian's outburst in a new light, she'd be furious with her.

After the shock had worn off, she'd gone over their conversation and admitted that she hadn't been completely honest. She'd made it sound as if the only reason she'd started to tell Jillian about herself and her family was because Roberta had told her to, which wasn't true. Roberta had given her the nudge she'd needed to do what she wanted to do, and it had been an intimidating step, something Jillian didn't appreciate. Sam was torn between leaving things as they were, and telling Jillian that she'd wanted to share more with her, that Roberta hadn't made her do it. She was torn between wanting to make sure Jillian was okay, and not wanting to show too much concern. She wanted Jillian to know that she cared, but she was worried that doing so would encourage Jillian's desire for more.

From this point forward, she'd walk a fine line, and she hated that. She'd just rediscovered the joy and value in having a trusted friend, only to have it snatched away, ironically because the friend cared too much. Now things would be tense and awkward; every word would have to be measured before it was spoken. Would they ever return to normal, whatever that was for them?

Sam didn't think so, but she didn't want to lose their friendship. She already missed Jillian, missed being able to call her and suggest they go get an ice cream. She'd miss verbally sparring when Jillian had deliberately said something provocative, miss her cynical rants, miss the comfortable silence in the car. *What would you do if the Fellowship went away? Would we stay in touch?* She understood now why Jillian had asked. Why hadn't she responded by saying, "Yes, I hope so"? Why had she stubbornly refused to answer?

Because the words that had immediately sprung to mind had scared her. They'd shattered the story she'd been telling herself: that the joint gifts forced her and Jillian to work together, and if they somehow went away, she and Jillian would go their separate ways. Sam would return to working alone, which she wanted, and she wouldn't miss Jillian much. Jillian would become like Brian and Warren, someone she occasionally crossed paths with on the island, someone she worked with once in a blue moon. She'd told herself that story over and over again, first when training Jillian had bound them together, and then when the joint gifts had. They'd become friends, but friends didn't practically live together, and going long periods without seeing a friend wasn't usually difficult.

Then Jillian had essentially asked, "If we weren't bound together, would you want to be in my life and have me in yours?" Sam had realized, in that instant, that somewhere along the line, the story had become a lie. But she couldn't voice the truth, because then it would be real, and out there, and she didn't know what it meant. What did it mean that she wanted Jillian around? What did it mean that she couldn't read tonight because she was upset, not because of Jillian's confession, per se, but because it had driven a wedge between them? The same fear that had stopped her from answering Jillian's questions kept her from answering her own. She didn't want to go there, and she didn't want to talk to Him about it.

What were the facts? They were bound by the joint gifts. They had to work together, so they had to be mature and professional and get past this. One of them had to take the first step. Sam wanted to know if Jillian was okay. She could project into her room, but because of the joint gifts, Jillian would sense her, and Sam didn't want to invade her privacy. Things were already bad enough between them. If she wanted to know how Jillian was doing, she'd have to ask.

She lifted her phone from the night stand. Jillian answered on the third ring. "Hey," Sam said. "I just wanted to see how you are."

"I'm fine," Jillian said.

Sam winced at the lack of vigour in Jillian's voice. "We have to discuss our next move. Will you be up for breakfast tomorrow around the usual time?"

Silence, then, "Sure. I'll probably look like hell, but whatever. See you tomorrow?"

Sam hesitated. She wanted to say it didn't matter what Jillian looked like, but would Jillian take that to mean she didn't care about her, or she cared a lot about her, or . . . ? "Yeah, see you tomorrow."

She disconnected with a sigh and picked up her book, determined to concentrate and read the next chapter. But she quickly put it down again and flicked on the TV, hoping it would take her mind off the woman in the next room.

* * * * *

JILLIAN CRINGED WHEN she walked into the hotel restaurant and spotted Sam sitting at one of the tables. Sam *would* be on time. Why had she agreed to this? *Because I'm an adult and can't hide from her.* After her outburst yesterday, she should be grateful that Sam was willing to have breakfast with her, but it was hard to be grateful when she felt like crap. The day would only go downhill from here. She hadn't reached the table yet, but humiliation and embarrassment were already hunching her shoulders. *Note to self: before confessing your undying love for someone, make sure you can get away from them for a long, long time if they don't respond in kind.*

She pulled out a chair and mumbled a hello, but didn't force a smile. She had her limits.

"Good morning," Sam said. She looked tired. She'd probably been up all night trying to figure out if she could somehow dump her sidekick despite the joint gifts. If she thought Jillian looked as if she'd been in a bar fight, she didn't say. Jillian wanted her to be rude, so she could hate her for a minute, but Sam was cut from the "if you don't have anything nice to say, don't say it" cloth. Jillian's tongue wasn't as disciplined, and her inner bitch wanted to assert itself today, lash out, make everyone as miserable as she felt.

On the one hand, she couldn't make things any worse. On the other, she wanted to salvage a friendship, eventually, when she was able to look at Sam without wilting. Best to only open her mouth when absolutely necessary and keep whatever she said short. Too bad she hadn't given herself the same advice twenty-four hours ago. She and Sam could be having their usual relaxed breakfast, instead of not knowing where to look.

When the waitress came over, Jillian wanted to hug her. A minute later, she was back to staring at the salt shaker.

"We have to talk to Michael's parents," Sam said. "I know we wanted to avoid doing it, but we can't sit around and wait for Abrams to call."

"I was thinking about your meeting with Abrams." Well, she'd thought about it for a few minutes this morning because she'd wanted to show that she was capable of getting back to work. Jillian was more cynical than Sam about Abrams' offer to help them out. Okay, Abrams' aunt was Sister Joan, but she was a reporter at heart. She hadn't insisted on an exclusive, but she must be hoping to get something out of the arrangement. "Her source might be a dead end. She might not even have a source."

Sam grimaced. "Why would she lie?"

Sam was funny. Sometimes she was suspicious of people, other times she gave them the benefit of the doubt right away. Actually, she wasn't funny, she was like everyone else. First impressions counted, and everyone's bullshit meter was calibrated differently. Sam was inclined to believe Abrams. Jillian hadn't been there, so she wasn't ready to trust her yet—maybe because today she didn't trust anyone. And even if Abrams turned out to be the most helpful and authentic reporter ever, Jillian would have to stay away from her. She couldn't risk the reporter remembering her. "She knows how to make people trust her, so they'll open up to her. I'm not saying she did that yesterday. I wasn't there. I'm just not ready to trust her one hundred percent."

"Good point, and all the more reason for us to explore other avenues. I called Emma last night. She arranged for us to see Michael's mother this afternoon, and his father tomorrow. Our flight leaves at 11:00. We're meeting her at 4:30."

Panic surged through Jillian. "I don't think I can do that today—meet with the parents of a kid who committed suicide."

Sam's face flushed. "I'm sorry. I should have realized."

"No, it's okay. I know I sound cavalier about my father's suicide sometimes. Any other time I wouldn't have a problem with seeing Michael's mother, but not today."

"I'll reschedule everything."

"No, don't do that," Jillian said, an idea quickly forming in her mind. "Well, reschedule the mother, but not the flight. But let me go alone. I'll stay overnight and see her tomorrow, or the soonest day she's available."

Sam's brow furrowed. "Why? We're supposed to see his father tomorrow."

"I'm thinking that maybe we can split up for this one. Rather than both of us going to see his mother and then his father, I'll see his mother and you see his father. It'll be more efficient that way. You saw Marcy Abrams alone."

"Because she can't see you. We don't have that problem with Michael's parents."

The waitress arrived with their teas. As Jillian poured her cup, she silently swore at the leaky metal pot. They could put a man on the freaking moon, but they couldn't make a little teapot that didn't dribble water. She plunked the pot down and met Sam's eyes, then quickly looked away. She wanted to be with her; she didn't want to be with her. A couple of days away from Sam would allow her to breathe. When she returned, she might be able to look at her without feeling like a first-class dolt.

"I'm not sure travelling alone would be the best thing for you to do right now," Sam said.

"I'm not helpless. We've been apart before. And I need to . . . be alone for a bit." She sighed. "It'll just be for a couple of days, or maybe a few, depending on when Michael's mother can see me."

Sam's forehead creased. "Running away isn't the answer."

Sam's words made her want to cry, not because they hurt, but because Sam had said them so gently. Jillian reminded herself not to read anything into Sam's concern. She was merely showing the usual concern anyone would show for someone they didn't hate, and hey, Deiforms were valuable. "I'm not running away. I just need to get away for a couple of days. I'll be back, as Arnold would say." Any other time, she would have used her best Terminator accent, but not today.

Sam lifted her hands in a gesture of surrender. "Okay. I'd prefer we go together, but if that's what you want."

It wasn't what she wanted. It was what she needed. "Thanks. I'll be careful."

The waitress rescued them from an awkward silence. It was okay not to speak when eating. Jillian looked down at her eggs, bacon, hash browns, and toast. She wasn't really hungry, but she'd force the meal down. Then she'd pack an overnight bag and drive to the airport. Later she might kick herself for insisting on going alone, but right now, the prospect of being by herself for a while, of wandering around the city near the hotel and pretending she wasn't the Deiform Jillian who was hopelessly in love with the Deiform Sam, lifted her spirits a bit.

Chapter Fourteen

A*FTER EATING DINNER* alone at the hotel, Jillian strolled to a nearby bookstore and browsed its religion section. She didn't regret coming to see Michael's mother alone, but she missed Sam. She'd kept expecting her to walk into the restaurant. Pathetic, considering she'd only left her a whole nine hours ago and would see her again within twenty-four hours. Michael's mother had agreed to meet at 1:00 tomorrow. Jillian would drive straight to the airport afterward.

She pulled out a book by an author she recognized and checked the copyright page. Published this year, and the title was unfamiliar. Good, she'd take it. She checked out and sauntered away from the hotel, stopping occasionally to gaze indifferently at a shop window display. Who was she trying to fool? Why did she want to appear as if she didn't have a care in the world?

For the first time, she wondered whether she should ditch this whole Fellowship thing. Instead of flying back to Grayhurst, she could fly home to Mom's, and tell her that she'd managed to escape her burning car, and as she'd watched the flames consume it, had decided to leave her life behind. At the time, she'd just been exonerated of two murders, and hey, she was about to go on desk duty at work, as directed by the agency's shrink. It was plausible. She'd seen stories on the news about missing people who were found twenty or thirty years later, living on the streets in Vancouver or married with kids in Thailand. Why not her?

Because she'd have to explain the burned body they'd found in her car, for one thing. Even if that wasn't the case, she was too freaking responsible for her own good, and the only thing she missed about her former life was Mom and Danny. Why the hell would she go back to it? *Running away isn't the answer. I know, Sam. I know.* But it was tempting. She could entertain the fantasy, pretend for a while that she wouldn't miss Sam, wouldn't hate herself for bailing on a life she'd come to believe in, wouldn't look over her shoulder every five seconds and end up dead in some hovel, maybe missing her head. Nope, it would be all rainbows and bunny rabbits.

She'd screwed up life number one. She did *not* want to destroy life number two, though she was doing a damn good job of trying. Sam had seemed genuinely concerned at breakfast. Their easy rapport had evaporated, but Sam wasn't angry. Maybe there was a chance they could rebuild their friendship, and the trust Jillian's impatience had shattered. If only she'd kept her big mouth shut.

She wasn't meant to have a relationship, or a friendship, for that matter. The only friendships she'd managed were fake. She had some type of death curse when it came to real ones. Okay, she was friendly with those on the island, but she didn't see them much. Give her a chance and she'd have Roberta, Ruth, Jeremy, and everyone else running for the hills.

She went into a clothing store, for something to do. As she studied the clothes worn by anorexic mannequins, she continued to ruminate. Sam used to be some rich kid who probably went to private school and drove her Mercedes to university. If not for the Fellowship, she wouldn't be rubbing elbows with a disgraced pastor's kid who would have been waiting tables if she hadn't gotten a scholarship. While Sam had hung out at the country club and stuffed her face with caviar, Jillian had worked her butt off to make the money she needed for textbooks and transit passes and clothes. Mom had denied herself and chipped in what she could, but . . .

Their pasts didn't matter, and this wasn't helping. She and Sam were on an even playing field now. Sam hadn't seen her family for twenty years. She wasn't an arrogant, selfish brat who looked down her nose at the peasants. It had never crossed Jillian's mind that she came from money. And she'd better think about something else, because this wasn't helping, either. She needed to convince herself that she shouldn't have feelings for Sam, damn it, not the other way around. She inwardly snorted. As if she could talk herself out of love.

She left the store but wasn't ready to return to the hotel. A minute later, the aroma wafting from a bakery made her stop and peer at the baked goods display. She was tempted, but no. Binging on cupcakes wouldn't make her feel better. Pondering whether to keep walking or go back to her room, she looked in the direction of the hotel, and tensed. The man staring into the window two stores away . . . she'd seen him before, in the hotel's lobby.

On Sam's advice, Jillian had developed the habit of scanning and remembering faces wherever she went. The guy wasn't looking at her, but the light was catching his profile in such a way that recognition stirred. He could be out for a stroll too, maybe to work through a problem or take in the evening air. She moved closer to the edge of the sidewalk and stooped to tighten one of her laces. He was in front of a lingerie store. He could have a wife or girlfriend back at the hotel. He'd been alone in the lobby, but that didn't mean anything.

She straightened and walked away from the hotel until she came to another clothing store. She gazed at the window, waiting for the man to pass her. When he didn't, she glanced back in the direction of the lingerie store. There he was, three stores down. Was he pretending to care about what was in the window, as she was doing?

Jillian continued to walk. She took the first right. He did the same. She crossed the street. He followed her. She stopped again. So did he. Okay, she had a tail, potentially a Beguiler. Her heart hadn't raced in the lobby, but maybe she hadn't been close enough to him. It was pounding right now, powered by adrenalin.

Just her freaking luck! How many times had she walked city streets with Sam? How long had she been on her own in Junior's freaking cult, albeit rarely alone? Today she'd been away from Sam for mere hours, and someone was after her. She'd thought Beguilers wouldn't bother with her again, not without a very good reason. She was trained. She'd thwarted them twice. Did they always know where she and Sam were? Did they monitor airline travel? Her hotel reservation had only been made last night. She'd seen the guy in the lobby not long after checking in. All of which she could think about later, after she'd dealt with her tail.

She continued up the street, looking for an alley or laneway. She and Sam had practiced a maneuver during her training. It was a tough one because time travelled so quickly when she was outside of it, but the alternative was to let the guy follow her back to her hotel, and then what? She'd have to sit up all night with her gun in her lap. Having slept little last night, she was already tired, and she wanted to find out why the guy was following her.

She spotted a laneway running between two stores and glanced over her shoulder. The guy was still behind her. She unzipped her jacket. *Turn, shift, watch, because he'll be on top of me in what feels like a second.* And she had to remember to drop the bookstore bag she was carrying. She turned into the laneway and shifted. Everything turned gray. Her follower suddenly appeared, walked past—she shifted back into time. In one motion, she dropped the bag and pulled her gun from its holster. "Stop where you are and put your hands on your head," she barked. "I have a gun pointed right at you."

He froze.

"Hands on your head. If they go anywhere else, I'll shoot."

He put his hands on top of his head.

"Turn around slowly."

He did so. She studied him. He stood about five feet away. Her heart was thumping, but not the panicked pounding a Beguiler would provoke. "Why are you following me?"

He started to drop his hands. "Jillian, I—"

"Hands on top of your head!" she snapped. "Now start talking. Why are you following me?"

"My name is Ben," he said, his hands firmly planted on his head. "I'm a Supporter with the Fellowship. I was told to keep an eye on you."

What?

"If you call your contact . . ."

She could hear the tremor in his voice. While she held her pistol steady with her right hand, she reached for her phone with her left. "One move, and I won't hesitate." She held out her phone and snapped his photo, then managed to bring up the right contact number while keeping her eye on him, though she didn't expect him to lunge at her. He was frightened.

"Yes," Emma said.

"It's Jillian. I have a man with me who says he belongs to the Fellowship and was assigned to keep an eye on me. His name is Ben. Can you confirm his story? I can send you his photo."

"Does he have brown hair and a goatee, average build, around five foot ten?"

"Yeah. That's impressive. Do you know all the Supporters by heart?"

Emma chuckled. "No, but I happened to be in here when Jeremy arranged his assignment. You can send me his photo if you want, but . . ."

"No, I don't think that's necessary."

"I thought you knew he'd be shadowing you."

"Why?"

"Because Sam asked for someone to back you up."

Huh? "When?"

"Around ten this morning."

After Jillian had insisted on making this trip alone. "Oh, uh, yeah, there must have been a misunderstanding. We discussed it, but I thought we'd decided against it. I guess I got it wrong."

"I hope he didn't frighten you."

Actually, she thought it was the other way around. Ben still stood with his hands on his head. He hadn't so much as twitched. "No harm done. If you speak to Sam, can you keep this call to yourself? I feel a bit stupid."

"Sure, no problem."

"I should go. I have a Supporter to apologize to." They said good-bye and disconnected. Jillian slipped her phone back into her pocket and holstered her gun. "I'm sorry. I didn't know you'd been assigned to me."

Ben slowly exhaled. He dropped his hands and shrugged. "Thanks for not shooting me." His grin looked forced.

She picked up her bag and glanced inside. It was a good thing she'd bought a hardcover. The book appeared unscathed. "Now that the cat's out of the bag, we might as well walk back to the hotel together."

They left the laneway and headed in the direction of the hotel. Ben laughed nervously. "I didn't know where you'd gone when I went into the laneway. You scared the crap out of me. I've heard about what you can do, but when I turned into the laneway and couldn't see you, it never crossed my mind that you'd . . . whatever you call it. I just kept going. I figured you must be in a shadow or something. Then, bam! I almost jumped out of my skin."

"Sorry," Jillian said again, her mind turning over what Emma had told her. Sam had put this guy on her. Why? Did she think Jillian couldn't take care of herself? Was Sam worried about her? *Don't go there!* It was damn hard not to. She wanted to, wanted to believe that Sam was sitting in her hotel room hoping her sidekick was all right, and not only because it would be a blow to the Fellowship to lose a Deiform. But if Sam wanted someone on her, why not tell her? If she'd suspected that Jillian would argue against it, she could have called her after she'd checked in and told her then. Why keep it a secret? Jillian wouldn't call her and ask. If she decided to tell Sam that she'd found out about her tail, she'd do it in person.

"I guess I'm not good at staying out of sight," Ben said sheepishly.

"I'm super paranoid about noticing people around me," Jillian said.

He pointed at her bag. "I saw you browsing the religion section at Indigo."

"Yeah. It's a birthday gift." Despite what had happened, she couldn't ignore Sam's upcoming fortieth birthday. She'd planned to take her out for dinner, but suggesting it would be awkward now. She turned to Ben. "Now that I know about you, I'll keep you informed about where I'm going. Best we not be seen together after we return to the hotel, though. It might spook the people I'm here to see." It was a lie, but she didn't want him in the car with her everywhere she went. She was fragile at the moment. The Supporter at her side didn't need to see a Deiform cry.

Driving the rental she'd picked up at the airport, Jillian pulled over a block away from her destination and killed the engine. Michael's mother lived in an apartment building around the corner. Seeing her a day later than originally planned wasn't going to make this any easier. Jillian wouldn't break down in front of the woman, but she'd rather not speak to her at all. What had been the alternative? To insist that Sam see both parents while she hid in her hotel room? To delay seeing them by a week?

A car cruised by. She resisted the impulse to wave at Ben and gripped the steering wheel. She wasn't sitting here sweating in a rented Toyota because of Sam's rejection, though it certainly didn't help. Today of all days, she needed to feel strong, not fragile. How often did she knowingly speak to others whose lives had been devastated by suicide? When she saw Michael's mother, inside she'd be saying, "I know how much it hurts. I know how it never goes away."

She'd never say the words out loud. It was the lingering shame, the doubt, the sorrow at being betrayed and the rage at being abandoned. The little voice inside that said she hadn't been good enough, pretty enough, smart enough to make him want to stay. He'd put the gun to his head in her bedroom, perhaps looking down at her. She hadn't been enough. Not enough. She'd tried to bury him deep inside, but he was always there. She saw him in the mirror. She hated him. She loved him. She'd never be rid of him.

Instead of seeing Michael's mother, she could have told Sam that she wanted to see his father. Had she chosen his mother because fathers and suicide were tied together for her in a way that made her want to punch something?

Needing to walk off her nervous energy, she got out of the car and checked the parking signs. Satisfied that she wouldn't get a ticket, she strode up the sidewalk. On her third time around the block—with Ben not far behind her, probably wondering what the hell she was doing—she finally squared her shoulders and entered the apartment building lobby. Claire Atkins must have been waiting for her, because the intercom crackled the second Jillian pressed her apartment buzzer. "It's Jillian Wright. I spoke to you on the phone."

"Come right up." The lobby door buzzed.

As Jillian climbed the stairs to the third floor, she wondered if Claire had been pacing the apartment, fretting about the prospect of discussing Michael with a stranger. To put her at ease, Jillian wished she could tell her about her own experience with the suicide of a family member, but it wasn't going to happen.

Claire was standing outside her apartment, her eyes too bright. Jillian saw her own anxiety in them. She stuck out her hand. "Jillian Wright. Thank you so much for agreeing to meet with me."

Claire's fingers barely grasped Jillian's. "I don't know if I can help," she said softly. "Tea or coffee?"

Jillian nodded. "Tea, please."

Claire went into the kitchen to prepare the tea she'd offered. Jillian sank onto the sofa. She could see Claire from where she was sitting, and couldn't help but think about Mom. Dad's suicide had driven a wedge between mother and daughter. Michael's had split up his parents. Had they blamed each other, accused the other one of not picking up on the warning signs, or worse, for driving their son to suicide?

Jillian hadn't blamed Mom. She'd been too busy blaming herself, and she'd been old enough to understand that Dad had betrayed and disappointed a lot of people. Nobody had driven him to suicide. He hadn't been running from his wife and daughter. Or had he? Sometimes she wished the bastard had left a note. Other times she was grateful he hadn't. It would have become an obsession, scrutinizing every word for a hidden meaning, and waffling between the note being the truth, a big lie, or drama. Well, one thing was for sure, if heaven existed, Mom didn't have to worry about bumping into him there. Pastor Campbell would be elsewhere.

"It'll just be a minute." Claire didn't have to raise her voice for Jillian to hear her. The cramped one-bedroom apartment barely had a hallway. The two doors Jillian had spotted on her way in must lead to the bedroom and bathroom. She glanced around the living room. Her eyes fell on a photograph sitting in a china cabinet. One of Michael's school photos, tucked away behind glass. He looked a few years older than he did in the photo hidden in Sister Catherine's cell. Was that what he'd looked like when life had pummeled him so much that he'd decided he'd had enough?

"Milk and sugar?" Claire asked.

"Milk, one sugar," Jillian said, not surprised that Claire had stayed in the kitchen while the water boiled, instead of joining her guest in the living room. The time she'd spent circling the block, Claire was now spending in the kitchen. Jillian could have spoken to her on the phone, but she agreed with Sam that the two homes could contain clues.

A minute later, Claire set a cup of tea on the coffee table. "Here you are."

"Thank you," Jillian murmured. She waited for Claire to sit down with her cup, then said, "As I mentioned on the phone, I'm here about Sister Catherine. She's been arrested for three murders in Grayhurst."

Claire's head bobbed. She had a fixed smile on her face that reminded Jillian of how Mom's smiles had looked in the few years following Dad's suicide. Danny had made her smiles genuine again—not her daughter. Sympathy surged through Jillian for Claire. *Shut up and stop feeling sorry for yourself.* Nobody had reached Michael's mother. She was still in hell.

"I don't know how I can help, but I'll try. You said she might have known Michael . . ."

Jesus, she's hoping I have answers. Jillian threw out any story she might have told about why she had a photo of Claire's dead son. "I'm working for Sister Catherine's defence team. We're trying to figure out why she's confessed to murders she didn't commit. We found a photo of Michael in her cell at the convent."

Claire's eyes widened. "Really? I have no idea why. Which photo?"

Jillian found it on her phone and showed it to Claire. "That's him in grade five," Claire said huskily. "I remember buying that shirt . . ." Her eyes reddened. Jillian turned away and looked at the photo in the china cabinet again. It was the only photo in the room. There were no family portraits on the wall, no albums in the bookcase, and Jillian suspected no photos on Claire's phone. Was Sam sitting in a similar living room? Probably not. Michael's father had remarried and had another child. Claire must be in her sixties now. There wouldn't be any more biological children for her, and she'd lived alone for almost twenty years. Jillian recognized herself. Between assignments, she'd sat in a living room like this one. If not for the Fellowship, she would have been Claire in twenty years.

Jillian turned her attention back to her. "Do you know why Sister Catherine would have had Michael's photo?"

Claire slowly shook her head. "Honestly, I have no idea."

It was one of the smaller school photos. Jillian couldn't recall how many each packet contained. Eight, maybe? Sixteen? "Do you remember who you gave his photos to?"

"The usual people. My parents, the in-laws, my sister and brother, Mark's sister . . . I still have a few."

"What about Michael? Did he give any away?"

"He could have. We didn't hide them."

Had he given one to Sister Catherine? Did the other family members still have their photos? "I gather he never mentioned a teacher named Mrs. Donovan."

"No." Claire stood. "Let me find the photos from that year." Without waiting for a reply from Jillian, she disappeared into the bedroom. Grateful for the break, Jillian sipped her tea and steeled herself. She hadn't asked the hard questions yet.

Claire returned holding a photo sheet from which several photos had been cut away. "We got twelve of these." She handed the sheet to Jillian. "There are eight gone. I can account for six. I don't know what happened to the other two. He might have given them to friends."

Jillian mentally counted the people Claire had mentioned. "Who did you give the sixth photo to?" she asked.

"Mark took it," Claire said.

Of course. Michael's father. She handed the sheet back to Claire and drew a deep breath. "Did you keep any of Michael's things?"

"A few things." Claire swallowed. "We gave most of his stuff away. Not right after—I mean . . ."

Jillian could see and hear Claire's guilt. She remembered the day Mom had finally emptied Dad's side of the closet, stuffing everything into garbage bags for Goodwill. It had taken her another month to clear out his home office. Everything had gone—the furniture, books, photos, even the carpet. Not long afterward, Jillian had come home from school to a for sale sign on the lawn. There had been no discussion, no, "Insurance companies don't pay when someone offs himself, so I can't afford the mortgage," no, "I just can't stand to live here anymore, and you need a new bedroom. You can't sleep on the sofa forever." They'd stayed in the apartment until she'd married Danny.

"I kept the things I thought were important to him," Claire said.

God, she hated this. "Can I see them? There might be something that connects him to Sister Catherine somehow."

"I doubt it, but yeah. Why not?" Claire went into the bedroom again, and this time came back carrying a cardboard box. She set it on the coffee table. Figuring Claire would be protective of Michael's possessions, Jillian picked up her tea and waited. Claire opened the box. "When Mark moved out, he took some of Mike's things," she said absently as she pulled out a folded sports jersey. She unfolded it and held it up for Jillian to see. The jersey looked too small to fit a fifteen year old. "He belonged to a team when he was ten," Claire said. "I was surprised that he'd kept it. He wasn't really into team sports. We would have paid for him to play the following year, but he didn't want to."

Claire refolded the jersey and put it on the cushion next to her, then reached into the box and pulled out a crumpled baseball cap that matched the jersey. After holding it long enough for Jillian to see it, she put it on top of the jersey. Next, another baseball cap. Her eyes teared up. She hugged the cap to her chest.

Jillian picked up her tea, then quickly put it down when the urge to fling it against the wall hit her. Why was she putting this poor woman through this? For a nun who'd either killed three men, or wouldn't open her damn mouth and help herself. Jillian wished she could go to the prison and give Sister Catherine a piece of her mind. Did she realize the pain she was causing? If she was innocent, it didn't matter what freaking reason she had for keeping her mouth shut. She wasn't being noble. She was being selfish.

"He was wearing this when he left that day," Claire whispered. "He went to school. We went to work. We found out later he wasn't in school after lunch. The coroner . . . he said it probably happened between 3:00 and 3:30 . . ." She squeezed her eyes shut. "I can still see him leaving that morning, because I've gone over it a thousand times. I didn't tell him I loved him. I would have, if I'd known." Her eyes opened. "We hadn't argued or anything. I thought he was all right. Mark and I had no idea . . ." She stared at Jillian. "I didn't tell him I loved him every morning. Most mornings were a scramble. But I always wonder . . . if I'd told him that morning . . ."

"It wouldn't have changed anything," Jillian said, not knowing whether that was true, but telling Claire what she needed to hear, even though it wouldn't make a difference. She'd still punish herself. *Guilt never runs out of ammunition.*

Claire shot to her feet and raced into the bathroom. When she returned, she was dabbing at one eye with a tissue. "God, I'm sorry. I thought I'd be able to hold it together. I'm making you uncomfortable."

"No, I'm sorry for making you do this." And you know what? To hell with Sister Catherine. She was an adult. If she was innocent and didn't want to rot in prison, she was perfectly capable of helping herself.

Jillian drained her tea. "I knew coming to see you would be a long shot. I shouldn't have bothered you with this."

"You have a job to do."

No, she was an asshole, and felt doubly worse that Claire was trying to make her feel better. She stood. "Thank you for—" Now that she could see into the box . . . "Is that a needlepoint?"

Claire nodded. She lifted the fabric and held it toward Jillian. "We had a lab," she said, explaining the embroidered Labrador that brought Puck and Raven to mind.

According to the nuns at the convent, Sister Catherine needlepointed. "Where did he get it?"

"He came home with it one day and said one of his friends at school had done it. He wouldn't say who, though." Claire smiled down at the needlepoint. "I thought maybe it was a girl who had a crush on him and that's why he didn't want to talk about it. You know how they are at that age. Everything's embarrassing, especially when talking to your mom."

The needlepoint was probably a coincidence. Then again, how many adolescent girls did needlepoint? It wasn't cool. "Thanks for showing it to me. When I saw it, it reminded me of my dogs."

"You have labs?"

"Two." She wouldn't mind being with them right now, instead of upsetting people for a nun she frankly didn't give a shit about at this point. "Anyway, I should go."

"If I think of anything, I'll let you know," Claire said.

"Thanks. And thanks for the tea."

Jillian left the apartment. When she reached the stairs, she turned to look back down the hallway and wasn't surprised to see Claire watching her. They waved to each other. Jillian almost said, "My father committed suicide. It wasn't your fault. It really wasn't your fault." But who would she be trying to reassure? She hurried down the stairs and burst from the apartment building.

In the car, she checked the time. *1:35.* Good, she had a few hours before her flight. She wasn't ready to sit in a cramped plane seat.

She'd done her shopping last night, but strolling around crowded stores appealed to her. She needed a distraction, so she could forget that she'd just forced a woman to relive her son's suicide because of Sister freaking Catherine. If the nun wanted to spend the rest of her life in prison, let her.

Chapter Fifteen

SAM REMAINED SILENT while Jillian paced and ranted about her visit with Michael's mother. She hadn't expected this when she'd come into Jillian's hotel room and asked her how the visit had gone. They'd both wanted to avoid dragging Michael's parents into the investigation, and her conversation with Michael's father hadn't been easy. But it hadn't upset her as much as it had Jillian. Maybe it hadn't been a good idea for her to interview a mother who'd lost her son to suicide, especially so soon after she'd confessed her feelings, and the awkward conversation that had hurt her.

"So to hell with Sister Catherine," Jillian said, swinging toward Sam. "If she's innocent, she can save herself. All she has to do is tell the police what she knows. If she doesn't want to do that, it's her choice. Let her stay in prison. What would it matter?"

"It would matter because the killer would still be out there," Sam said levelly.

"And she freaking-well knows who it is!" Jillian looked as if she were about to explode. But then she sank onto the end of the bed and let out a long, heartfelt sigh. "If she's innocent—well, no, she's not innocent. At the very least, she's protecting a killer and making us upset innocent people. She doesn't need us. She can open her mouth any time she wants. It galls, Sam. It galls that we're running around trying to help her, when all she has to do is open her mouth."

Sam leaned forward. "You need to reframe this in your mind. I know Roberta said she's innocent, and so it seems like we're trying to help her, but we're not. If she's innocent, someone is getting away with murder. Think about it as getting justice for the victims. Don't think about it as helping Sister Catherine."

Jillian shrugged and looked at her lap. "I'll try."

Sam wouldn't harp on it. She wasn't happy with the nun either, and she wasn't convinced that Michael Atkins was connected to whatever Roberta had sensed when she'd seen the news report about Sister Catherine. While investigating the murders, they might have stumbled onto an unrelated situation, like when an X-ray picked up something that had nothing to do with a patient's symptoms. But until they ran out of leads, they'd keep digging. When they returned to the island, Sam wanted to be able to tell Roberta they'd examined every angle.

While ranting, Jillian had said something interesting. "You mentioned a needlepoint . . ."

Jillian lifted her head. "Yeah, of a dog. The nuns mentioned that Sister Catherine does needlepoint."

"Did you—"

"No, I didn't ask her to let me have it," Jillian snapped. "She doesn't have much left of him, and I was on my way out when I saw it."

"I was going to ask if you took a photo of it," Sam said mildly.

"Oh. Well, no. Maybe I should have, but I just wanted to get out of there. And really, do we need it? It was of a dog—a lab."

Sam pulled out her phone and brought up the contact information for Sister Catherine's ex-husband. Donovan picked up. "Hello."

"Hi, it's Sam Wright. I'm the PI that came to see you at your office."

"Yes, of course. What can I do for you?"

"Did Catherine do needlepoint when you were together?"

"All the time. Her hands were always moving."

"Did she like to do needlepoints of dogs?"

Silence, then, "I don't know. I didn't pay much attention to it, to be honest."

"What did she do with the needlepoints when they were finished?"

"Uh, gave them to the church, I think, or charity, or something. There may have been a few around the house." He paused. "It was a long time ago. Why do you want to know about her needlepoints?"

"I came across one and was wondering if she'd done it. Anyway, thanks for your time," Sam said, wanting to be rid of him. "Bye."

She hung up. "Maybe Sister Catherine did it, maybe she didn't. Donovan says she gave most of her needlepoints to the church or to charities. Michael could have gotten his hands on it indirectly."

"Why would an adolescent boy want a needlepoint?" Jillian stood and folded her arms. "Even if we knew it was Sister Catherine's and she gave it to him, what would it tell us? We wouldn't be any further ahead, apart from knowing for sure that they knew each other." She peered down at Sam. "Did you find out anything from his father?"

"No."

"So making them relive all the crap got us a big fat nowhere."

"We had to do it."

"Sure we did," Jillian muttered. She moved to the window and spun around. "What now?"

"Marcy Abrams called me earlier. She's arriving tomorrow. She'll talk to her guy, then call me."

"Hopefully she won't want to see you tomorrow."

"Why?"

Jillian frowned. "You know why," she said quietly.

Suddenly Sam felt uncomfortable. Jillian must have read her file. Had that happened before or after she'd confessed her feelings? Either way, it was time to leave. "She might not call tomorrow. We'll see." She stood up and stretched. "I'm tired. Breakfast?"

"Yeah. Breakfast."

When Sam was at the door, Jillian said, "By the way, I busted your guy."

Sam turned around. "What guy?"

Jillian gave her a pointed look. "The Supporter you put on me. Tell Roberta, or whoever needs to know, that he should be doing something other than following people. Nice guy, but he sucks at it."

"I put him on you because I knew you, uh . . ." Sam hated this. "You were distracted when we had breakfast, and I figured—I thought—"

Jillian held up her hand. "It's okay. I just wish you'd told me, because I scared the crap out of him when I pulled that shifting maneuver we practiced."

Pride surged through Sam. "You got him that way?"

Jillian nodded. "He was easy to spot."

She wanted to tell Jillian she'd done well, but . . . "I'll talk to Roberta about finding him something more suited to whatever skills he has."

"Good. And don't worry. I won't think you're in love with me because you don't want the Beguilers to get their hands on me."

Sam quickly pulled open the door. "See you tomorrow." In the corridor, she stared at the door that had closed behind her. She should knock, go back in, tell Jillian she'd done well, with Michael's mother and protecting herself. This wall between them . . . she didn't want it.

She knows I'll turn forty tomorrow. Jillian must have finally read her file. She'd repeatedly said that she wanted to hear it from the horse's mouth, but something had changed. She was no longer interested in finding out what was behind the facts. Sam had hated it when Jillian had pressed her about her past life. Now she missed the questions. No, she missed someone wanting to know her. She missed having someone treat her like a normal human being. For Jillian, the gifts had never mattered. For everyone else, they were all that did.

Sam disconnected from her phone conversation with Marcy Abrams and picked up her knitting. Abrams had something for them, but would it be enough to keep them on the case? Sam would find out when she had dinner with her tomorrow night. Before then, she'd fill her time with more knitting and reading. It was getting tedious. Her time at a church this morning had started the day off well, but since then she'd felt at a loose end.

Someone knocked at her room door. *"It's me."*

She let Jillian in. "Happy birthday," Jillian said.

Sam stared at the gift-wrapped package Jillian held out. When Jillian hadn't said anything about her birthday at breakfast, Sam had hoped to get through the day without it coming up. "You didn't have to get me anything."

"Yes, I did. Open it."

She took the gift and self-consciously unwrapped what she could tell was a book.

"I hope you haven't read it. I've been paying attention, but I haven't been around long enough to know everything you've read.

I chose something released in the past year that I haven't seen you with."

Sam read the title of the book, written by a popular Christian commentator. "Thank you. I haven't read it. It looks interesting."

"Good."

They looked at each other. Sam struggled for something to say. "You know it's my fortieth birthday today, so I guess you read my file."

"No, I haven't."

"You haven't?" Sam said, surprise—and elation—raising her voice an octave.

"No. Roberta told me a while back that you were going to turn forty on your next biological birthday. I asked her when."

"Oh."

"She only told me because I was worried I'd missed it."

"I'm not upset with her." Sam set the book on the desk. What now? "Marcy Abrams just called. Her guy gave her something. I'm having dinner with her downstairs tomorrow."

Jillian frowned. "She couldn't tell you over the phone?"

"She insisted on meeting in person."

"Maybe she thinks her phone is tapped."

"I want you nearby. I don't like it when I have to eat at a pre-arranged time and place."

"You're afraid someone might slip something into your food."

Sam nodded.

"We eat at the hotel restaurant all the time."

"But we're together, and we go whenever we feel like it. It's not prearranged."

"But . . ." Jillian blinked at her. "Okay, but there's a problem. Abrams can't see me."

"You can show up after us, sit where she won't see you."

"I'll take a newspaper to hide behind."

"That would work."

Jillian shoved her hands into her pockets. "Speaking of dinner, I was planning to suggest that we go for dinner, somewhere nice. I still want to. I'm not sure . . ." Her voice trailed off. "It would be to celebrate your birthday. If you want to, I won't read anything into it."

Sam wished she still had the book in her hands. She'd like to go. The alternative would be to eat alone in her room and think about her family. She thought about them often, but her birthday was always the worst. They must think about her today. She wished she could tell them she was all right, and that she missed them terribly.

Jillian looked down at her feet. "Not a good idea?" She lifted her head and smiled, but failed to mask her humiliation.

Sam's stomach knotted. She hated seeing Jillian like this, looking embarrassed and defeated. But if she went to dinner with her, would that help her, or make the situation worse? She wanted to feel relaxed with her, to pick up where they'd left off, but Jillian could take it the wrong way, despite insisting that she wouldn't. "I don't think it would be a good idea right now," she said, going with the answer that felt less risky. "But thank you for asking."

Jillian's smile was frozen on her face. "Sure. I should go."

Sam wanted to say, "Stick around for a while," but said, "Thank you for the book."

After the door had closed behind Jillian, she glanced around her empty hotel room and sighed. *Happy birthday.*

SAM CLASPED HER hands on the table and smiled at Marcy Abrams. Why had she agreed to meet her for dinner? She should have insisted that Marcy give her the information over the phone, and only agreed to this if Marcy had refused. Without menus to hide behind, the silence at the table was loud. What would they talk about for the next hour?

She tensed when the waitress approached their table. This waitress had served her a couple of times before, when she was here with Jillian. Would the woman wonder why Sam was sitting with Marcy and Jillian was sitting alone at another table? Would she say something? Maybe Sam should have suggested another restaurant, but she'd wanted to stay close to the hotel.

"Good evening," the waitress said with a smile. She set two menus on the table. "What would you like to drink?" If she recognized Sam, she didn't let on.

Sam's shoulders relaxed, but a minute later, they were stiff again as she struggled to make small talk with Marcy. If she'd gone to dinner with Jillian last night, would it have been less awkward? Last week, definitely. Lapses in their conversations hadn't felt uncomfortable. The minutes hadn't crawled by. But things had changed. Sam didn't feel weird when they stuck to discussing the case, but there wasn't much to talk about right now. Still, she wished she'd had dinner with Jillian last night. It had been her fortieth birthday. They had to work together. And being with Jillian would have been better than sitting in her hotel room brooding. Oh well, it was too late now.

"I'm here, in case you didn't see me come in," Jillian said.

Sam's spirits rose. Hearing Jillian's familiar voice in her head eased her anxiety. *"I see you."* Jillian was sitting at a table in Sam's line of sight, and nowhere near the washrooms or along the path to the exit.

The waitress returned with two glasses of water and took their order. *"We just ordered,"* Sam said to Jillian.

"If I see you facedown in your plate, I'll spring into action."

Despite knowing that Jillian was teasing her about her paranoia, Sam would have chuckled, if not for Marcy sitting across the table from her.

Marcy sipped her water and eyed Sam over the rim of her glass. "So, how long have you been a PI?"

"About six years," Sam said, reciting the information she'd reviewed before coming down to the lobby.

Marcy's eyes narrowed. "You're not based in Grayhurst. Why did the church hire you? You *are* working for the church, right?"

"Is what I tell you going to end up on the news?"

"No. This isn't a business dinner, and I don't want to piss you off."

"You want your exclusive."

Marcy quirked a brow. "You haven't answered my question."

"We've worked for the church before. It wanted a firm it could trust. The Sister Catherine situation is sensitive."

Marcy snorted. "I'll say. Imagine the reaction when the powers that be found out that a nun had confessed to three murders."

"Speaking of the murders, what did you find out?"

"Down to business, I see. Well, why not? Let's get it out of the way. Then we can relax for the rest of the evening." Marcy leaned forward and lowered her voice. "According to my friend, there were rumours of an investigation around the time Michael Atkins committed suicide. It involved child pornography. The whispers mentioned two men. Joseph Fowler, a municipal politician at the time, and Peter Steele, an attorney who often defends dodgy clients. The authorities were building a case, and then it suddenly went away. He thinks the prosecutor's office was pressured to drop it, or the witnesses decided not to testify, if you get my drift."

Jeremy had poked around in the police files. He hadn't come across a child pornography case. "I spoke to a retired cop. He didn't mention any investigation around Michael Atkins' death."

"Did he belong to the Grayhurst force?"

"Yeah."

Marcy nodded. "It wasn't them. It was the RCMP. I'm sure the Grayhurst cops heard something about it, though, at least at the higher levels."

"How reliable is your friend?"

"He's reliable."

"There's no file? No paper trail about a killed investigation?"

"I don't know. I don't have access to the RCMP's files, and neither does he."

"Did he mention Brandon MacIntosh?"

"No. But you'd said that MacIntosh might have signed an agreement that bought his silence. Witnesses suddenly deciding not to testify . . ."

They still hadn't connected Sister Catherine to Michael, but when they'd confronted Brandon about him, he'd said he couldn't talk about it. Michael had to have been involved in the case Brandon couldn't speak about. In fact, Brandon wouldn't speak about Michael at all. How sweeping was the agreement he'd signed? If the witnesses had been threatened, was Brandon still afraid? Were the men involved that powerful?

At least she and Jillian hadn't hit a dead end. They had two names, and Jeremy might find something in the RCMP's database. "Where are Fowler and Steele now?"

"Fowler passed away a few years ago. Steele still practices here."

"I'll have to pay him a visit."

"Be careful. When I said he defends dodgy clients, I meant the types who wouldn't think twice about getting rid of someone they don't like. My friend gave me the impression that Steele is tight with those he represents."

Had Steele been directly involved in the child pornography ring, or had it been one of his clients? Sam wasn't worried about him coming after her. They'd snoop through his files when he wasn't around. "Thanks. This is helpful."

"I can see how it might explain Michael Atkins' suicide, if he was one of the victims. But I don't see how it helps Sister Catherine."

"I don't, either. Not yet. But we're chasing down everything that could possibly be related."

"I suppose desperate times call for desperate measures," Marcy murmured. "You're running out of time."

Yes and no. Despite Sister Catherine's determination to be convicted, if evidence came to light that exonerated her, she'd eventually be released. But who would be looking for that evidence? Roberta couldn't keep them on the case forever. Once they'd exhausted every lead, it would be time to move on.

The waitress arrived with their food. Sam sprinkled salt on her fries. "Did you always want to be a reporter?" she asked Marcy.

While they ate, she continued to ask Marcy about her work, hoping to keep the conversation focused on her. When Marcy asked her a question about herself, she kept the answer short and turned back to Marcy's work. She wanted to finish dinner and get back to her room, so she could call Jeremy, and figure out their next move with Jillian.

Marcy dabbed at her mouth with a napkin. "That was pretty good. I'll have to remember this restaurant next time I'm here." She smiled at Sam. "We can stay here and have a drink, but I was thinking we could move on to somewhere else."

"Somewhere else?" Sam said, confused.

"Yes. I know a club downtown. I thought we could go there."

A club downtown? Why would they go to a club downtown? "Uh . . ."

"Oh, shit, I hope I haven't put my foot in it." Marcy grimaced. "Is my gaydar not working?"

What?

"I was pretty sure we both ride the same bus. I'm sorry if I offended you."

"No, you didn't. You're right. I just—" Why was this happening to her? Twenty years of working for the Fellowship and only once had someone asked her on a date, a man who'd worked in a records office she'd had to visit several times over the course of an investigation. She was rarely in the same place long enough for anyone to notice her much, not that it mattered tonight. She'd seen Marcy only once before.

Why are You doing this to me? She'd learned to pay attention to seeming coincidences and sudden clusters of similar circumstances, especially unusual ones. First Jillian, now Marcy. What did He want her to see? "I, um . . ." She looked past Marcy. Jillian was the only one in the restaurant dining alone. "I'm seeing someone," Sam said.

Marcy groaned. "Just my luck. Is it serious?"

"Yeah. Sorry."

"Gosh, don't apologize. If I didn't have a job," she raised her right forefinger," that I love, and that didn't pretty much own my life, I'd be with someone, too. I'm not into wrecking other people's relationships, so I accept your polite refusal."

Sam couldn't help but smile. "Thank you."

"On that note, I should go." Marcy beckoned to their waitress. They settled their bills. Sam would normally have charged hers to her room, but she didn't want Marcy to find out her room number that easily. Then again, the woman was sharp. She probably already knew it.

"If I hear anything else, I'll call you," Marcy said as they strolled into the lobby. "Don't forget my exclusive."

"I won't."

Sam went to the lobby window and watched Marcy stride across the parking lot to her car and drive away. Then she returned to the restaurant and sat across from Jillian.

Jillian set her knife and fork on her empty plate. "So?"

"Still no connection between Sister Catherine and Michael, but she gave me the names of two people who might have been wrapped up in a child pornography case the RCMP was building. They suddenly dropped it, maybe because one of the men was a municipal politician and the other a crooked attorney."

"Not to be contrary, but are we sure we're not picking up stuff that has nothing to do with Sister Catherine? Did Brandon MacIntosh's name come up?"

"No."

Jillian blew out a sigh.

"I know, we could be chasing down leads that aren't related, but it's all we've got."

"When do we draw the line?"

Sam picked up the unused napkin on her side of the table and unfolded it. "Let's look into the two names she gave us and see if they lead anywhere. If they don't pan out, I think we should call it a day. Oh, and let's try to confirm that Brandon signed an agreement and see if we can find his copy. Then we've tied up everything we know about."

"Who are the men?"

"Harry Fowler and Pete Steele. Fowler's dead, so we should start with Steele, the attorney. As for Brandon, I was thinking that one of us could suddenly be interested in buying a house. The other one can check out his place."

"He won't give either of us the time of day. He'll figure we're just trying to talk to him again."

"Not if someone else makes the appointment and shows up with you."

Jillian raised her brows. "You want me to be the one to brave Brandon again while you poke around. Okay. Who will I go house hunting with?"

"A Supporter. Maybe your boyfriend. We'll set it up." Sam pulled out her phone. "I'm looking for the address of Steele's law office. We should go take a look around."

"Now?"

"Yeah."

"What about the RCMP? Did Jeremy check their files?"

"No. I'll give him a call when we're somewhere more private."

The waitress came over. Jillian signed off on the charge to her room and sipped from her half-full water glass. Sam folded the napkin, then unfolded it again.

"I guess my chaperoning duties are complete," Jillian said lightly.

They certainly were. From now on, it would be phone-only contact with Marcy Abrams.

Chapter Sixteen

Jᴵᴸᴸᴵᴬᴺ ᴸᴱᴬᴺᴱᴰ ꜰᴏʀᴡᴬʀᴰ in the passenger seat so she could see Steele's law office. Steele and Associates occupied a one-storey building on a commercial street. "There aren't any lights on. Do you want to quickly double-check that nobody's there?"

"Yeah." Sam leaned back in the driver's seat and closed her eyes.

Jillian didn't go along for the ride. She'd have to touch Sam, and she wasn't sure how Sam would feel about that now. Plus, with no light, there wouldn't be anything interesting to see, but Sam should be able to discern whether anybody was inside working in the glow of a desk lamp or other light source they couldn't see from out here.

Colour returned to Sam's cheeks a few minutes later. "Nobody's there, but there's a security system I've dealt with before. His office space isn't very large. Why don't I go in while you stay out here and keep watch?"

"Sure."

Sam got out of the car. After grabbing her knapsack from the trunk, she sprinted across the street and disappeared up the laneway that ran between Steele's building and its neighbour.

Jillian glanced around. At this time of night, there was hardly any foot traffic, but she rounded the car and got into the driver's seat, so nobody would wonder where the driver was.

Five minutes passed, then ten. One person had strode by on her side of the road and only two cars had driven past her; otherwise the area that would be bustling during the day was a ghost town. She checked her watch for the third time. Sam would be rifling through Steele's files, hoping to—

A car pulled up to the curb in front of Steele's office. Three men hopped out and gathered on the sidewalk near the car's passenger door. *Shit.* She grabbed frantically for her phone.

The three men went to the entrance to Steele's office. One pulled out a set of keys. Forget the phone; they'd be inside the office in mere seconds. If Sam was near the front door . . . She could shift, but she'd be stuck inside until the coast was clear, and she might not be fast enough for them not to see.

The man with the keys swung the door open. Jillian couldn't see anyone strolling up either sidewalk, and a quick look in the side-view mirror confirmed that no cars were coming her way or approaching from behind. She visualized Sam standing on the road, just outside the driver's door. *Come on.*

She jumped when Sam materialized outside the door, holding her phone and a penlight. Jillian lowered the window. "I don't think that'll ever stop freaking me out."

Sam stared down at her, bewilderment in her eyes. "What's going on?"

Jillian jerked her chin toward Steele's office. "You were about to be busted. I didn't have time to phone you and you were too far away for telepathy. Get in."

Sam rounded the car, slipped her knapsack off her back, and dropped into the passenger seat. She craned her neck to look at Steele's office as Jillian pulled away. "I could have shifted," she murmured, pulling off the latex gloves she wore.

"Yes, but they would have seen, and if anything appears out of place, who knows how long they would have stayed there. They might have posted someone inside to guard the place. The problem with shifting is that we have to return within twenty-four hours."

Sam nodded, but Jillian could tell that her mind was elsewhere. "Did you leave anything out of place?"

"I don't think so. I'd just shut a cabinet drawer."

"Did you find anything?"

"I saw some familiar names in the few files I managed to see before you yanked me out, and there were lots of framed photos on the wall with what looked like important people. I took photos of everything."

"Which names?"

"Nobody to do with Sister Catherine. Public figures."

Great. "There wasn't a file labelled child pornography, I suppose."

"No."

She hated this case.

"But we may be on to something. It wasn't a total loss."

Jillian wanted to look at Sam, but kept her eyes on the road. "Why?"

"Boris Vasiliev was in one of the photos. He looked younger, but I'm sure it was him."

One of the victims. "With Steele?"

"And two other people I didn't recognize. We need to find out who they are. From the clothing, I'd guess it was taken in the late eighties."

"Around the time Michael killed himself."

"Yeah."

Jillian moistened her lips. "You know who can probably tell you who the other two people are."

"I don't want to have dinner with her again. We didn't have much to talk about."

"Email her the photo. If she insists on meeting in person, refuse."

"She *would* be the quickest way to find out who they are." Sam was silent for a moment. "I'll run it by Jeremy first. If he doesn't come up with anything, I'll email it to her."

That didn't make sense. Jeremy would have to use facial recognition software, which could take a while and might not get a hit. "Email it to her before Jeremy. There's a good chance she'll recognize everyone right away."

"All right, I'll email it to her," Sam growled.

Jillian glanced at her. Was her very presence irritating Sam now? "Well, this is good news, right? We have a potential connection between Vasiliev and Steele, which could mean Vasiliev was implicated in the dropped investigation."

"Or he just happened to know the mayor, or ran into him and posed for a photo. It looked like it was taken at some type of publicity event. We can't even say the mayor knew Steele or Vasiliev. I said we may be on to something, not that we are."

She hated this case. "Well, let's hope—"

Sam's phone rang. She picked up. "Yeah." Silence, then, "Yeah, okay, I'll tell her."

"What?" Jillian said.

"You have an appointment to meet Brandon MacIntosh tomorrow. Your boyfriend will meet you in the hotel lobby at noon. You're to go to lunch first, then meet Brandon at 2:00."

"Why? Was that Roberta?"

"Yeah."

Why hadn't Roberta called her? Habit, or would she always see Sam as the more experienced Deiform, and therefore the leader? "Did she say why we have to go to lunch?"

"No."

Maybe she wanted people to see them doing something together, just in case Brandon questioned their relationship. But why would he? Even if he did, they wouldn't have witnesses from the restaurant with them when they went house hunting. "Did she say who it is? My boyfriend?"

"No, just that it's a Supporter. She said Jeremy will send you more info tomorrow morning."

Another thought struck Jillian. "She probably wants us to warm up and develop a rapport before we meet Brandon. If we were to see him five minutes after meeting each other, he might figure I'm doing exactly what I'll be doing. Pretending I'm buying a house with a fake boyfriend."

"Better you than me."

Jillian couldn't imagine Sam pretending to be with anyone. Except her. Though in her fantasies, nobody was pretending. Would it ever end? How could it, when she couldn't get away from Sam for longer than a day or two? The constant ache, and the irrational hope that one day Sam would open her eyes and realize they'd be great together, would always be there.

"IT'S SOME BUSINESSMAN in the photo with the mayor and Vasiliev," Sam said, peering at her phone.

Jillian looked up from the cereal the waitress had set on the table five minutes ago. "Marcy already replied?"

Sam nodded.

"Who, exactly?"

"Daniel Prince. Some tech guy. According to Marcy, he ran a BBS in the eighties."

"BBS?"

"Bulletin board system."

"Bulletin boards?" Jillian said, envisioning a series of boards with papers tacked to them, and figuring she must be missing something.

"They were popular before the masses came onto the Internet. Think an electronic meeting place, where people could chat, read news, that sort of thing."

Jillian raised her brows at Sam.

"When I was a teenager, I hung out on them. There were a few Christian ones."

"Oh." She hadn't, but then she hadn't had her own computer at home. Mom couldn't afford one.

"We should talk to this guy. What if Vasiliev and the others hung out on the same board?"

"What if they posted child pornography?" Jillian said. "I bet Internet traffic wasn't monitored as diligently as it is today."

"I bet you're right."

They smiled at each other. Sam quickly looked at her phone. Jillian stared at her cereal.

"I'll try to arrange a meeting with Prince this afternoon, while you're out with your boyfriend," Sam said.

"I thought you were going to Brandon's house."

"I'll do that first. Keep him busy."

Jillian grunted. "We've gone from nothing to a solid lead, and maybe Brandon will give me something. Things are looking up. Maybe Roberta is onto something, after all."

"Or maybe Vasiliev didn't use a BBS and just happened to have his photo taken with Steele, the former mayor, and Prince at a fundraiser or some other event."

"If that turns out to be true, we're done, right? Because we have nothing else. Assuming Prince can see you today, tonight we're either still on this case and getting somewhere, or we're heading home. Like I said, things are looking up."

"I'll call Prince." Sam punched in a number and stuck her phone against her ear.

"Marcy included his phone number?"

Sam nodded.

Efficient and smart. Jillian could almost have a crush on Marcy, if she wasn't already in love with the woman across the table from her. She listened to Sam leave a message on Prince's voicemail, then her phone beeped. It was Jillian's turn to peer at her phone. "It's an email from Jeremy," she said, opening it. "It must be about the boyfriend I'll meet for—" Her jaw dropped.

"What is it?" Sam asked.

She looked up. "It's Andy. I'm meeting Andy."

"Andy . . ." Sam's brow furrowed. "You mean the guy who was in the soul healers, the one we flipped to keep him from, uh . . ."

"Turning me in. Yeah." Jillian studied his photo. His hair was shorter, but otherwise he looked pretty much the same as the last time she'd seen him. She reread the short email. "Roberta is forcing us to have lunch so we can clear the air."

"And then pretend you're a couple. Sounds like fun."

"No kidding." She dreaded seeing him, but at the same time, wanted to talk to him. Since that night at Junior's cabin, she'd wondered what had happened to him. Sometimes she felt worse about having deceived him than she did about shooting Junior, but then she remembered him sitting there watching Junior stroke Jane's face and doing nothing to stop him from killing her, and she didn't feel so bad anymore.

JILLIAN WATCHED THE floor number change as the elevator descended to the lobby. She'd smile at him, shake his hand, and make polite conversation until they'd ordered. Then she'd ask what he'd been doing since the Fellowship had given him sanctuary in exchange for his silence.

The doors swooshed open. Jillian strode into the lobby and spotted him right away. He must have been watching for her, because he immediately stood and waved. She forced a broad smile. When she reached him, she noticed that his smile was as wide as hers. She stuck out her hand. "How are you, Andy?"

His grasp was strong. "I'm doing well. How are you?"

"I'm fine. Do you want to go to the hotel restaurant, or somewhere else? There are a few places just up the street."

"The hotel restaurant is fine. Lead the way."

"Sun's out today," she said as they walked.

"I heard it might rain tomorrow."

She nodded and searched for something else to say, but she already felt awkward. They were discussing the weather? Jesus. Fortunately the restaurant was just off the lobby. They were quickly seated, and hid behind their menus until the waitress took them away. Then they did a great job of avoiding each other's eyes until Andy said, "They chose me because someone apparently told them we have chemistry."

Jillian couldn't help but chuckle. "Probably Ruth."

"Ruth?"

"You've met her. You knew her as my mother."

"Oh. I didn't know that. They only tell me about people when I have to work with them." He studied his hands. "I didn't think I'd see you again."

"I wasn't sure. I never know who I'll end up working with—well, except for Sam. Did they tell you about Sam? Do you remember her?"

He snorted. "How could I forget her? The last time I saw her, she was pointing a gun at me."

After shooting Junior, Jillian had passed out and hadn't come around until she was on the plane on her way to the island, but Sam had given her the gist of what had happened. "I thought you were in the car with us for a while."

"I was, until we met up with who I'd now refer to as other Supporters. She put her gun in my face and told me to get out and go with the guy who'd pulled the door open."

"She didn't force you to join the Fellowship."

"No. I knew that life as I knew it was over. I could either go to prison or accept the offer she'd made. I had nothing else to do, nowhere else to go, and I was in a fog. So was everyone else. We all did what she told us to do."

Once they'd cut the head off the snake, its body had lost its purpose. When faced with a group, going for the leader first was often the best way to deal with a confrontation, especially when outnumbered, as Ruth and Sam had been that night. The fact that they were armed and had relieved the others of their weapons had helped.

"The man we'd followed for years had just been shot and killed, right in front of us," Andy said.

Jillian winced. "Yeah, well—"

"I didn't know who you really were, not then, anyway. I thought you were real."

"I am real."

He shook his head. "You weren't who I thought you were. Neither was your mother. Neither was your friend. I trusted you."

Jillian's hands clenched. "Give me a break! What do you think you were doing? You wanted to put my mother into a home, so I'd use my power of attorney to sell her house and hand over all her money, and mine. How many people did you do that to?"

Andy spread out his hands. "I honestly believed I was doing a good thing."

"How? How could you have thought that giving money to Junior and Jackson was a good thing? What about Amanda? What about Jane? You just sat there."

His shoulders hunched. "I know. That's why I don't blame you for shooting him."

Jillian wanted to smack him. "Well, thank you. Thank you very much." She blew out an exasperated sigh. "Look, I wish I wasn't forced to shoot him, but I was trying to save everyone's asses after I'd been punched in the face and bashed my head on the floor. If Ruth and Sam hadn't shown up, what do you think would have happened?"

When Andy didn't answer, she answered for him. "Jane would be dead, and who knows when Junior would have snapped and blown us all to kingdom come. Did you know he'd rigged the place? No, because as far as Junior was concerned, you were expendable." She tapped her chest. "We broke up the cult. We got everyone out and tipped off the cops to those graves. If there had been a way to do it without lying to everyone, I'm sure we would have taken it. Be grateful that Sam stuck that gun in your face. We could both be in prison, but instead we can actually do some good."

"You're right," he said hoarsely.

Yeah, but she could have been gentler. It wasn't long ago that she'd questioned the Fellowship's methods and wrestled with whether the ends justified the means. Sometimes she still did. "I'm sorry.

I shouldn't have gone off like that. You were in a cult. You weren't thinking straight. You—"

She broke off when the waitress arrived and set their plates down. "Thank you," she murmured.

"I just sat there, watching him," Andy said, when the waitress was gone. "If you hadn't done something, Jane would have died." He barked a laugh. "I would have told myself it was for her own good. How could I have done that? I didn't even help you. When you stood up to Junior, I didn't help." He stared down at his plate.

Jillian swallowed. She wouldn't tell him that she believed the Fellowship had taken him in because he'd been the weakest link, and the most redeemable. The others were cold-hearted survivors. There would have been no doubt that they'd lie to the police to save their own skins. But Andy . . . his guilt would have had him spilling his guts. The Fellowship would have cleaned up the mess and kept her out of the authorities' hands, but it had taken the easier route. But that didn't erase what she'd done. Andy was sitting in front of her because she'd shot Junior. She was the last person who should be lighting into him. "Can we leave the soul healers behind us? We're having lunch so we can clear the air. I don't know about you, but I've aired enough. I don't hold anything against you. I hope you don't hold anything against me."

He curtly shook his head. "Junior, my life, the soul healers . . . I'm not angry about that anymore. But I can't—couldn't—" he took a breath "—I can't help feeling betrayed. By you."

Jillian couldn't blame him. She'd used his attraction to her to manipulate him. "I didn't deliberately choose you. You were the coach who picked up the phone when I happened to call. I knew that behind the cult bullshit, there was a decent guy who fell in with the wrong group." But they were here to clear the air. "I'll admit that I used you a couple of times to make contact with Ruth. I didn't like doing it, but I did what I had to do. I was going after a murderer and a fraud. I'm sorry you got caught in the middle."

His face softened. "Thanks. I appreciate it. Your apology."

The air did feel a little lighter, now that she'd gotten a few things off her chest. She picked up her fork. "Our lunches are getting cold."

Andy dipped one of his fries into the ketchup he'd squirted onto his plate and scanned the immediate area, then lowered his voice. "So you're a Deiform."

"Yeah."

"It must be an honour, to have been chosen by God."

Jillian chewed her mouthful of hamburger and pondered what to say. Telling him she was an atheist would feel confrontational, especially after the conversation they'd just had. She didn't want to go out of her way to constantly make a point, either. She had the gifts. Did it matter if everyone in the Fellowship except her believed they were divine in origin? She swallowed her hamburger. "You thought you were God's chosen when you were in the soul healers."

"Everyone believed the Soul Master received his powers from God."

"Powers?"

Andy smiled ruefully. "I know. I don't know how I believed it, either."

"I thought everyone believed Junior was a god, but I'll admit that I tuned out a lot of the idol worship."

He chuckled. "So, I guess I should be polite and ask. How is she? Samantha?"

Jillian froze. "Don't call her that. The Beguilers call her that. Call her Sam."

Andy's brows shot up. "So they're real? The Beguilers?"

"Oh yeah, they're real."

"Have you seen one?"

"Yes, and I don't want to talk about it." She sipped her water. "Ruth is a Deiform, too. My mother."

"Is she your real mother?"

"No." Her real mother was probably sitting in front of the TV watching a talk show. Jillian ached to see her, to be with someone who loved her, even though she hadn't said so very often. If she could, she'd be at Mom's right now, curled up in the guest bedroom, hoping the pain would go away. "I assume you're officially dead?" she said to Andy. It would be the only way to ensure that he never breathed a word about Junior's death to the police.

He nodded. "I know you are, too. When you told me about Ruth, I thought maybe your mother joined the Fellowship with you."

"No. I left her behind." And they'd better change the subject. "I assume you know why we're meeting Brandon MacIntosh and pretending we want to buy a house?"

"I'm not sure I have all the details about the case, but I've got the gist."

"Let's make sure we're on the same page."

While she and Andy were house hunting, Sam would take a look around Brandon's house and talk to Daniel Prince. They'd either have a solid lead to discuss over dinner, or they'd still have bits of information they couldn't connect together. Was there something there, or were they chasing shadows?

JILLIAN POCKETED HER phone and flashed Andy a smile. "Sam, catching me up on what she's up to." Right now, she was inside Brandon's house. This charade with him had better not be a waste of time. Jillian would rather have Sam's back. She pointed at the house with the for sale sign on its lawn. "I wonder why he told us to meet him here. This house would be way too big for two people."

"I told him we'll eventually start a family," Andy said.

Oh. "Well, you did good. He'll show us places that'll take more than five minutes to walk through."

She'd wait until the third or fourth house before she brought up the agreement Brandon might have signed. Doing so could bring an abrupt end to their house tour, but all she hoped to do was confirm that a non-disclosure agreement existed, so they'd have something concrete. Right now, all they had were guesses, a bunch of dots that weren't connected.

A sedan pulled up to the curb. Jillian chuckled to herself. The last time she'd laid eyes on that car, it had been screeching away.

Brandon hopped out, rounded the car, and strode up to Andy with his hand outstretched. "Brandon MacIntosh."

Andy pumped Brandon's hand. "Andy Nichols."

Brandon turned to Jillian. She sensed his hesitation and stuck out her hand. "Nice to see you again, Brandon."

He shook, but she could see the skepticism in his eyes. She pointed to the house. "This is a good start."

Brandon grunted. "Let's take a look inside." He strode up the path. Jillian glanced at Andy. They fell into step behind him.

Chapter Seventeen

SAM FINISHED READING the information Jeremy had sent about Daniel Prince and got out of the parked car. She'd found nothing at Brandon's. If an agreement existed, Brandon kept it elsewhere, or it had been in the form of a verbal threat. One avenue down. Next, Prince.

Perhaps Marcy had been trying to be kind when she'd called him a businessman. Prince had a string of failed businesses behind him, all in the technology sector. His latest venture was an Internet cafe. Given the rise of mobile devices, Sam doubted this latest business would survive, a prediction that felt firmer when she entered the cafe and saw only one person sitting at a computer. The woman—teenager—at the cash was hunched over her phone, her thumbs tapping away.

Sam approached the counter and cleared her throat.

The woman lifted her head. "Yeah?"

"I'm here to see Daniel Prince."

"He's in the back," she said, pointing that way. Her head dipped again.

Sam strode past the empty workstations and peered into the only other room she could see. Daniel Prince's hair had grayed and his face was no longer smooth, but otherwise he looked pretty much the same as he did in the picture hanging on Steele's wall. She knocked on the open door.

Prince looked away from the computer monitor on his desk. "You Sam Wright?" he asked.

"Yeah."

"Well, come on in and sit down. What's this about? You mentioned my BBS on the phone. I haven't thought about that for years."

Sam sat in the only other chair in the cramped office. "I'm doing some work on the triple murder case." She handed him a business card. "I heard that one of the victims, Boris Vasiliev, used your BBS. In fact, I heard you were friends," she said, deciding to get to the point quickly.

Prince stared at her business card. "I wouldn't say we were friends."

"But he used your BBS."

"He did," Prince said, surprising Sam. For some reason, she'd expected him to deny it. "I only know that because we occasionally ran into each other. But we never hung out together."

"But you're sure he used your system?"

"Boris knew I ran the BBS, so he mentioned that he used it." Prince slipped Sam's business card into a drawer. "I think one of the other murder victims may have logged in, too. I can't be sure, though. The BBS was free to use, and people didn't use their real names on the board. They used handles."

Sam nodded. "I used to hang out on a BBS."

His brows shot up. "Really? Those were the days, eh? Then the web came along and the masses got on board. It's all cats and memes now, unless you know where to hang out."

"Why do you think one of the other victims might have used your BBS?"

Prince shrugged. "I saw him with Boris a few times. I heard them say something that made me think they were meeting up on my turf. I can't remember exactly what he said. We're talking twenty years ago."

Sam kept her excitement from her face. This was the first time she'd heard about a potential connection between any of the victims. "Which victim are we talking about?"

"Dave Mahoney."

"Have you told the police this information?" Sam asked, knowing he hadn't.

Prince shook his head.

"Why not?"

"I can't prove it. Like I said, everyone used handles. And we're talking over twenty years ago. I can't see there being any connection between them being on my BBS and being murdered years later."

"Really? You don't think it's interesting that two guys who used the same BBS were both murdered within the same week?"

"I'm not a cop," Prince said with a sheepish smile.

"Maybe whoever killed them also used your BBS."

Prince's eyes widened. "I hadn't thought of that."

Sure, he hadn't. He must think she was an idiot. He hadn't gone to the cops because he didn't want them to look into him. Sam didn't believe he was the killer, but he was definitely into something shady. His tailored suit, Rolex watch, and manicured nails looked out of place in the shabby office. The money wasn't coming from the Internet cafe. At the same time, he wasn't involved in whatever Vasiliev and Mahoney had been doing, either years ago or in the present day. If he believed Sister Catherine was the killer, he'd be worried that she'd spill the beans about whatever he was involved in now, or what had taken place on his BBS back then. And if he thought her innocent, he'd be wondering if the real killer would come after him.

Prince appeared relaxed. He wasn't worried about anything, including money and the possibility that his latest business would fail. But he must have known about what was going on, all those years ago. Either that, or he'd been a hands-off BBS operator. "The guy who ran the BBS I hung out on was always tinkering with the software and sticking his nose into conversations. Even when he wasn't, we all knew he monitored our discussions." She forced a chuckle. "I bet you did, too."

"What happened on my BBS stayed on my BBS," Prince said, not really responding to what she'd said.

"Look, I don't care what you're involved in now, and I won't implicate you in anything your users did on your BBS. I want to find out whether the police have the right killer."

Prince straightened. "You think they don't?"

"I'm ensuring they do. You can either help me, or help the cops. I think it's possible that Vasiliev and Mahoney used your BBS for something unsavoury," she said, not wanting to suggest that whatever had taken place was illegal. "You must have some idea of what it was."

"No," he said, shaking his head.

"Do you have anything that might help me figure out what they were doing, and whether the third victim also hung out on your BBS?" Assuming Mahoney did meet Vasiliev there.

"Why don't you just let it lie?" Prince stared at his perfect fingernails. "The police have their woman. Let things rest."

"I can't do that. So either you help me, or I tell the police that you can help strengthen their case. I won't use anything you give me against you. I can't say the same for the cops."

"They used handles. I have nothing that ties real names to the handles."

Sam narrowed her eyes. "But you have something. If there's no easy way to identify who the BBS users were, then why not let me take a look at what you have. I'll be very focused in terms of what I care about. Once I find it, I'll stop looking. The cops, on the other hand . . ."

Prince lifted his hands. "Okay, all right. I don't have anything here. If you come back in an hour, I may have something for you."

It could be a gun to her head, but she wanted whatever he had. She looked at her watch. "I'll be back at 3:15." She stood.

Prince put his feet on his desk and locked eyes with her. "You go to the cops, and I'll make your life difficult," he said, his cold eyes and menacing tone contrasting with the easy-going personality he'd projected a second ago.

"I'm a private investigator. If I betrayed informants, I wouldn't be able to do my job."

"You'd likely be dead."

Sam nodded, understanding Prince's message. "See you at 3:15."

Outside, she called Jillian and was surprised when she picked up. Sam had intended to leave her a message.

"I told him I had to take it and stepped outside," Jillian explained.

Sam filled her in about Prince.

"Are you sure you should go back alone?" Jillian said. "Call him and tell him you can't make it until tonight. We'll go together."

"I doubt he's planning a nasty surprise." Plus, she used to go to these sorts of meetings alone. Having Jillian along would be nice, but it wasn't necessary. "He won't kill me, but any information he gives me might be bogus."

"Call me after you've met with him. If I haven't heard from you by 4:00, I'll cut this short and go to the Internet cafe."

Sam wanted to say, "Yes, Mom," but that would be insensitive right now, and she didn't want to mock Jillian's concern. "I'll call you by then."

"Thanks."

Sam hung up and looked up the street, then headed for the bookstore she'd noticed as she'd searched for a parking spot.

JILLIAN FOLLOWED BRANDON up the path to the fourth house they'd see and waited while he fiddled with the lockbox hanging on the door handle. A minute later, she and Andy followed him into a spacious hallway. She breathed in the scent of fresh paint.

"As you can see, the owners have already moved out." Brandon looked up at the ceiling. "All the rooms on the ground floor have these high ceilings, giving them—" He broke off and looked at Jillian. "Is this for real?"

"What do you mean?" she asked, knowing what he meant.

"Out of all the real estate agents you could call, you call me. I only came because it would have looked bad to refuse to meet with someone who'd left a long message with the office about how much he wants to buy a house with his girlfriend and really wants to work with me. I couldn't exactly tell them—"

Change of plan. "Couldn't tell them you were worried I'd bring up Michael Atkins and what happened back then? Listen, all I want to know is whether you signed a non-disclosure agreement when a child porn investigation was dropped. That's it. I don't want details. I don't want to know how you were involved. I just want confirmation that the investigation existed and someone made it go away."

"That's all?"

"If you can tell me how Michael was connected to Sister Catherine, that would help, too."

Brandon shifted his attention to Andy. "Who are you?"

"Her boyfriend. She asked me to help her out." He threw his arm around Jillian and squeezed her. "She didn't think you'd meet with her if she was coming alone."

"She got that right." Brandon muttered something under his breath and went to brush by Jillian.

She grasped his arm. "Brandon, please help. There may be an innocent woman sitting in jail, and who knows, maybe whoever was involved back then could be brought to justice."

He frowned. "She's not innocent. The nun confessed."

"Do you know why?" Jillian had another thought. "Do you know her?" They'd been focusing on Michael.

"No, but who confesses to three murders they didn't commit? She's either guilty, or needs help."

"She wasn't guilty of whatever happened to you back then."

His mouth pressed into a thin line. "Nothing happened to me back then." Defiant eyes met Jillian's, but the vein in his temple ticked.

"Don't you want them brought to justice?" she asked quietly, wishing Andy would take his arm off her shoulders.

"It's too late."

"They can't go to prison, but there are other ways to make them pay," Andy said, finally lifting his arm.

Jillian nodded. "Their reputations can be ruined, they can be—"

Brandon shook his head. "Two are dead."

She quickly seized on a potential connection to Sister Catherine. "Let me guess. They're two of the three people Sister Catherine has confessed to murdering."

He hesitated, then nodded.

"So there was an investigation?"

He nodded again, then glanced around the hallway, as if afraid that someone was listening. "All I know is that we were told not to talk to anyone about anything, or it would be the last thing we did."

"Who threatened you?"

Brandon shook his head.

"Was Michael Atkins involved?"

"I don't want to talk about Michael."

She wanted to press him, but didn't want to spook him. "Was Sister Catherine?"

"No."

"Did Michael know Sister Catherine?"

"No."

"She used to be a teacher. Mrs. Donovan."

"He didn't know her. Do you know why he committed suicide?"

"No," Jillian said.

"Well, neither do I. Neither does anyone else. I'd seen him that morning, and he was fine. He was making plans. It never made sense, that's all I'm saying. These people . . ." He swallowed. "I shouldn't have said anything. Go. I don't want to be seen with you. Don't contact me again."

"Thanks," Jillian murmured. She motioned for Andy to leave with her. "We got what we came for."

Andy's brow furrowed. "Did we?"

"We know the police were investigating and the victims were told to keep their mouths shut." She couldn't wait to tell Sam.

"What now?" Andy asked.

Jillian opened the car door and slid into the driver's seat. "We're done for the afternoon. Let's go back up Sam."

Chapter Eighteen

J ILLIAN LEANED AGAINST a pole outside the Internet cafe, waiting for Sam. Andy was pretending to read the menu posted in a restaurant window. When they'd met up with Sam outside the cafe, she'd insisted on going in alone, but had promised to keep Jillian in the loop telepathically.

"There's nobody else here and he hasn't pulled a gun on me," Sam said.

Jillian's shoulders relaxed. *"Good."* Today was turning out to be very productive, indeed, assuming Prince handed over something that would help them.

Five minutes later, Sam emerged from the cafe carrying a cardboard box. "What's in it?" Jillian asked. Andy hovered nearby.

Sam put the box down on the sidewalk and lifted one of the lid's flaps. Jillian peered inside. She raised her brows at the two stacks of five-and-a-half-inch floppy disks. "I haven't seen one of those in ages."

Andy took a peek. "Do you have anything that can read them?"

Sam didn't look at him. "Not here." She pulled out her phone, then changed her mind and shoved it back into her pocket. "Have you ever been to the island?" she asked Andy.

"No. I've heard about it, though."

"Today's your lucky day. I want you to take this box to Jeremy on the island. I was going to call a Supporter to do it, and then I realized we have one right here."

"How do I get there?"

"I'll call a pilot." Sam pulled out her phone again and wandered away from them.

Jillian turned to Andy. "You'll love the island. Try to persuade Roberta to let you stay a night."

He pulled a sad face. "I thought we'd have dinner together."

"We're on a deadline. Sister Catherine's court case is coming up."

He looked in Sam's direction. "She said she'll call a pilot. I'm going on a private plane?"

"Yeah. You can take my car. I'll ride back to the hotel with Sam." She gave him directions to the airfield, then said to Sam, *"You don't have to rush him away. Are you sure we won't need him again?"*

"If we do, we'll ask for him to come back." Sam returned to Jillian's side and slid her phone into her pocket. Her eyes flicked to Andy. *"I get the feeling he'll hang around if we don't give him a reason to leave. The chemistry is still there for him."*

Jillian wasn't sure Sam was right. Then again, Andy hadn't seemed in a hurry to go. *"Okay, let me say good-bye to him. He's taking my car. I've already given him directions."*

"Meet me at the car, then. It's parked up the block." Sam looked at Andy. "You should be at the airfield for 5:30. Have a good trip, and don't let that box out of your sight. It was nice seeing you again." She strolled away.

Andy stared after her. "It was nice seeing me again?"

"Her sense of humour is a little dry," Jillian said, not sure whether Sam had been polite or half kidding. Probably both. "I'm glad we had a chance to clear the air. I've wondered what happened to you after that night. I know it must have been a shock, suddenly having your life turned upside down like that, and everything you believed ripped away."

"I've wondered about you, too. I was angry, but . . . I, uh, I could call you."

Jillian grimaced. "I don't think that would be a good idea. I'm pretty much always in the middle of an investigation."

"You could call me when you're not."

Damn, he was pleading with his eyes. They might have to work together again. She'd lied to him before, big time, because she'd had to. There was no reason to keep lying to him now. "Look, there's something else you should know about me. I'm gay. I bat for the other team."

His eyes widened. "Seriously?"

"Yeah, seriously."

"I didn't—I mean . . ." He lifted his hands and dropped them to his sides. "I can't seem to get anything right."

"No, no, you're a nice guy. I like you. I could be friends with you. But that's all."

"The old, 'you're a nice guy, but' speech." Andy's smile looked strained. "Thanks for telling me. I won't keep checking my phone."

"The only calls I make these days are related to whatever I'm working on. I'm dead, too, remember."

"Yeah, I guess neither of us will be settling down with anyone."

"There are other dead women in the Fellowship," Jillian said. They both chuckled.

Andy's brows drew together. "Wait. Are you and Sam together?"

Jillian wished. She forced another chuckle. "No. We're stuck together because we share a set of gifts that require both of us for them to work."

"Really?"

"Really. Look, if we see each other again, and I'm thinking we probably will at some point, ask me to tell you about it. You have a plane to catch."

He looked as if he wanted to say more, then he crouched to pick up the box. "I hope we do work together again. Take care of yourself."

She patted his arm. "You too. Oh, and here." She fished the car key from her pocket, then realized he couldn't take the key from her just yet. "I'll walk you to the car."

When they reached it, she unlocked the trunk for him. "Don't lose that box. It's our only lead," she said, watching him settle the box inside the trunk.

He slammed the trunk shut and held out his hand for the key. Wanting to avoid any awkwardness, she dropped the key into his open palm and walked away, giving him a quick wave. The car's engine roared to life behind her. She waved again when Andy drove past her, and smiled when he beeped the car's horn. She *did* like him. He was a nice guy. Unfortunately he had feelings for someone he couldn't have. *Join the freaking club, buddy.* The one nobody wanted to belong to.

Jillian slipped into the passenger seat of Sam's car and fastened her seatbelt. "I came out to him."

Sam gave her a curious look. "How'd he take it?"

"What could he say? It wasn't what he wanted to hear, but now he doesn't have to wonder." Not that it would make him feel any better, but she'd done the right thing. Everyone danced around to spare feelings, but it was kinder to let someone know than to string them along. Okay, not everyone danced. Sam hadn't had any problem telling her that there would never be anything more than friendship between them. Jillian wanted to give her points for honesty, but it was difficult to pat someone on the back for ripping your heart out. In case Sam was thinking about how she'd recently had to tell the woman in the passenger seat that she wasn't interested, Jillian said, "You know what they say. The truth will set you free."

Sam quirked a brow. "You know you just quoted John 8:32, right?"

Had she? Well, John 8:32 could take a flying leap. The truth *could* set you free. Other times it beat the shit out of your heart and made you feel like crap, thank you very much. "What do you think is on the disks?"

"Who knows? Maybe nothing. He could have dumped a bunch of meaningless files on us, to get rid of me. What happened with Brandon? You called earlier than I thought you would."

"He figured we weren't interested in house hunting, but it wasn't a total loss. Two of the murder victims were definitely being investigated back then. I think the cops dropped it because none of the porn victims would talk to them. Brandon said they were told to keep their mouths shut. The pornographers must have threatened to beat the shit out of them, or worse. He's still terrified they'll come after him. The bad news is that Sister Catherine wasn't involved, and Michael didn't know her. He said he didn't know whether Michael was involved in the investigation."

"I thought they were hanging out together." Sam pursed her lips. "Then again, it's common for teenagers who are being sexually abused to keep it to themselves. If they're not afraid to talk about it, they're ashamed. It's possible they were both being abused and never told each other."

"He also said that he'd seen Michael the morning of the suicide. In his opinion, Michael wasn't suicidal. But kids can be really good at hiding pain, and as you said, if he was ashamed or frightened . . ."

Sam nodded. "You and Andy did great, but it doesn't put us any further ahead. Still no connection between him and Sister Catherine, or whatever the murder victims were up to and Sister Catherine. We still have nothing to suggest she's innocent. Let's hope the disks give us something."

Inside Sam's hotel room, Jillian watched a Supporter wheel in the last of the banker's boxes he was delivering. While Sam said goodbye to him, she eyed the twelve boxes. The moment the hotel door swung shut, she said, "You've got to be kidding me. Did Jeremy do a search for the names we know?"

Sam nodded. "Nothing. Dig in, I guess." She lifted the lid off the nearest box.

Jillian chose another one and pulled out a stack of papers that amounted to about five percent of the box's contents. When Sam had said she'd asked for hard copies of the files so she wouldn't have to stare at a screen for hours on end, Jillian had thought she was exaggerating. Apparently not. It was going to be a long day.

Three hours later, she wanted to throw the boxes out the window. They were filled with transcripts of conversations that had taken place on Prince's BBS. Given that the board had operated for a couple of years, twelve boxes would be a tiny percentage of the discussions. Why had Prince given Sam these? "What did you discuss on the BBS you belonged to?" she asked Sam. "Were the conversations this inane?" And then there were the acronyms. She'd had to look a few of them up on the Internet and was keeping a running translation.

Sam lifted her head and rubbed one of her eyes. "We discussed the Bible."

"Honestly, I'd rather read those transcripts than these."

Sam's mouth turned up at the corners. "Let's do another half hour and then go for dinner."

Jillian forced her eyes back to the page she'd been reading.

Little Star: i like the red ones the best

Bluebird: really? i like the brown ones

Bluebird: brb. pizza's here
Trigger: i want a slice
Little Star: me too
Bluebird: back
Little Star: wb
Trigger: wb
Trigger: afk
Bluebird: yummy heres a virtual slice for you. enjoy
Little Star: ouch. i just burned my tongue
Bluebird: rotflmaoastc

Jillian checked her crib sheet. Rolling on the floor laughing my ass off and scaring the cat. Okay. Would someone please put her out of her misery before she flung herself out the window? At least these three weren't having cybersex. She'd read enough of that this afternoon to want to poke out her eyeballs and bleach her brain.

Bluebird: the delivery guy was hot
Little Star: you should have . . .

She looked up when Sam's pen clicked. Sam circled something on the paper in front of her, then put it aside and rifled through the pages she'd already read. "Did you find something?" Jillian asked.

"Maybe." Sam continued to search through her finished pile. A few minutes later, she lay five pages next to each other on the bed.

Jillian stood and peered at the papers. Sam had circled three handles.

"They're always on together, and I think they're using some type of code." Sam pointed to a line. "This doesn't make any sense."

Jillian read it. *Harley D: drop pkg rush 442 pic.*

"That's sort of repeated on each of these pages, sometimes several times. Look here, and here."

Jillian's eyes followed Sam's finger. *Harley D: drop pkg reg 442 pic.* On another page: *Pluto: pick pkg rush 518 vid* and *BionicMan: drop pkg long 798 vid.*

"There's more of the same, and other types of sentences that don't make sense."

"Three handles, three murder victims," Jillian said. "It sounds like they're talking about photos and videos, but . . . maybe the numbers are coded locations?"

"If it is the three victims, they can't tell us. Look here." Sam stuck another page under Jillian's nose. "Prince broke in. They were paying him off."

BionicMan: pick pkg reg 442 pic

[Admin]: you know what guys, im sick of this crap. i wish youd fuckin take it somewhere else. this isnt your fuckin playground

Pluto: how much more do you want

[Admin]: you sick piece of shit

BionicMan: how much asshole?

Harley D: cut the bs p you don't care as long as you get the $$

BionicMan: hypocrit

[Admin]: f you

[Admin]: its business man give me the same as last time

There was more posturing until the three users agreed to pay Prince more money. "I wonder why he gave us the transcripts. He obviously knew what was going on," Jillian said.

"What was going on?" Sam asked, but not as a challenge. "Nobody can say for sure what they were arranging on there, and if they're who we think they are, they're all dead. Prince didn't want me pointing the cops in his direction, that's all. He's not worried about what happened on his BBS back then, but about what he's up to today."

"Okay, so let's say we're right, and BionicMan, Harley D, and Pluto are the three victims and they were using the BBS to coordinate sharing their collections." Ugh.

"They could have been arranging photo and video shoots, too," Sam pointed out.

Double ugh. "Where does Sister Catherine come in? Did she know this was going on back then? Is that why she killed them? Or if she didn't kill them, who is she covering for?"

"One of the victims," Sam stated. "Not the murder victims. The boys."

"Okay, but why wait so long? And if she *is* covering for one of the boys, why would she do that? Why would she ruin her reputation and throw away the rest of her life?"

Sam chewed her lip. "Guilt." She paced. "How about this. Sister Catherine was a teacher. Let's say she somehow found out that some of her students were being sexually abused by the three victims. On top of that, the abusers were sharing photos and videos of whatever they were doing. Maybe she's the reason for the investigation. Maybe she went to the authorities."

"But someone powerful got them to sweep it under the rug."

Sam frowned. "Maybe not. There's another possibility."

"I'm all ears."

"What if Michael didn't commit suicide? Everyone says it came out of the blue and he was fine that day. I know that doesn't mean everything was fine, but what if he was murdered because he was key to the investigation?"

Excitement surged through Jillian. "Maybe he was going to testify for the prosecution!" She wanted to high-five Sam. "If it's true, we still need to figure out the Sister Catherine angle. You know, why we're looking into this in the first place."

"I'll call Jeremy and see if he can dig up Michael's autopsy report, and the police report, too. You'll go back to the school where Sister Catherine taught and dig a little deeper. I know Michael didn't go there. Neither did Brandon, but . . ."

"It's definitely worth going back. Last time I focused on Michael's photo." Something was niggling at her. "Remember one of the nuns mentioned that Sister Catherine was agitated when she saw a column in the newspaper about the first victim? We thought maybe she'd recognized the victim, but maybe it was more than that. Maybe she suspected who'd killed him. It's hard to believe that someone could feel so guilty that she'd arrange to take the rap, though."

"Guilt can be powerful," Sam said.

"So can the need for revenge. If we're on the right track, the killer waited years to blow his abusers away." Jillian couldn't stop herself from hoping the sons of bitches had suffered.

Chapter Nineteen

Principal John Duncan ushered Jillian into his office and motioned for her to sit. "More research, eh? How can I help?"

Jillian waited for him to sit down. "Sister Catherine taught grades nine and ten here, correct?"

His brow furrowed. "Yes."

"Did she do any tutoring on the side, or anything else that may have involved boys around fourteen or fifteen years old?"

Duncan took a moment to think about it. "Well, she . . ." He shook his head. "No, they would have been too young." He frowned in concentration, then his eyes lit up. "I think she might have helped out with the drama club at Eastside High."

"Why? Why not do something here?"

"Oh, it was here, or at least it involved some of our students. I can see you're confused," Duncan said with a smile. "Sometimes the teacher over at Eastside needed more students for one of her plays. They don't have a drama club there anymore, but until about ten years ago, the annual play was a community effort. A few other schools also participated."

Sam had visited Eastside. "Sister Catherine led the drama charge for this school?"

"Yes."

"I assume there were joint rehearsals."

"Oh yes. For a good few months before the performance."

"Who did she work with at Eastside High?"

"Jean Shipton. You should talk to her. She's still there."

Jillian stood. "Thank you. I'll go see her."

"I'll look forward to your book," Duncan said.

She flashed him a smile that faded as soon as she'd left his office. Outside, she called Sam. "Apparently Sister Catherine was involved in a drama club at Eastside High."

Sam grunted. "Nobody mentioned it when I was there, but the person I spoke to was pretty tight-lipped. She checked their files and told me Sister Catherine hadn't taught there, which we already knew. She let me look through class photos but wasn't interested in helping me beyond that. She was also in her early twenties, so she didn't know anything about what was going on in the eighties. I didn't press because we had no reason to think Sister Catherine had a connection to the school. We were trying to find out who Michael was. Do you want me to go back?"

"No, let me. Maybe the book angle will loosen her up."

"Okay."

"Anything from Jeremy?"

"We have the files. We're having someone take a look at the autopsy report. I'm looking at the police report now."

They said good-bye.

Fifteen minutes later, Jillian smiled at the twenty-something woman Sam had dealt with. "A book?" the woman breathed, after Jillian had given her the usual spiel. "And you're sure the nun helped out here after school?"

Jillian nodded. "She worked with Jean Shipton."

"Mrs. Shipton." The woman picked up her phone. "She's probably in class, but I'll call the teacher's lounge. Have a seat."

Jillian sat in one of the chairs outside the principal's office, something she'd never done as a kid. Nope, she'd been one of the good kids. It wouldn't have done to have the pastor's daughter acting out in class and sent to the principal's office. She'd had to be the perfect angel.

The office clerk hung up. "She won't be available until recess, and that's over an hour away. Do you want to come back?"

"Sure."

"If you give me your cell number, I'll call you. In case I forget, she'll be down around 1:45."

After reciting her number, Jillian headed to the Tim Hortons she'd spotted on the corner. As she stared out the window and sipped her tea, she chuckled about how Sam the PI had been given the cold shoulder, but Jillian the author was receiving the royal treatment. Their PI licences opened a lot of doors for them, but they could also make people clam up.

Her phone rang as she was strolling back to the school. It was the helpful twenty-something. Mrs. Shipton was waiting for her. The teacher must have raced to the office, because it was only 1:40.

"So you're writing a book about Sister Catherine," Shipton said, after the twenty-something had ushered them into a tiny office and they'd shaken hands. "Well, I knew her as Cathy. Could have knocked me over with a feather when I found out she was taking vows. I didn't even know she was religious."

"I was told that she ran the drama club with you."

"Mmm." Shipton's eyes grew wistful. "We had a lot of fun, doing that. The kids did, too. They all wanted to be the next Hollywood star, I suppose."

"Did, uh, Cathy take a special interest in any of the boys?"

Shipton drew back. "What do you mean, special interest?"

"Not what you're thinking," Jillian said quickly. "Did she have to coach any of the boys more than the others, or did she . . ." Oh, to hell with it. "What I'm trying to get at is whether any of the boys might have confided in her. I've been given the impression that she loved teaching and really nurtured her students. If she helped any of them with problems outside of school, I'd like to interview them."

"Oh. All right, then. Let me think." Shipton tapped her chin. "I can't say that she spent more time with any of the boys. She always tried to give everyone equal attention. You don't end up doing that, no matter how hard you try, but she didn't neglect anyone, or spend much more time with anyone in particular."

Great. Another brick wall.

"Maybe they'd tell you differently, though. I haven't kept track of everyone, but I know where two of the boys are." She smiled. "Well, they're men now, aren't they? Some of them have their own children, including the two I know about. One has a son who goes here now, and the other a daughter. That's how I know they're still in Grayhurst." She nudged Jillian's arm. "Interesting story with one of them. He used to try our patience when rehearsing. Always acting out and telling us we were wrong. Mouthing off for no reason. Interesting thing was, he was a model student until he started grade nine. We came this close to throwing him out of the club." Shipton made a one-inch gap with her thumb and index finger. "But then as suddenly as he'd become a handful, he calmed down."

"Interesting," Jillian said politely.

"But here's the interesting bit. His son did the same thing. Last year, he started acting up in class and being aggressive to the other students. He punched another boy. He was mouthing off to all his teachers. He started smoking. He was suspended twice. We had his father in here so many times, I lost count. I don't know what Shawn did, but a few weeks later, his son's attitude changed, and now it's as if he never acted out. His marks have improved, and he's so much more pleasant to be around."

"When did this happen?" Jillian asked, an idea taking shape.

"I can't remember when it started, but Ryan—the son—he's been his usual self for about a month now."

Jillian's breath quickened. "What's the father's name?" she asked. "I'd like to interview him about Cathy. I want to talk to someone who was in the drama club. His history will make for a more interesting story."

"Shawn Mitchell. That's the father." Shipton moistened her lips. "Why are you only interested in the boys? It was a co-ed club."

"Someone else told me that Cathy had helped a couple of boys out with problems at home, but couldn't remember their names."

"Oh. Well, I don't know anything about that. All I can tell you is that she didn't treat anyone differently when I was with her."

"Thank you for your time. You've been very helpful."

"Really? I didn't say much."

True, but Shipton may have provided the missing piece that allowed Jillian to answer all the questions she and Sam had asked yesterday when going through the BBS transcripts.

The twenty-something gave her Shawn Mitchell's address and phone number without a word of protest. Jillian left the school eager to get back to the hotel, so she could tell Sam that she might have identified the killer.

WHEN SAM OPENED her hotel room door, Jillian started talking. "What if he didn't wait years and he didn't do it for revenge," she said, brushing past Sam and whirling to face her. "What if he did it because the men who'd abused him were doing the same to his son?"

Sam gestured for Jillian to slow down. "Start at the beginning."

"According to Jean Shipton, one of the boys in the drama club has a son who now attends the same school. Both of them had a period when they acted out. Both suddenly calmed down. The son started to behave again soon after the murders."

"So you're thinking that they acted out because they were being sexually abused and the son calmed down because the father killed their mutual abusers?"

"Yeah, and the father calmed down because the investigation spooked the abusers and stopped the abuse. When they figured it was safe to start up again, the father was too old."

Sam cocked her head to the left, then to the right. "Okay, it sounds plausible, but how does Sister Catherine fit in?"

Damn Sister Catherine. "I don't know. Maybe she doesn't. Maybe we stumbled across something unrelated."

"No. If your hypothesis is true, it's too coincidental that Sister Catherine was one of the leaders of the father's drama club. Let's keep digging. Call Jeremy and have him get everything he can on the father."

Used to Sam barking orders, Jillian said, "Okay. Did you hear anything about Michael's autopsy?"

"Yeah. Our expert can't say he committed suicide, but also can't say that he didn't. He was hanging in the closet. He didn't leave a note. There was nothing in the autopsy report to suggest someone killed him, but there was nothing to eliminate it, either."

"Nothing like, he couldn't have done it because he was left-handed, or the rope was too short—"

"Stocking."

"Okay, stocking, or . . . I don't know." Jillian blew out a sigh. "We have a working explanation, but not a shred of concrete evidence to support it."

"We can't explain why Sister Catherine confessed."

Jillian sank onto the bed. "You have to go see her again."

"I will. But first we have to look into the father and his son."

"The father's name is Shawn Mitchell." Jillian pulled out her phone and called Jeremy.

⋆ ⋆ ⋆ ⋆ ⋆

SITTING IN THE car's passenger seat, Jillian clasped her hands on her lap and watched the colour return to Sam's cheeks. "Anyone home?" she asked, when Sam opened her eyes.

"Emma was right. They're at Ryan's hockey game. You didn't tag along?"

"No. I have to touch you to tag along."

Sam looked at Jillian for a moment. She drew breath, but then shook her head and got out of the car. Jillian scrambled after her. "Let's both go in. Two of us can search the place faster than one. We know around what time they'll be home, so I don't need to keep watch."

Sam didn't reply. They walked the half block to the Mitchell residence and ducked into the backyard. Sam snapped a latex glove onto her left hand and pulled out her phone with her right. She didn't have to tell Jillian that she was calling Emma. "Okay, we're at the back door." She waited, then tried the door knob. The door swung open. "We're in. I'll call you when I want you to reactivate the alarm. If any of the Mitchell cell phones move, let us know." She disconnected and stepped inside the house.

Jillian followed her in and glanced around the cozy family room. Drawn to the framed photos on the wall, she gazed at Shawn Mitchell, his wife, and their two sons. If she was judging the ages of the subjects correctly, one photo appeared fairly recent. Everyone was smiling, even though Ryan may have been enduring abuse and his father had killed three men, depending on exactly when the photo had been taken.

Everyone always smiled. She'd looked like the happiest girl alive in all her school photos after Dad's suicide. *Don't let them see you sweat. Don't let them see you cry.* Every photo was a lie, and not because they'd been air brushed.

Now photos were digital. Many would be lost. When people were feeling nostalgic and wanted to travel back in time, there would be gaps in their history. They'd fill in the blanks with smiling faces, not tears.

She turned around. Sam was searching through a cabinet stuffed with video games. "I'll see if he has a study," Jillian said, figuring that if Mitchell had hung onto anything incriminating, he'd probably hide it in his study or man cave. "I'll check the garage, too," she added.

Sam grunted.

Jillian wanted to apologize for what she'd said in the car, but doing so could make things worse. Over the past few days it had almost felt comfortable working with her, but only because they'd been busy. She'd blown it, really blown it.

She found Mitchell's home office in the basement, and was sifting through his filing cabinet when she heard Sam coming down the stairs. Sam strode into the office and thrust an open photo album under Jillian's nose. "Who's that?"

She stared down at it. The man on the left was a younger Shawn Mitchell in a graduation gown and cap. The woman beaming proudly to his right, the one he had his arm around . . . She sucked in her breath. "It's Sister Catherine."

"She went to his university graduation," Sam said, unable to contain a smile. "We finally found something."

Jillian's elation that they'd uncovered a connection between Sister Catherine and their prime murder suspect was tempered by her desire to hug the woman in front of her. Would the longing and the disappointment ever go away? She'd thought rejection would do it, but no. Only never seeing Sam would do it, so she'd have to get used to the ache in her chest and focus on their investigations. "He went to university in Ottawa. She had to travel there."

"Yeah, but not from here. He graduated when she was living in Kingston after her divorce. But the key thing is that they kept in touch, or at least they did before she entered the convent. I'll see if I can find anything more recent."

Jillian waited until she could hear Sam thumping up the stairs, then returned to searching the filing cabinet. The top and second drawers were filled with household bills, insurance papers, and old tax returns. Mitchell had kept every piece of paper from the last ten years. The guy wasn't a fan of digital bills and bank statements.

The bottom drawer held more of the same. When she pushed it shut, something inside it bumped against the back of the drawer. Jillian opened it again and pushed all the files toward the front. Excitement surged through her. She lifted the stack of envelopes that had been hidden underneath the files and carefully removed the rubber band that held the envelopes together. Letters to Shawn Mitchell. No return name or address. The envelopes weren't sealed. She opened one and pulled out the single sheet it held.

Dear Shawn,

I'm sorry I haven't answered your last two letters. I didn't mean to frighten you. I haven't written because I've been staying at St. Joseph's convent. I had to withdraw for a bit, to try to stop all the clamour inside my mind and outside my window. I haven't been in touch with anyone during the last three months. Just the nuns, and I've come to a decision. I'm entering the convent. I can't stay in this world anymore. I need God. I need peace.

I'll be able to write to people, but this will be my last letter to you. We have to let each other go. You have a wife, and a child on the way. I have to focus on God, on forgiveness. Our relationship is keeping us in the past. We have to break free. We have to reclaim our lives.

I'm sorry I couldn't help you. I tried, but I wasn't powerful enough. I let you down. I believe God will do what I couldn't. I have to believe, to make sense of it.

Take care of your wife and your son. Protect them.

I'm sorry.

Cathy.

Jillian read the letter again. Had Sister Catherine and Shawn been lovers? She raced up the stairs. "I hit the jackpot." She held out Sister Catherine's final letter. "Read this."

Sam looked up from a photo album and took the letter.

"There's a stack of them. Letters."

"Just a sec," Sam said, her eyes on the letter.

"Sorry," Jillian murmured. "I'll let you finish reading." When Sam lowered the letter, Jillian said, "Do you think they were lovers?"

"I don't know. Relationship could mean friendship."

Was she trying to make a point?

"He moved to Ottawa for university and didn't come back until after she was in the convent," Sam continued. "She never lived in Ottawa. When would they have gotten together?"

"Did you find more photos of them?"

"Yes, but they were all taken at his graduation. His future wife was there. She didn't look upset."

"Maybe she didn't know or suspect. Hopefully these will tell us more." Jillian looked at the stack of letters she held, then glanced at her watch. "Forget the albums. Let's go through these."

"You start. I'll search the rest of the house." Sam slid the photo album back into a bookcase. "Did you finish his office?"

"I checked the desk and the filing cabinet. I didn't look for a safe or check anything else."

Sam nodded and strode from the room. Jillian pulled out her phone and snapped a photo of Sister Catherine's last letter. She carefully folded the sheet and put it back into the envelope, then moved to the next letter on the stack. Worried about running out of time, she only skimmed the rest of the letters. Nothing jumped out at her to suggest that Sister Catherine had been carrying on with a former student, but a more careful read was in order.

When she finished, she put the letters back where she'd found them and slowly pushed the drawer shut. She found Sam in an upstairs bedroom. "You finished his study, right?"

Sam nodded.

Jillian checked her watch again. "We should go soon."

"Only the garage is left."

"You haven't found anything else?"

"No."

They went down to the garage. Fortunately the Mitchell family wasn't using it for storage. It only took them a few minutes to check a couple of plastic tubs in the back corner. Nothing. Jillian doubted he'd buried anything in the backyard, but they did a cursory search on the way out. The ground didn't appear disturbed.

"I suppose it was too much to expect to find his blood-splattered clothing," she said.

"We're still not sure he did it. Now we know for sure that he's connected to Sister Catherine, but we don't have anything connecting him to the murders. If our theory is right, it could have been either of them." Sam was silent for a moment. "In the letter, she sounded like whatever happened was still haunting her. Maybe she killed them."

"So what's our next move? Talk to him, or her?"

"Him."

"Maybe something in the letters will help us."

Sam nodded and pulled the driver's door open. "I'm getting tired of the hotel. Let's hope we're closing in on what really happened, so we can go home."

Jillian forced a smile. The island wouldn't be the same. The cloud that had hung over her since she'd spilled her guts to Sam would darken her favourite places and take the bounce out of her step. *But you know what they say. Better to know the truth than to delude yourself.* Yeah? Bullshit. Next time she'd stick with "ignorance is bliss."

JILLIAN CLOSED THE file containing the letter she'd just read and opened the next one. Sister Catherine and Shawn had definitely been close, but not "between the sheets" close. Events from the past had bound them together, but unfortunately Sister Catherine danced around whatever had happened, always referring to what they considered a joint failure in vague terms.

Someone tapped on her hotel room door. "It's dinner," she said to Sam, who was reading another letter on her phone. Now that they were homing in on the killer, neither had wanted to take a break, but they were hungry.

Jillian opened the door and paid the pizza guy. "It smells good," she said, putting the pizza on the desk and flipping the box lid open. No response. She turned around. "Sam?"

"He has a cottage," Sam murmured.

"What?"

Sam lifted her head. "He has a cottage. There could be something there. I'll call Jeremy."

Jillian slid a piece of pizza onto a napkin. "We could head out there tomorrow."

"No. It's near Glenwood."

"That's four hours away by car."

"Yeah. Let's have Supporters take this one. They can search the place tomorrow. We'll ambush Mitchell on his way out of work."

Jillian agreed that they didn't have to be the ones to search the cottage, but had Sam suggested it to avoid a long car ride with her? "Sure. Sounds like a plan."

She bit into her pizza and listened to Sam's side of the conversation with Jeremy. Okay, she was saying that sending Supporters would mean they could confront Mitchell tomorrow when he left work, but was it true?

Sam disconnected.

"You have to wonder why they moved back to Grayhurst, especially in Mitchell's case," Jillian said.

"The rest of his family is here." Sam shrugged. "I don't know. Maybe he thought he'd worked through it."

"But his kids . . ."

"He probably thought he could protect them, or maybe he didn't imagine that the same abusers would go after his son."

Plus, it didn't matter where one lived. Nowhere was safe. Jillian wasn't paranoid, but there were pedophiles preying on children in every city. She pointed to the pizza. "Eat." Then she returned to her laptop and continued reading the letter from Sister Catherine, a.k.a. Cathy. Was she covering for Mitchell, or had she killed for him?

Chapter Twenty

Jillian shoved her hands into her pockets and kept her eye on the entrance to the office building where Shawn Mitchell worked. The Supporters had come through. They'd found a memory stick containing recent photographs of the victims under a floorboard in one of the cottage's bedrooms. Sam had told them to leave it there. The cottage would now be under surveillance, in case Mitchell returned to get rid of the stick, which he might feel compelled to do after the conversation she and Sam were about to have with him.

"It's almost 5:00," she murmured to Sam. People were streaming from the building. Fortunately it didn't have underground parking. They were standing near Mitchell's car. "There he is," she said, pointing.

Sam straightened. "Don't forget to let me do the talking at first."

Jillian nodded. She'd start recording the conversation with her phone and hope that Mitchell would be too focused on Sam to notice. He might let something slip that they didn't pick up on right away.

"Shawn Mitchell," Sam said loudly when he approached his car.

He looked in their direction.

"I'm Sam Wright. I'm working with Sister Catherine's defence team. This is my associate, Jillian. We have a few questions we'd like to ask you."

He backed away from Sam and tripped over his feet.

Sam caught his elbow. "Are you okay?" Jillian slid her phone from her jacket pocket and hit Record, then slipped it out of sight again. *"I'm recording,"* she mentally said to Sam.

"I'm good. Sorry." Mitchell moistened his lips. "Who did you say you are?"

"A private investigator working with Sister Catherine's defence team. We understand that you kept in touch with her until she entered the convent."

The blood drained from his face. For a moment, Jillian thought he was going to faint. "Do you mind if I smoke?" He pulled a pack of cigarettes and a lighter from his pocket before Sam could reply, lit his cigarette, and took a long drag. "How do you know we kept in touch?"

"She told me."

Mitchell tapped away the ash from the cigarette's tip and sucked more deadly chemicals into his lungs.

"He's not what I expected," Sam said. *"The guy's a wreck. I'm not going to hold back. We just might get a confession."* "We know about the photos at your cottage," she said to Mitchell. "We know about what your abusers were doing to your son."

He winced.

"I understand why you did it, but I don't understand why you're going to let Sister Catherine rot in jail for the rest of her life."

He jerkily shook his head. "She wanted to," he said hoarsely.

Jillian wanted to jump in and ask a question, but didn't want to disrupt Sam's flow.

"Why?" Sam asked. "Why would she want to confess to murders she didn't commit?"

"What do you mean?"

"You said she wanted to."

Mitchell's eyes darted to Jillian, then back to Sam. "She wanted to kill them."

Sam's brows shot up. "You're saying *she* murdered them?"

He paused to take another drag. "We don't see them as murders. We had to stop them. They deserved it."

"Why didn't you go to the police?"

His smile looked ghoulish. "The police? The courts? We tried that last time. Then Mike Atkins died, and those fuckers were free to do what they wanted." His mouth twisted. "They weren't stupid. They went underground for a while. But sickos like that, they can't stop. They can't resist. But they made a mistake when they went after my son. They won't be going after anyone else's son now."

"What did you do to make Sister Catherine confess? Do you have something on her? Did you threaten her?"

His eyes widened. "She willingly confessed."

"But she didn't do it," Sam pressed.

"Look at me. Do you think I could do it?" The cigarette burned away between his trembling fingers. He looked at it, then dropped it to the sidewalk and squished it with his foot. "I have a family. I show up at work every day. But those fuckers . . . they took so much from me, and then they were doing it to my son? I don't want to go to jail. Cathy, she doesn't want me to go to jail. When she found out they were abusing my son, she came up with a plan. She didn't try to talk me out of it. If she'd said something, told me she didn't want to do it . . ."

Jillian wanted to roll her eyes. So it was Sister Catherine's fault. Please. She wasn't a fan of the woman, but "the nun made me do it" worked just as well for her as blaming the devil.

"If she planned to murder them, why would she try to talk *you* out of it?" Sam asked. "Wouldn't it be the other way around?"

Mitchell stared at his feet.

Sam looked at Jillian, then focused on Mitchell. "You know what I think? You murdered three men in cold blood and you're letting a friend throw her life away so you don't have to go to prison." She snorted. "You're as bad as the men who abused you."

Mitchell lunged at Sam. Jillian reached for her concealed pistol, then relaxed her hand when Mitchell glared at Sam, but stepped back.

"Do you think I want Cathy to be in prison?" he asked, his voice strained. "I feel guilty about her. I don't feel guilty about protecting my son and getting rid of three filthy pedophiles."

"So you did do it."

"No. I knew and didn't stop her. Anyone in my place would have done the same."

"Go to the police. I'm sure a jury will understand. The prosecution might cut a deal."

"I told you, I'm through dealing with the police. And the others know that as long as I'm free, I could come after them."

"Others?" Jillian blurted.

Mitchell's eyes flicked to her. "Do you think there are only three sickos in Grayhurst? We promised each other we'd stop after we took care of the ones who abused me and my son. But there are more, and I hope they're looking over their shoulders. As long as they know I'm out here—"

"They won't stop," Sam said. "They can't. You said so yourself. They might resist for a while, but . . ."

He drew a shaky breath and stared into the distance. "Some other boy's father will have to blow them away."

"Tip off the police anonymously."

"No. The others might have pictures and videos of my son. He could get dragged into it." His eyes focused on Sam again. "They're not going to make him feel like he did something wrong, like he's the sick one."

"Do you have the names of these other pedophiles?" Sam asked levelly, but Jillian could sense that she really, really wanted the names.

Mitchell nodded.

"Tell me who they are."

"So you can tell the police? No. We saved my son. That's all that matters to me."

"You can't mean that. Do you really want someone else's son to go through what you and your son did?"

"I can't go to prison." He lifted his chin defiantly. "It shouldn't be a crime to take out the garbage."

"Tell that to Sister Catherine. She's the one who'll be locked away. She's the one whose reputation is shattered."

"She wanted to do it," he said, but his voice quavered. "She understands. She wants me to have a life, to be there for my family."

"I'm getting frustrated," Sam said. *"You try."*

Jillian stepped in. "We have enough evidence to show that *you* killed them, not Sister Catherine," she said, lying.

"No. She did it. Her prints are on the gun. There's nothing tying me to the murders. I won't talk, and neither will she. She'll deny anything you say about me."

"We have the memory stick with the photos."

"She gave it to me. She asked me to hide it."

Bullshit. When would a nun have had the time to photograph the victims?

"Turning yourself in would be the right thing to do," Sam said.

Mitchell's certainty that Sister Catherine would stick to her story seemed to have given him back his courage. "Cathy is where she wants to be, doing what she wants to do. She'll never implicate me, and I won't go back on what we agreed." He pulled out his car key. The car beeped when he unlocked the doors. "I've said all I'm going to say."

They didn't try to stop him. Jillian watched him speed away, then turned to Sam. "We have what we need for Roberta."

Sam sighed and shook her head. "No, we don't."

In their parked car, Jillian listened to the recorded conversation with Mitchell. After he'd sped off, they'd returned to the car but hadn't gone anywhere. Mitchell had answered some questions and created new ones.

"I've said all I'm going to say." A car door slammed. An engine started.
"We have what we need for Roberta."
A sigh. "No, we don't."

She twisted to look at Sam, who was in the driver's seat. "Sometimes it sounds like he's confessing, and other times he's pointing the finger at her. But I'm pretty sure he did it."

"Both of them did it. One of them pulled the trigger, but both of them did it."

"I think he pulled the trigger."

"Why?"

"Because he said things like, 'She didn't try to talk me out of it,' and 'Some other boy's father is going to have to blow them away.'"

"He said they planned it together. They're both guilty, no matter who actually killed them."

"But remember what Sister Susan said about Sister Catherine freaking out when she saw the news of the first murder in the paper? Why would she freak out if she'd killed the first one? I think she only got involved after the first murder. When she saw the paper, her mind went right to Mitchell and what had happened all those years ago. Sister Susan said she saw her with a man the next day. I bet it was Mitchell. I bet that's when she offered to take the rap for him."

"But why would she think of Mitchell? Other boys were abused back then."

"True." But Sister Catherine had kept in touch with Mitchell until she'd entered the convent. Seeing the newspaper article would have dredged up the past. "Maybe she didn't meet with him because she suspected him of doing it. Maybe she met with him to make sure he was okay. She would have known that the news of the murder would take him back to when he was being abused. Maybe she only found out he'd done it when she saw him. The guy must have been a basket case. Look at how he was just now."

Sam nodded thoughtfully. "You should go back and show Sister Susan a photo of him."

"I will."

"We have nothing tying him to the murders, and she's just as guilty as he is. Assuming you're right about her seeing the newspaper and putting two and two together, she didn't go to the police. She stood by while he murdered the other two."

"Or they were in it together from the beginning. I think he started it with the first murder and she came on board after that, but am I one hundred percent sure?" Jillian slowly shook her head. "No."

Sam frowned. "Roberta was wrong. Sister Catherine may be innocent of murder, but she's not innocent. She's at least an accessory for the other two."

"We can throw Mitchell to the cops. They'll charge him with being an accessory and investigate further."

"But he won't give them the names of the other pedophiles he mentioned. That's what we're here for. It's not really about Sister Catherine." Sam chewed her lip. "I'm betting Mitchell told her about the other pedophiles. We have to make her give us the names."

Jillian smiled. "What are you going to do, go visit her and slap her around?"

Sam's eyes brightened. "No, I'm going to use the leverage we've got. Who does she care about?"

"Mitchell." Jillian understood what Sam intended to do. "We'll tell her we'll give the recording to the police unless she gives us the names."

"She'll want to keep Mitchell out of it."

"But we *are* going to give Mitchell to the police, right? We can't let him get away with it, as much as we might like to," Jillian said.

"We can't give them the recording. They'll want to know who's talking to him. We'll be long gone. Even if we weren't, we can't have the police digging into our backgrounds. We can't go to court."

"But we can point them in Mitchell's direction," Jillian said.

"We could, but he won't tell them the names of the other pedophiles. We need Sister Catherine to talk. I'll give her my word that we'll keep Mitchell out of it if she gives us the names."

"But we'd be letting a killer go free, or an accomplice. No, a killer. I think he did it. I think she kept her mouth shut and then took the rap. So yeah, we'd be letting a triple murderer walk."

"It won't be the first time we've had to make a choice like this. If I tell Sister Catherine we'll keep Mitchell out of it, then we have to keep him out of it. I won't outright lie."

"How do you know he won't kill again?"

"You saw him. Do you think he'll do it again?"

"If one of those pedophiles goes after his son, sure," Jillian said.

"But that won't happen if we get the names."

"Assuming they're convicted."

"He won't kill an innocent person, and I doubt his son is in danger. According to him, the other pedophiles believe he was involved in the murders. Maybe he told them. He knew they wouldn't go to the police."

Jillian wanted to argue that Mitchell had to go to prison because vigilantism wasn't right, no matter how heinous the crime, but the Fellowship took the law into its own hands all the time. She despised hypocrites and wouldn't become one. If it were her, she'd tip off the cops after she had the names, regardless of what she'd promised Sister Catherine. But apparently that would be over the line for Sam. Jillian wanted Mitchell *and* the pedophiles, but she could go along with Sam and sleep at night. "Okay. If you give her your word, we'll leave Mitchell out of it."

"Good. I think we should both go and see Sister Catherine. But before we do, go see Sister Susan. I'll tell the Supporters watching Mitchell's cottage that he might swing by for the photos. I don't think he will, but if he does, we'll want to know what he does with them." Sam's voice lifted. "This could be over tomorrow."

Yeah, and it would be back to the island. Would Sam still want to jam together? Would she avoid the annoying woman she was bound to until Roberta sent them away again? Their working relationship had survived Jillian's embarrassing revelation, but there was a barrier between them now. Her impatience had derailed a growing friendship. The island would deepen her pain over its loss.

Chapter Twenty-One

J ILLIAN TRIED NOT to fidget as she waited for Sister Catherine to enter the prison's interview room. The windowless box reminded her of the room she'd sat in at the courthouse while she waited for her arraignment for the murders of Jim and Joanna to begin. She'd thought her life had changed when the cops had arrested her in the underground parking garage at work, but the real turning point had been that day, when the Fellowship had busted her out of jail and never let go. She'd met Sam that evening. Looking back, she'd felt drawn to her almost instantly, and here they were.

She gave Sam a sidelong glance. Sam was staring at the wall across from them, her eyes distant. Was she thinking about their imminent conversation with Sister Catherine, or wishing she wasn't stuck in an airless room with someone who had put herself before their friendship?

"Let's hope she speaks more than a sentence or two this time," Jillian said, to fill the silence. Her meeting with Sister Susan that morning had firmed up her belief that Mitchell had killed the three men, and Sister Catherine had confessed to keep him out of jail. Sister Susan was certain that she'd seen Sister Catherine with the man after the first murder, and though she couldn't say for sure that the man matched the photo Jillian showed her, she said it was possible. Perhaps Sister Catherine and Mitchell had met before the first murder without anyone seeing them, but even if they had, Jillian still believed Mitchell was the culprit. He had a strong motive. Sister Catherine didn't, or at least they hadn't uncovered one.

She jerked her head toward the door when another door clanged shut nearby. Sister Catherine shuffled into the room, followed by a guard. Jillian studied the nun she'd only seen in photos. The woman had an air of defiance about her. The moment the guard removed her handcuffs, she folded her arms and tapped her foot.

After the guard had closed the door behind him, Sam leaned forward. "Thank you for agreeing to see me. This is Jillian Wright, my associate. Since your attorney isn't present, she's here as a witness."

Jillian nodded to the nun, who ignored her.

"I didn't want your attorney here because I know you're determined to go to prison for the murders. Because of that, I didn't think you'd appreciate him listening to what I'm about to say." Sam swiped to a photo on her phone and turned the device around so Sister Catherine could see. "I've spoken to Shawn Mitchell. I know he killed the three men, and you're sitting here because you don't want to see him go to prison."

Sister Catherine's eyes flicked to the phone. She swallowed.

"Here's something else you might be interested in." Sam played the recording Jillian had sent her.

"I understand why you did it, but I don't understand why you're going to let Sister Catherine rot in jail for the rest of her life."

"She wanted to."

"Why? Why would she want to confess to murders she didn't commit?"

"What do you mean?"

"You said she wanted to."

"She wanted to kill them."

"You're saying she murdered them?"

"We don't see them as murders. We had to stop them. They deserved it."

"Why didn't you go to the police?"

"The police? The courts? We tried that last time. Then Mike Atkins died, and those fuckers were free to do what they wanted. They weren't stupid. They went underground for a while. But sickos like that, they can't stop. They can't resist. But they made a mistake when they went after my son. They won't be going after anyone else's son now."

Sister Catherine shifted in her chair.

"What did you do to make Sister Catherine confess? Do you have something on her? Did you threaten her?"

"She willingly confessed."

"But she didn't do it."

"Look at me. Do you think I could do it?" Silence, then, "I have a family. I show up at work every day. But those fuckers . . . they took so much from me, and then they were doing it to my son? I don't want to go to jail. Cathy, she doesn't want me to go to jail. When she found out they were abusing my son, she came up with a plan. She didn't try to talk me out of it. If she'd said something, told me she didn't want to do it . . ."

"Turn it off," Sister Catherine snapped.

"If she planned to murder them, why would she try to talk you out of it? Wouldn't it be the other way around?" A pause. "You know what I think? You murdered three men in cold blood and you're letting a friend throw her life away so you don't have to go to prison." A snort. "You're as bad as the men who abused you."

A scuffle, followed by silence. "Do you think I want Cathy to be in prison? I feel guilty about her. I don't feel guilty about protecting my son and getting rid of three filthy pedophiles."

"Turn it off!"

Sam stopped the recording. "It's over, Sister. When I give this—"

"He's trying to protect me," Sister Catherine said. "I did it. I killed them."

Jillian resisted the urge to look at Sam. "Maybe you did," Sam said mildly. "I was asked by the church to prove your innocence. I now have another suspect, one who wavers between confessing to the murders and absolving you, and insisting that you did it. That's good enough for reasonable doubt. When the police bring Shawn M—"

Sister Catherine shot up from her chair. Jillian's heart pounded, but she willed herself to remain still. "Don't you dare involve him," the nun said through clenched teeth. "He isn't responsible."

"He killed them," Sam said.

"I murdered them." Sister Catherine slapped her chest with her right hand. "Me."

Sam shrugged. "Maybe that's true, but this will certainly be enough for reasonable doubt, and once the police question Mitchell, who knows what he'll say."

Sister Catherine sank back into her chair. "Don't," she whispered. "I'm begging you. He's already gone through so much. Bringing him into this . . . he doesn't deserve it. It will ruin his life. His family . . ." She drew a shaky breath.

"Perhaps we can come to some type of agreement."

The nun's eyes sharpened with interest. "What do you mean?"

"If you answer all my questions, maybe I'll lose this recording."

"Why would you do that?"

"Because Mitchell also said this." Sam forwarded the recording to the section she wanted to play.

"I told you, I'm through dealing with the police. And the others know that as long as I'm free, I could come after them."

"Others?"

"Do you think there are only three sickos in Grayhurst? We promised each other we'd stop after we took care of the ones who abused me and my son. But there are more, and I hope they're looking over their shoulders. As long as they know I'm out here—"

"They won't stop. They can't. You said so yourself. They might resist for a while, but . . ."

"Some other boy's father will have to blow them away."

"Tip off the police anonymously."

"No. The others might have pictures and videos of my son. He could get dragged into it."

Sam stopped the playback. "I want the names of those other pedophiles. If you tell me their names and answer a few other questions, I won't give the recording to the police."

"I don't know who they are," Sister Catherine said quickly.

"Yes, you do."

The nun didn't flinch.

"Who are they?" Sam asked, her voice hard.

"I don't know."

"Why would you protect pedophiles?"

Sister Catherine's eyes flashed. "You don't know anything. You come in here and judge me from your lofty perch, when you don't know anything."

"I don't know anything because you won't tell me anything. Tell me. Why did you do it? Who are the other pedophiles? Why does Shawn sometimes sound like he's confessing to the murders?"

The nun's mouth pressed into a thin line.

"Fine. I'll give this recording to the police, then." Sam pushed back her chair. "Thank you for meeting with us."

Jillian followed her lead. They were almost at the door when Sister Catherine said, "No, wait!"

Sam returned to the table but remained standing. She looked down at Sister Catherine. "Are you going to tell me the names?"

"What good will it do if I give them to you? They'll just get off, like they did last time."

"Tell me about last time. Give me your side of the story." When Sister Catherine curtly shook her head, Sam said, "Let me tell it, then. You met Shawn Mitchell when you were involved with the after-school drama club. You found out he was being sexually abused by several pedophiles. It got worse. He wasn't the only one. The RCMP opened an investigation. For some reason, perhaps because it lost a key witness or was pressured from above, it dropped the case, but the abuse stopped, until the pedophiles felt safe again. I don't know when they started up, but at some point, they abused Shawn Mitchell's son, and that led to their violent deaths. Now, the murders may have sent other pedophiles underground, but they'll eventually resurface, just like the three dead ones did."

Sam shifted her weight. "Maybe you don't want to tell me the names because nothing was done last time, and you figure it will be the same this time. Maybe you're worried about retribution against Shawn and his family. But if you give me the names, there's a chance they'll be stopped. If you don't, there's no chance of that happening. The same thing that happened to Shawn, and Brandon, and Michael, will happen to other children. Is that what you want? Is that what Shawn wants? Just give me the names."

"The others know that if they dare touch another boy, they will pay," Sister Catherine spat. "They got the message."

"How will they pay? You killed the others, and you'll be in prison for the rest of your life."

Sister Catherine's face flushed.

"*Got her,*" Jillian said to Sam.

Sam sank into the chair again. Jillian stayed where she was. The nun was focused on Sam.

"Shawn killed them," Sam stated. "Give me the names and answer a few questions, and I won't say a word to the police or give them the recording. You know that getting those pedophiles off the street, or at least trying to," she said, when Sister Catherine drew breath, "is the right thing to do. You have to live with yourself."

The nun snorted. "You think I'm concerned about living with myself? Why do you think I entered the convent? Why do you think I'm here? Because of what I did back then. I promised those children that I would take care of it. I went to the RCMP. I got them to open the investigation. And what happened?" Her eyes welled with tears. "They did nothing. They said the stories were contradictory, that there was no solid evidence. But I knew it was because Michael Atkins had died."

"Nobody pressured them to drop the investigation, like a politician or someone else powerful?"

"Not initially. Michael Atkins had agreed to meet with them. I was told he was working up the courage to tell his parents, and then he killed himself—supposedly. Suddenly the RCMP didn't have a case. I don't know if they were worried about someone getting to the other boys, or if they believed that Michael was the only one willing to go on record with evidence that would make their case, and when he died, they had nothing again. I did hear a rumour that someone had told them it would be best to shelve the investigation and spare everyone more pain. The police would be keeping an eye on the abusers, blah, blah, blah." Sister Catherine's mouth twisted. "If it was true, I wonder if whoever made the call was a pedophile himself, or protecting a family member. Sick. Sick."

"What about Shawn? Couldn't he have helped the RCMP?"

"He didn't want to get involved. I'd told him, told all of them, that I'd take care of it. I'd promised them."

Jillian couldn't believe it. Freaking Shawn Mitchell, blaming Cathy, the police, everyone around him! If he'd had the courage to tell his story . . . Michael might have died because he'd been willing to face his abusers.

"So you knew Michael?" Sam said.

Sister Catherine shook her head. "I knew of him. I knew he was another victim, but he wasn't one of the boys I was trying to help."

"But you had his photo."

"When he died, people left cards and candles and things at a little memorial outside his house. Someone had left the photo." Sister

Catherine grimaced. "I took it. I kept it to remind myself of what a mess I'd made of everything."

Sam clasped her hands on the table. "You can't blame yourself. You did what you could."

"If that were true, Michael Atkins would still be alive. Those boys wouldn't have lost faith in the justice system. Shawn's son wouldn't have suffered."

"It wasn't your fault. You can't control everything."

"I should have defied everyone and gone public. I should have . . ." Sister Catherine shook her head.

"You have to forgive yourself. Jesus died on the cross for you."

"I can't." The nun bit her lip and lowered her head. She appeared truly sorrowful.

Sam studied her. "You didn't kill those men."

Sister Catherine lifted her head. She wiped away a tear. "Yes, I did. I killed them."

Jillian's hands clenched. So it was going to be like that, then.

Sam must have reached the same conclusion. "Then you'll go to prison for murder, but what about those other pedophiles? Don't let the other boys suffer. Things have changed since Shawn was abused. Give me the names of the pedophiles you know about. I promise I'll do what I can to bring them to justice."

"And you won't tell the police about Shawn?"

"No, I won't."

Sister Catherine rubbed her forehead.

"Tell me. You'll sleep better at night."

"I won't, but I don't need anything more on my conscience. If anything happens to Shawn or his family, you'll be responsible."

Sam nodded, but Jillian couldn't tell whether she agreed with the nun's statement.

Sister Catherine closed her eyes. *"Give her a minute,"* Sam said. What felt like five minutes ticked by. The nun opened her eyes. Sam readied her phone and raised her brows.

Jillian let out her pent breath when Sister Catherine reeled off four names. Sam tapped them into her phone. "Thank you," she said when she'd finished. "Now, we're going to walk out of this room. Are you sure you don't want to change your mind about your confession?"

"I killed them," Sister Catherine said.

"Okay." Sam pushed back her chair and strode to Jillian's side. She turned around. "I can't guarantee that when the police interview the pedophiles, Shawn's name won't come up."

Sister Catherine's eyes widened.

"But he didn't murder anyone, so I'm sure he'll be all right. It won't matter how long they interrogate him. Five, ten hours, locked in a room. No matter how hard they press him, if he didn't do it and answers their questions honestly, he'll have nothing to worry about." She banged on the door.

Sister Catherine slowly rose. "You are rotten to the core," she shrieked. "You don't care about the boys. You just care about doing your job."

The guard swung the door open.

"You had the nerve to bring up Jesus?" the nun shouted. "You know nothing of Jesus. Burn in hell!"

Jillian wanted to slap the nun silly. She glanced at Sam. "Are you okay?" she asked as they walked to the prison entrance.

Sam nodded. "I'm fine." She paused. "I shouldn't have said that to her, but she rubs me the wrong way. She stood by and let him murder two men, maybe three, and she doesn't seem bothered by it at all. I know they were pedophiles, but still. It's cold."

"I think you were quite restrained," Jillian said. "I would have been a hell of a lot ruder."

"I don't know what she thinks she's accomplishing by protecting Mitchell. The guy's a wreck. He wants to confess."

"So you think he did it?"

"Yeah. Do you still think he did it?" Sam asked Jillian. "Pulled the trigger, I mean."

"I do. She's much more cool and calculating than he is. If it was her, why would she involve him? Look at how terrified she is that the police will haul him in. If she was the killer, she would have kept him out of it."

Sam grunted.

"The little bits of evidence we managed to uncover point to him, too. Though I wanted to kick myself when she said she hadn't known Michael."

Sam chuckled. "Me too, but the photo started us down the right path. We wouldn't have gotten anywhere without it."

True. They'd been heading back to the island when Sister Lynn had called and asked to meet with Jillian. "I have to admit, I haven't thought about what might happen when the police round up the others, assuming they do."

"They'll at least talk to them, but hopefully they'll do more than that and find whatever they need to charge them."

When they reached the car, Sam pulled out her phone. "When you were with Sister Susan this morning, I called Sister Catherine's attorney. I'm going to send him the names and tell him about the photos at Mitchell's cottage." She tapped on her phone. "I'll sum up what Sister Catherine just told us, too."

"You said you wouldn't tip off the police about Mitchell."

"I'm not. I'm tipping off her lawyer, and he's not getting the recording."

"You're splitting hairs, but I don't care. I want Mitchell and the pedophiles."

"Me too," Sam said, still hunched over her phone.

Of course she did. Why had Jillian ever thought that Sam would be satisfied with only one or the other? "Why didn't you tell me you were going to tell her lawyer about Mitchell?" See, this was why she should have kept her mouth shut about her feelings. Sam was keeping her out of the loop again.

"Because I wasn't sure how things were going to go with Sister Catherine. She might have told us to go ahead and tell the police about Mitchell." Sam briefly looked up from the email she was composing. "Plus, I'm telling you now."

Yeah, sure. Damn it! What had happened to being patient? She wasn't freaking twelve. Sam had started to open up, to trust, and then Jillian's big mouth had blown it because she'd wanted right now what she couldn't have right now. Life sucked. "Even if Mitchell confesses, Sister Catherine will insist she did it."

"Probably." Sam continued to tap away on her phone for a few minutes, then looked up. "There, I just hit Send." She pocketed her phone. "Greenwood should have enough for reasonable doubt that Sister Catherine acted alone. Whether he'll be able to get the murder charges dropped, who knows?"

Frankly, Jillian didn't care. "She didn't stop Mitchell. They were both responsible for two murders, at least, and she didn't go to the police about the first."

"I expect they'll both do time, but how the police and courts deal with them isn't our problem." Sam opened the driver's side door. She smiled. "We're done. We have a plane to catch."

Jillian returned Sam's smile, but she wasn't looking forward to going home. Her favourite places would remind her of rejection and stupidity.

Chapter Twenty-Two

JILLIAN FOLLOWED SAM into the library and watched her hug Roberta. When it was her turn, she embraced Roberta without cringing. She still wasn't into touchy-feely stuff, but returning to the island really did feel like coming home to family.

Roberta sank into her chair. "It's good to have you both back."

"We were away longer than we expected to be," Jillian said. Then she wished she hadn't said it. They'd expected the investigation to be short because they'd been skeptical of Roberta's certainty that Sister Catherine was innocent. Had they been right? The nun wasn't innocent, but she wasn't guilty of the charges she was facing—strictly speaking.

"Has anything happened?" Sam asked.

"Sister Catherine's attorney acted quickly." Roberta looked up at them. "Sit down."

Jillian grabbed the nearest chair, but Sam shook her head.

Roberta continued. "They brought in Shawn Mitchell about half an hour ago."

"I guess we'll see if he confesses," Jillian murmured.

Roberta nodded. "As for the pedophiles, I assume they'll do some preliminary investigation before they question them. They'll want their ducks in a row."

"They won't want to spook them." Sam scratched her nose. "I'll see you at dinner, then. I haven't played a note since we left. I want to practice before tomorrow's service."

"It'll be good to have you back at the organ." Roberta's voice dropped. "Jeremy isn't the same."

"He's getting better. I'll see you later." Sam caught Jillian's eye as she strode away, but didn't say good-bye to her.

Jillian sighed.

"Is everything all right between you two?" Roberta asked.

Damn, she hadn't meant to be so loud. "Everything's fine." She studied her hands. "This case was a tough one. I understand why they did it. At the same time, if everyone took the law into their own hands, it would be chaos."

"But you sympathized."

Jillian felt her shoulders relax. She took a second to consider her answer. "To be honest, I didn't like her."

"Sister Catherine?"

"Yeah. I think she saw what she was doing as protecting Mitchell and his son. But I think she was doing it for herself, to assuage her guilt."

Roberta's eyes narrowed. "She had nothing to feel guilty about."

"I know, but I can't feel sorry for her. She was so cold about it all. The only time she showed any emotion was when she spoke about Mitchell."

"We don't have to like the people we help, not that we helped her much." Roberta smoothed her skirt. "I was in the ballpark, though."

Jillian's smile was genuine. "Yes, you were." She should leave the library now, but what would she do? She wanted to run into Sam, and dreaded running into her.

"Is something else troubling you?" Roberta asked.

Yeah, that everyone in this place was psychic. "Just that I can't help but think about us when I think about what Sister Catherine and Mitchell did."

"What do you mean?"

"Vigilantism. We take the law into our own hands. I shot Junior, and then we buried him." Literally and figuratively. "We took out that rapist."

"You shot Junior in self-defence. As for the rapist, we only stepped in after all the legal channels had been exhausted. We always try to nudge the authorities along first and hope the legal system works." Roberta paused. "There are occasions when we commit a crime, but never for revenge. Sometimes we know about things we can't pass on to the authorities."

"Because we don't have any evidence to support what we know?" Jillian said lightly. "I suppose telling them that our Guide knows wouldn't cut it."

Roberta's mouth twitched. "Sometimes that's the case. Other times we can't give the authorities what we have because it would raise too many questions and bring us unwanted attention."

As the recording of Shawn Mitchell would have done. "I'm not trying to be difficult."

"I know. I'd worry about you if it didn't sometimes bother you that we live outside the world and don't always operate in accordance with its laws."

They lapsed into silence. Jillian stood. "I should go." She couldn't cling to Roberta forever. "I took my guitar with me but didn't play it once. I miss it, and who knows how long we'll be here this time."

"We could use a guitar in our services. Well, someone to play one, to be more accurate."

She was tempted, not because she believed, but because she needed to belong right now. She'd wished she could go to the services; they were important to everyone who mattered to her. And hey, atheists did go to church. Sometimes they were the ones behind the pulpit.

"We won't mob you and force you to declare your belief in the Lord," Roberta said.

"I know. I . . . maybe. I'll think about it."

If Roberta was surprised, she didn't show it. "You're always welcome. And you're always welcome to come chat with me. I enjoy talking to you."

Damn it. She should forget about trying to pretend with Roberta. Somehow the woman always knew. "I enjoy talking to you, too. I'll see you later."

Now what? Normally she'd be itching to walk the island's paths again, but not this time. She went to her bedroom, closed the door, and stared at the four walls.

Jillian sat on her bed strumming her guitar, but her heart wasn't in it. She kept straining to listen for footsteps, even though hearing them would worsen her dour mood. Sam would go into her bedroom and shut the door, but at least Jillian would be able to go outside without worrying about running into her. She'd only been in her bedroom for an hour and she already hated being confined. *You're doing it to yourself. Nobody locked you in here.*

How old was she again? She should talk to Sam, tell her that she wanted their friendship back. Right. She'd known, *known*, that if she opened her mouth about her feelings, it would ruin everything. *So why? Why?* She had nobody but herself to blame. She didn't deserve Sam's friendship, but she wanted it. She'd had it, until Sam hadn't opened up fast enough for her. Had she always been this selfish and demanding when she wanted to get close to someone? She couldn't remember; it had been so long ago. She'd spent most of her adult life pretending to be someone else and only getting chummy with a woman when she wanted to get information out of her, and never *that* chummy. A sympathetic ear, a nod at the right time, a gentle pat on the hand . . . not this. Not love.

Sam had also spent most of her life being Sam somebody-or-other, rather than Sam McDougall. Yeah, she worked for God. If they'd gotten together, Jillian would always have played second fiddle to a powerful imaginary friend. It was bad enough when one half of a couple felt as if they didn't come first. Imagine being second to someone you couldn't see, hear, and touch. Sam would have used Him as an excuse. *"Sorry, Jillian, not today, God wants me to do something else." "Jillian, I wish I could, but, you know." "I agree with you, Jillian, but I have to obey the Lord."* Yeah, it would have been great when the three of them had an intimate dinner or went for a stroll.

Nope, it wasn't working. She blew out some air, then would have smashed her guitar against the wall, if she didn't like it so much and Sam hadn't gone with her to choose it. Okay, they were bound together for the rest of their lives. How long could Sam stick to discussing nothing but whatever they were investigating? Well, she'd worked alone for twenty years and it had taken her months to answer a personal question without making Jillian feel as if she were being rude, so . . . Jillian rested the guitar at her feet, for its own protection.

It was time to act her age. They were both adults. If Sam didn't want to rekindle their friendship, if she didn't miss it, then Jillian wanted to know. Wondering and waiting wasn't working for her. And that little voice telling her that impatience was what had gotten her into this in the first place? It could take a flying leap. She couldn't spend months making small talk, not this time. They were beyond that now, whether Sam liked it or not. Jillian just wanted to clear the air, apologize again, make sure Sam knew that it was okay to have a personal conversation and show interest in her sidekick's life. Jillian wouldn't take it as a sign that they were going to ride off into the sunset together.

Wanting to find Sam before she lost her nerve, Jillian headed for the door, but then paused and grabbed her guitar. She slung the instrument onto her back and walked to the chapel, her resolve increasing with every step, along with her butterflies.

Music didn't reach her ears as she approached the chapel, but that could mean Sam was practicing at the piano, rather than at the organ. She entered the chapel and peeked into the sanctuary. Yep, Sam was at the piano.

Jillian hovered outside the sanctuary, suddenly unsure. *Keep going.* She had nothing to lose. What could Sam do? Refuse to discuss investigations with her? She didn't want Sam to hate her. At the same time, if wanting to clear the air turned Sam against her, then Sam wasn't worth it. Jillian was confident that she'd hear her out. She might not be thrilled, but she'd listen.

The piano sat to the right of the altar. Jillian took a deep breath and strode up the aisle. Halfway down it, Sam stopped playing in the middle of a piece. Jillian self-consciously closed the distance between them. She bit her lip. "I'm sorry for interrupting, but I really need to talk to you. Is there any chance we can clear the air and try to repair whatever damage I did? Can we talk about it?"

Sam blinked at her, then picked a piece of lint off her jeans. "Okay."

Jillian chuckled nervously. "Not here. I feel like I'm at a disadvantage."

Sam's expression didn't change, but she got up from the piano. They left the chapel in silence. When they'd walked a short distance, Jillian forced herself to open her mouth. "Look, I know I blew it, okay. I knew that telling you would be a mistake. I kept telling myself to be patient." No, no, that implied they'd get together in the future. She'd hoped they would, but . . . Why did she have to babble when she was nervous? "I should have been patient, waited for my feelings to run their course," she said quickly.

"Do you think your feelings will peter out?" Sam asked.

The question surprised Jillian. "I—I, yeah, I mean . . ." Damn it. She'd wanted this conversation. They might never talk about this again. She needed to be honest. "I don't know. I assume they will. Eventually. Maybe. Or maybe not. I don't know. I've felt this way for a while and they haven't, but . . ." She trailed off.

"Why do you have your guitar?" Sam asked.

Jillian stopped walking and turned to her. She patted the instrument on her back. "In case I chickened out when you'd already spotted me. Plan B was to tell you that I was wondering if we could play together for a bit."

"You were going to say that you wanted to play together . . . in the chapel." Sam's tone said it all.

"Yeah, it was lame." Hope tugged at her. Sam was teasing. Jillian swallowed. "I miss this. I didn't say anything for the longest time because I didn't want to lose this. I don't deserve it, but I want it back."

"Why don't you think you deserve it?"

"Because I was selfish."

Sam's brows drew together. "You were just being honest."

"Sometimes honesty isn't the best policy, like when it costs you a friend." Jillian looked down at her feet for a moment, then lifted her head. "Can we get past this? Can we go back to the way it was before I opened my mouth?"

"No."

"Sam, we work together. Hell, we live to—"

Sam lifted her hand. "It can't be the same, because everything's out in the open now. But it will be pretty miserable for both of us if we can't be friends." She hooked her thumbs through the belt loops on her jeans. "I've missed it, too. I've wanted to have this conversation, but . . ." She lifted her shoulders.

Jillian wanted to press her, but held back. She was out of the penalty box! Did she want to risk going right back into it?

"I wasn't sure what to say." Sam freed her thumbs and motioned for them to walk. Jillian fell into step with her and fought her raging curiosity. One wrong question could end the conversation.

"I've thought a lot about what you said. About how you feel." Sam shoved her hands into her pockets. "I didn't tell you this, but when I met Marcy Abrams, she wanted to go to a nightclub after dinner. A lesbian nightclub. With me. Together."

Jillian's jaw dropped.

"When she," Sam hesitated a beat, "flirted with me, it made me uncomfortable."

Jillian grunted, wondering what the hell this had to do with anything. If Sam told her she regretted not taking Marcy up on her offer, Jillian would have to nod and take it. Being friends meant discussing stuff like this. She liked it when Sam opened up to her, right? And if they were going to be close, she couldn't expect Sam to avoid certain topics because it might hurt her feelings.

"When you told me how you felt, it made me angry. I should have been gentler." Sam turned to Jillian. "I'm sorry."

"It's okay. Really. I should be the one apologizing. I said some terrible things, and then I dropped a bomb on you."

"The thing is . . ." Sam grimaced. "When you told me, I didn't realize it at the time, but it scared me. That's why I was horrible to you."

"Marcy didn't scare you?"

Sam shook her head. "I don't care about Marcy, in the sense that she's not a part of my life." Her voice softened. "I value our friendship. I don't think you understand how much I do."

"You were mad at me because I put what I wanted before what we already had. I get that. I've been mad at myself for the same thing, and terrified that we're never going to be comfortable with each other again." She wanted to give Sam's arm a reassuring touch, but knew better. Now they were both walking with their hands in their pockets. "Our friendship means a hell of a lot to me, too. I didn't mean to give you the impression that it doesn't."

"That's good." Sam pulled her hands from her pockets and folded her arms. "Things will be less tense." She gave Jillian a tight smile. "I should get back to the piano. I'm rusty."

Anxiety snaked through Jillian. "Yeah, sure," she said.

Sam strode away.

Confused, Jillian remained where she was and stared at Sam's back. She hadn't said anything Sam hadn't said, so what the hell?

Was everything Sam had said bogus? Did she want to get past what Jillian had told her, but couldn't? Jillian wanted to go after her, then she stiffened when Sam whirled. Oh, shit.

Sam stopped in front of her. She clasped her hands and stood awkwardly.

"What did I say that upset you?" Jillian said, struggling to keep her exasperation from her voice. "I'm glad you came back. I don't want anything hanging over us."

Sam looked down at her hands, then unclasped them and slipped them into her back pockets. She rocked on her heels. "It's not you, it's me."

Jillian barked a laugh. "That's never good."

"I feel I should tell you something, but . . ." Sam's mouth pressed into a thin line. "I don't know what's best for you."

"For me? I'm a big girl, Sam, even though I behave like a child sometimes. Tell me what's on your mind and let me decide what's best for me." Despite her brave words, she dreaded what Sam would say, and braced herself.

Sam met Jillian's eyes. "I wish I'd gone to dinner with you on my fortieth. It was silly not to. I regret saying no."

"Then let's go to dinner," Jillian said, her effort to keep her elation out of her voice making her sound flat.

"It's too late."

"No, it isn't. You didn't turn forty that long ago. Let's go, and to a swanky restaurant."

Sam's mouth turned up at the corners.

"We'll go next time we're" —Jillian waved her arm at nothing— "out there. And you know the rules around birthday dinners, right? No work talk. None."

When Sam didn't say anything, Jillian wanted to kick herself. Damn it, she was doing it again.

"A swanky restaurant," Sam drawled. She chewed her lip. "What are you going to see this dinner as? A date?"

Jillian opened her mouth to reply with an emphatic no, then bit her tongue. Sam hadn't reminded her not to see it as a date. Interesting. "What will you see it as?"

Sam took her time answering. "I don't know." She scratched her cheek. "When Marcy suggested that we go to a club, I told her I was seeing someone."

Jillian had no idea how to respond to that. Was Sam thinking out loud, or trying to tell her something? *Don't blow it again.* This time she wouldn't follow her heart off the cliff.

"All I know is that I want to go to dinner with you," Sam said.

"Then we'll go." Jillian wagged her finger. "I'm holding you to it. No backing out."

"I won't back out. I wouldn't do that to you."

Jillian believed her. Maybe Sam had been right and a dinner without shop talk wasn't such a good idea, because Jillian wanted to hug her and squeeze her so tightly that she'd beg for air.

Sam looked in the direction of the chapel. "I should get back."

"You should. Go."

"I'm glad we had this conversation."

"Me too."

"But I should go."

"Yes. Go."

They smiled at each other. Sam walked away. This time, she didn't turn back.

Jillian waited until she couldn't see her anymore, then took a moment to let it sink in. Was it her imagination, or was the sun shining more brightly? She headed away from the chapel. There was only one place to go.

On the way, she wanted to bust out some dance moves. Maybe she was getting carried away, but it had sounded to her like Sam hadn't shut the door on being more than friends. Hell, since Jillian had confessed her feelings, Sam had been diligent about holding her at arm's length. She wouldn't suddenly stop doing that unless she was no longer worried that Jillian would take something she said or did the wrong way.

Then again, Sam could have decided that Jillian had gotten the message. Nah. Maybe she was interpreting their conversation the way she wanted to, but she didn't believe Sam would have brought up dinner, agreed to it, and admitted that she *wanted* to go to dinner with her, if the thought of being more than friends hadn't crossed her mind. Come on, she'd asked whether it would be a date, and hadn't said it wouldn't be. She had to have known how it would come across. She wouldn't have been so careless if there was no chance, none, not even when hell froze over.

This time, patience. Patience, patience, patience! They wouldn't wake up between tangled sheets the morning after Sam's birthday dinner. Hell, they wouldn't even kiss. But that was okay. Jillian believed they were on their way. Being in a car with Sam and travelling ten kilometres an hour meant they'd eventually reach their destination. It was better than standing on the side of the road by herself.

She clambered onto her favourite rock, slipped her guitar off her back, and sat cross-legged. In a minute, she'd play one of the hymns she and Sam loved, but first, she'd gaze out at the crystal blue water. The island, her home . . . what a beautiful place it was.

BREAKING NEWS at World News Five:

The news anchor looked solemnly into the camera. "The jury delivered its verdicts today in a case that has split Grayhurst down the middle. Six months ago, three men were brutally murdered, and a local nun confessed to the crime. But then police arrested father-of-two Shawn Mitchell, and suddenly the case wasn't so clear-cut, because he also confessed to the crimes. So, who did it? The father, or the nun? Our very own Marcy Abrams was the first to break the news of Shawn Mitchell's arrest and was given exclusive access to Sister Catherine's attorney, Dave Greenwood. She was at the courthouse when the verdicts came in. Marcy."

"Thank you, Carol. It took the jury three days to sort through the evidence they heard during a trial that lasted almost a month. Sister Catherine and Shawn Mitchell were tried together, but even though both had confessed to the crimes, they pleaded not guilty at the advice of their legal counsel. From the outset, the authorities believed that only one had pulled the trigger, but as witness after witness was called to the stand, it became obvious that the other had played a role in the murders that shocked the city.

"We learned that the two accused used to be teacher and student, and that the murders were related to events that took place in Grayhurst over twenty years ago, but we don't know the details. The press and public were barred from the courtroom for the portion of the trial that related to past events, but we learned from a reliable source that they concerned the sexual abuse of several boys, and that Mitchell was one of the victims."

"So what did the jury decide?" Carol asked.

"The jury rejected the first degree murder charges, instead convicting Sister Catherine of second degree murder. As for Mitchell, the seven women and five men refused to convict him of murder, but did find him guilty of an accessory charge, one of the options the judge had offered them during his instructions."

"Were people surprised by the verdicts, Marcy?"

"Some were, but most of those who sat through the trial expected that Sister Catherine would be convicted of a more serious charge than Mitchell. The nun and former teacher didn't show any remorse, or any emotion at all, during the trial—in stark contrast to Mitchell, who often broke down as he listened to testimony. Perhaps the only surprise was that Mitchell was convicted of only the lesser charge, but some would say he shouldn't have been convicted at all. The case of the father and the nun, as some have dubbed it, was a real whodunit, but at the end of the day, what the jury believed was all that mattered."

"Will there be an appeal?"

"According to Dave Greenwood, Sister Catherine's attorney, they won't be appealing. Mitchell's attorney wouldn't speak to reporters, but given the outcome of the trial, which must have been better than what they'd hoped for, I doubt they'll appeal. The evidence was compelling," Marcy replied.

"And what are you hearing about a possible connection between this case and the four men arrested several months ago for crimes related to sexual abuse and child pornography?"

"The authorities aren't confirming or denying anything, but sources tell me that evidence uncovered during the investigation of the murders led to the arrest of the four men, and as a result of that, to arrests in other cities."

"What started as a murder investigation may have also cracked a major child pornography ring."

Marcy nodded. "That's right, Carol. As Chief Duncan said at the press conference held shortly after the arrests of the four local men, Grayhurst's children are much safer because the men are off the streets, and the same applies to other communities in several provinces."

"Thank you, Marcy." Carol turned back to the camera and intoned, "Safer indeed."

Other Titles by Sarah Ettritch

Threaded Through Time
The Daros Chronicles
The Salbine Sisters
The Rymellan Series
The Missing Comatose Woman

If you'd like to be notified when the next Deiform Fellowship book is released, sign up for the notification list at Sarah's website: www.sarahettritch.com

Thanks for reading!

www.ingramcontent.com/pod-product-compliance
Lightning Source LLC
Chambersburg PA
CBHW050527190726
48284CB00003B/974